William Harrison

Mona miscellany

a selection of proverbs, sayings, ballads, customs, superstitions, and...

William Harrison

Mona miscellany
a selection of proverbs, sayings, ballads, customs, superstitions, and...

ISBN/EAN: 9783744780513

Printed in Europe, USA, Canada, Australia, Japan

Cover: Foto ©Andreas Hilbeck / pixelio.de

More available books at **www.hansebooks.com**

The Manx Society

ESTABLISHED IN THE YEAR

MDCCCLVIII

VOL. XXI.

DOUGLAS, ISLE OF MAN
PRINTED FOR THE MANX SOCIETY
MDCCCLXXIII

N.B.—Members at a distance are requested to acknowledge their copies to the Honorary Secretary, Mr. Paul Bridson, Atholl Street, Douglas, to whom also their Subscriptions may be remitted.

Printed by R. & R. CLARK, *Edinburgh*.

MONA MISCELLANY

" Here's metal more attractive—And this our life,
    Finds tongues in trees, books in the running brooks,
    Sermons in stones, and good in everything."

SHAKSPEARE.

" Mekyll and littil olde and zynge,
    Herkyns alle to my talkyne."

OLD MS.

MONA MISCELLANY

A SELECTION OF

PROVERBS, SAYINGS, BALLADS,

CUSTOMS, SUPERSTITIONS, AND LEGENDS,

PECULIAR TO THE ISLE OF MAN

COLLECTED AND EDITED

By WILLIAM HARRISON,

AUTHOR OF 'BIBLIOTHECA MONENSIS.'

SECOND SERIES

DOUGLAS, ISLE OF MAN

PRINTED FOR THE MANX SOCIETY

MDCCCLXXIII

Printed by R. & R. CLARK, *Edinburgh.*

PREFACE.

THE Council of the Manx Society having expressed a wish that the editor should make a further selection from his store of the folk lore of the Island of Man, to form a second series to that which appeared in the 16th volume of their publications in 1869, he has been induced to prepare the present volume, in the hope that it may be received as favourably as its predecessor. He was led to expect that he would have received some aid from members of the Society who had documents of a similar nature in their possession, but he has been disappointed, with the single exception of one, to whom he now wishes to express his warmest thanks for the great interest he has taken in the present volume, and the valuable assistance he has rendered in making it as perfect in its details as possible, although not wishing to be mentioned by name.

To the Rev. John Thomas Clarke, who was ever ready to assist in procuring Manx songs which otherwise would have been lost, as well as to Mr. John Quirk, of Cairn ny Greïe, for his willingness to give them an English dress, the Editor also begs his acknowledgments and thanks.

There are, doubtless, many Manx songs that might still be rescued from oblivion that would throw light upon many a long-forgotten fact, if some one could be found capable and diligent enough to collect them. It may be said that many of these are only of a very homely nature and rude verse, yet what are the generality of ballads ?—written for the day, nevertheless may contain truths that otherwise would have escaped the notice of the historian of after years. As such, those given in these volumes, it is hoped, will be found useful, if not for their elegance of diction, yet for the truths that may be found in them.

A specimen of a Manx *carval* is given in the present collection, with an English version of the same, on the "Bad women mentioned in Scripture," which the Editor believes has not hitherto been translated. It would have been easy to have given many of these *carvals*, which may be termed a literature entirely peculiar to the Manx people, consisting chiefly of ballads on sacred subjects which have been handed down in writing to the present time, and are yet to be found in many an out-of-the-way mountain farm-house, preserved in smoke-dried volumes redolent of peat. A collection of these would some years hence form quite a literary curiosity, many of them possessing considerable merit, but are yearly becoming more difficult to procure, either from being altogether lost, or the unwillingness of the peasantry to part with their treasured manuscripts. Most of these carvals are from 50 to 150 years old, and amongst the favourites may be mentioned "Joseph's History," "Susannah's History," "The Nativity," "The Holy War," "David and Goliah," "Samson's History," "Birth of Christ," with the specimens that have been given in the present collection.

The editor has every reason to believe that the two volumes of "Mona Miscellany" contain the largest collection of the "Folk Lore" of the Isle of Man that is to be met with, and which the author of the term (Mr. Thoms, for many years the editor of *Notes and Queries*) defines to include "Popular superstitions, ballads, legends, and generally, as the name implies, the lore of the people."

In the present volume the editor has the pleasure of giving a copy of the scarce print of the shipwreck of the herring fleet in Douglas Bay in 1787, mentioned in the first series of *Mona Miscellany*, as also a plate of the curious silver cross formerly in the possession of Mylecharaine, which he hopes will be found an acceptable addition.

WILLIAM HARRISON.

Rock Mount, *July* 1873.

CONTENTS.

CUSTOMS AND SUPERSTITIONS.

PECULIARITIES IN NUMERATION, CURRENCY, WEIGHTS, MEASURES, DIVISIONS OF LAND, AND QUANTITIES.

PROVERBS AND SAYINGS.

"Fill up another to the brim, and laugh."

PROVERBS AND SAYINGS.

Miscellaneous Proverbs.

These Miscellaneous Proverbs, which are here brought before the Members of the Manx Society, are given more for the purpose of showing the Manx mode of expressing the sentiment than as belonging exclusively to the Isle of Man. No doubt many of them will be found to be of a world-wide use, for the thoughts and modes of expression of most people will naturally partake of some similarity, varying only in the peculiar idiom of that nation which makes use of them. Some of these, however, may be more applicable to Manxmen, and may probably be ascribed to their paternity. Their language is so rich, full of meaning and expression, that it frequently conveys much more than can be expressed in a bald translation ; and if, as it has been remarked, "that it is a doomed language," it is well to embalm some of their sayings in their native tongue before it entirely passes into oblivion.

"*Cha jagh moylley ghooinney hene ricau foddey voish e ghorrys.*"
"Self-praise travels no distance, or is no recommendation."

"*My ta keim sy laair, bee keim sy lhiy.*"
"An amble in the mare is also in the colt."

B

"*Kiangle myr noid,
    As yiow myr carrey.*"
"As an enemy bind,
    And a friend you'll find."

"*Cha boght as lugh killagh.*"
"As poor as a church mouse."

"*Tra ta fer laccal ben, cha vel eh laccal agh ben,
    Agh tra ta ben eehey, téh laccal ymmodee glen.*"
"When a man wants a wife, he wants but a wife ;
    But when he has got a wife, he wants a great deal."

"*Crén doaie tórt ?*"
"How fare you ?"

"*Woish y lave gys y veeal.*"
"From hand to mouth."

"*Lhig y my hraa, or Lhiggey Shaghey.*"
"One who lets by ; one who puts off."
Spoken contemptuously of an idle fellow.

"*Tra hig yn laa, hig yn choyrle lesh.*"
"When the day comes, its counsel will come with it."
"Every day has its night, every weal its woe."—*Danish
Proverb.*

"*Laik lhiat ve marish y chioltane ; agh tán camagh ayd
    camagh ny goair.*"
"Thou wouldest fain be numbered with the flock ; but
thy bleat is the bleat of the goat."

"*Goll sheese ny lhargagh.*"
"Going down the declivity."
Spoken of one who is declining or failing in health.

" *Shooyll ny thicyn.*"
" Going on the houses"—that is, begging.*

" *T'ou cha daaney as clagh vane.*"
" Thou art as impudent as a white stone."

" *T'ou cha daaney as assag.*"
" Thou art as bold as a weasel."

" *Boayl nagh vel aggle cha vel grayse.*"
" Where there is no fear there is no grace."

" *Eshyn nagh gow rish briw erbee téh deyrey eh hene.*"
" He who will acknowledge no judge condemns himself."

" *T'ad beaghey bwoailley er kayt as bwoailley er moddey.*"
" They live like cat and dog."

" *Shegin goaill ny cairkyn marish y cheh.*"
" We must take the horns with the hide."

" *Kione mooar er y veggan cheilley, as kione beg gyn veg edyr. Towse cheilley rish.*"
" A great head with little wit, and a little head without any."
The Spaniards say, " Long hair and little brains."

" *Bwoaill choud as ta'n yiarn cheh.*"
" Strike while the iron is hot."

People must be plied when they are in a good humour or mood.

" *Cre yiow jeh'n chayt agh y chrackan.*"
" What can you get of the cat but the skin."

---

* For a notice of the Manx mode of treatment of beggars, see *Mona Miscellany*, first series, p. 34 ; but as their hospitality has been so frequently abused by strangers, it is now falling into disuse.

"*Faggys ta my lheiney agh ny sniessey ta my chrackan.*"
"Near is my shirt, but nearer is my skin."
The Spaniard says, "The shirt is nearer than the coat."

"*Myr sniessey da'n chraue s'miljey yn cill.*"
"The nearer the bone the sweeter the flesh."

"*Commee obbyr commee bee.*"
"Sharing work, sharing meat."

"*Coontey ny heïn roish ta ny hoohyn guirt.*"
"Counting the chickens in the eggs."
"Count not your chickens before they be hatched."

"*Cha dooar ricau drogh reaynee corran mie.*"
"A bad reaper never got a good sickle."

This is similar to the proverb, "A bad workman quarrels with his tools."

"*Eshyn yiow skeilley, yiow eh craid.*"
"He who gets imposed upon is mocked."

"*Ta cree dooie ny share na kione croutagh.*"
"Better is a kind heart than a crafty head."

"*Tu dooinney creeney mennick jannoo carrey jeh e noid.*"
"A wise man often conciliates his enemy."

"*Myr smoo siyr smoo cumrail.*"
"The more haste the more hinderance."

"*Hig daill gys ceck.*"
"Credit will come to payment."

"*Roshee daill y dorrys.*"
"Credit shall reach the door."

"*Cha dennee ricau yn soogh y shang.*"
"The full belly never feels for the hunger'd."

" *Cha stamp rieau yn dow doo er e chass.*"
" The black ox never stamps on his own foot."

" *Moyll y droghad myr heu harrish.*"
" Praise the bridge as you find it."
Another mode of expression is, " Praise not the ford till
you are safe over."

" *Un eam gys bee, as jees gys obbyr.*"
" One call to meat, and two to work."

" *Eddyr daa stoyl ta toyn er laare.*"
" Between two stools is a fall."
The Scotch say, " Betwixt twa stools the doup fa's down."

" *Ta bee eeit jarroodit.*"
" Eaten bread is forgotten."
It is also said, " A good turn is soon forgotten."

" *Cha nee yn wooa smoo eieys smoo vlicaunys.*"
" It is not the cow which shouts most milks the best."

" *Dy chooilley ghooinney er e hon hene, as Jee son ain ooilley.*"
" Every man for himself, and God for us all."
The Spaniard says, " Every one in his own house, and God
in all of them."

" *Laa er-meshtey as laa er ushtey.*"
" A day tipsy, a day watery."
It is also said, " A drunken night makes a cloudy morning."

" *Cha vel fer erbee cha bouyr, as eshyn nagh jean clashtyn.*"
" None so deaf as he who will not hear."

" *Siyn folmey smoo sheean nee.*"
" Empty vessels make the most noise."
Its opposite : " The deepest streams flow with the least noise."

" *Ta fooillagh naarcydagh ny smelley na ce scammyltagh.*"
" Shameful leaving is worse than shameful eating."

" *Geeck cabbyl marroo.*"
" Paying for a dead horse."

" *Eskyn nagh bee mie rish e gharran, shegin da yn phollan
y chur lesh er e ruin.*"
" He who will not be kind to his pony must bring the
saddle on his own back."

" *Cha daink lesh y gheay, nagh ragh lesh yn ushtcy.*"
" What comes with the wind goes with the water."

" *Tra ta'n gheay sy villey yiow shiu magh yn Ghlass ghuilley.*"
" When the wind is in the tree you will find the Lockman."

" *Daa Ghrogh eeck tayn geeck rolaue, as dyn geeck edyr.*"
" Two bad pays, pay beforehand, and no pay at all."

" *Gien nonney gortey.*"
" Feast or famine."

" *Freayl y craue glass.*"
" Keeping the bone green."

" *Surree eh yn flout, my yiow eh yn Glout.*"
" He will suffer the scoff if he'll get the prog."

" *Gow coyrl bleb son keayrt.*"
" Take the advice of a fool for once."

" *Gowee bleb rish e royllcy, as cha
Gow dooinney creeney rish e phlaiynt.*"
" A fool will receive praise, and a wise man will not re-
ceive rebuke."

" *Yn ogha gyllagh toyn losht da'n aiee.*"
" As the devil correcting sin."

"*Cha vow laue ny haaue veg.*"
"The idle hand gets nothing."

"*Eshyn ghuirrys skeilley hayr ys skeilley.*"
"He who broods evil shall be overtaken by it."
Or, "He who opens a ditch for another shall fall into it
himself."

"*Haghyr eh ny share na hiollee eh.*"
"It happened better than he deserved."

"*Goll thie yn ghoayr dy hirrey ollan.*"
"Going to the goat's house to seek for wool."

"*Lhig dy chooilley ushag guirr e hoohyn hene.*"
"Let every bird hatch its own eggs."

"*Lhig dy chooilley vuck reuyrey jee hene.*"
"Let every pig dig for herself."

There are numerous proverbs inculcating this sentiment,
that every man should be independent of his neighbour, as
the common saying, "Let every *tub* stand on its own bottom."
The French say, "*Chacun ira au moulin avec son propre sac.*"
"Every one must go to the mill with his own sack ;" that is,
bear his own burden. Some say, "Let every man soap his
own beard." "Let every pedlar carry his own burden."

"*Ta chengey ny host ny share na olk y ghra.*"
"The silent tongue is better than evil speaking."

"*Lhig da'n innagh lhie er y chione s'jerree.*"
"Let the woof rest upon the last end."

"*Eshyn lhieys marish moddee, irrys eh marish jarganyn.*"
"He who will lie down with dogs will rise up with fleas."

"*Jean traagh choud as ta'n ghrian soilshean.*"
"Make hay while the sun shines."

" *Ta rouyr chebbyn mic leodaghey mitchoor.*"
" Too many good offers disgust the rogue."

" *Cha daink ricau yn baase gyn leshtal.*"
" Death never came without an excuse."

" *Ta booa vie ny gha as drogh lheiy ee.*"
" Many a good cow hath but a bad calf."

" *Ta dty lhiasagh dty ghoarn.*"
" Thy recompense is in thine own hand."

" *Share goll dy lhie fegooish shibber na girree ayns lhiastynys.*"
" Better to go to bed supperless than to get up in debt."

" *Lhiat myr hoilloo.*"
" Success as thou deserves."

" *Litcheragh goll dy lhie, Litcheragh dy irree,*
As Litcheragh dy gholl dys y cheeill jedoonee."
" Lazy go to bed, lazy to rise ;
And lazy attending church on the Sabbath."

" *Yn loam leigh yn loam chair.*"
" The clean law, clean injustice."

" *Ta ny moddee er chur nyn gione sy phot.*"
" The dogs have put their head in the pot."

" *Rouyr moddee, as beggan craucyn.*"
" More dogs than bones."

" *My yial dy moll.*"
" How promise, how deceive."

The meaning is, that the man who is too ready to promise is often the first to forget his promise, or to deceive."

" *Mollee yn molteyr oo my oddys eh.*"
" The impostor will cheat you if he can."

"*Yiow moyrn lhieggey.*"
"Pride will have a fall."

"*Cha vel eh cheet jesh da moyrn, dy yannoo red erbee ta
laccal leshtal.*"
"It does not become pride to do what needs an apology."

"*Cadley ny moddee tra ta my mraane creearey.*"
"Dogs sleep when the women are sifting."

"*Mie Mannin, mie N'herin.*"
"Good in Mann, good in Ireland."

"*Share yn olk shione dooin, na yn olk nagh nhione dooin.*"
"Better the evil we know than the evil we do not know."

"*Cha bee breagery credit, ga dy ninsh eh y n'irriney.*"
"A liar will not be believed tho' he speaks the truth."

"*Obbyr dyn shirrey obbyr dyn booise.*"
"A gift unasked is a thankless gift."
Also it is said, "Proffer'd service stinks."

"*Tra tou jannoo yn trie jean yn oarlagh.*"
"When giving the foot, give the inch."

"*Obbyr laa yn ghuilley buigh or obbyr laue.*"
"The day work of the yellow lad—hand work."

"*Cha nee tra ta'n cheyrrey gee yn ouw te cheet r'ee.*"
"It is not when the sheep eats the marsh-penny-wort it
tells a tale."

It means slow poison is certain death.

"*Laa'l parlane, daa honn goll'sy nane.*"
"St. Bartholomew—two masses in one."

"*Ta daa Pharick jannoo un ghimmagh.*"
"Two small lobsters make a big one."

" *Boayl ta giocc ta kcck, as boayl ta mraanc ta plcat.*"
" Where there are geese there's dirt, and where there are
women there's talking."
It is also said, " Where there are women and geese there
wants no noise."

" *Tasht prughag as cc lughag.*"
" Store miser, and eat mouse."

" *Ta'n rcd ta goit dy mic,*
Ny sharc na'n rcd ta jcant dy mic."
" What's taken well is better than what's well done."

" *Cha ncc cshyn ta rcd bcg cchcy ta boght,*
Ayh cshyn ta yccarrcc mooaranc."
" It is not the man who has little that's poor,
But he who has all, yet pines after more."

" *Slaa sahll cr toyn muck roauyr.*"
" Daub grease upon the rump of a fat pig."
The Scotch say, " Every man flams the fat sow's a—."

" *Quoi erbcc s'bcayn cha bcayn y chcnndiaght.*"
" Whoever is durable, the aged will not be durable."

" *S'bcayn dagh olk.*"
" Every evil is durable."

" *S'banglancagh yn phy'agh.*"
" How branchy is the person."

Branchy, full of branches ; said of a person who professes
to know a great deal—a boaster ; one who assumes to have a
knowledge of all branches of science, etc. " How branchy
the fellow is !"

" *S'booiagh yn roght cr yn reggan.*"
" How willing is the beggar of the least alms."

" *Ta fuill ny s'chee ra ushtey.*"
" Blood is thicker than water."

" *Ta un cheyrey screbbagh mhilley yn slane shioltane.*"
" One scabby sheep infects the flock."

" *Tra scuirrys y laue dy choyrt scuirrys yn veeal dy roylley.*"
" When the hand ceases to give the tongue ceases to praise."

" *Myr s'doo yn feeagh yiow eh sheshey.*"
" Black as is the raven, he'll get a partner."

" *S'giare y jough na yn skeeal.*"
" A short story, but a long drink."

Is said when a person is desired to cease in his story and
pass the bottle.

" *Shaghyn dagh olk.*"
" Avoid all evil."

" *Sheayn dty hie as dty aaght ta'n fer-ghriaght ec dty ghorrys.*"
" Peace on thy house and lodging, the officer of justice is
at thy door."

" *Ta shehey chammah as ayrn.*"
" A companion is as good as a share."

" *Dy ve aashagh syn oie, monney shibber nagh ee ;*
Er nonney n'oo plaiynt ec laccal dty laynt."
" To be easy in bed, you must lightly be fed,
Or else you'll complain of your health being slain."

" *Shibber eddrym lhiabbee ghlen.*"
" A light supper makes an easy bed."

" *Myr sniessey da'n oie slhee mitchoor.*"
" The nearer the night, the more rogues."

" *S'loam ta laare y valley vargee.*"
" How empty the floor of the town market."

" *Tu kecayll ommidjys ny sloo ny t'ee ee dooinney creeney dy*
     reayll."
" Wisdom is folly unless a wise man guides it."

" *Guilley smuggagh dooinney glen,*
     Inneen smuggagh sluht dy ven."
" A snotty boy makes a clean man :
     A snotty girl a slattern of a woman."

" *S'mie ve daaney agh s'olk ve ro ghaaney."*
" 'Tis good to be forward, but bad to be too impudent."

" *Eshyn smoo hayrys, smoo vees echey."*
" The more a man catches the more he'll have."

" *Cha smooinee ricau er yn olk naght ren."*
" A man never thinks of the evil he did not do."

" *My s'olā ayn smessey ass."*
" If bad in, worse out."

" *T'an breagerey molley yn sonderey."*
" The liar will cheat even the miser."

" *Sooree ghiare, yn tooree share."*
" A short courtship is the best courtship."

" *Ta'n chied sponnag lowit."*
" The first error is overlook'd."

" *Tra sreaie yn chloie, share faayail jeh."*
" When the play is the merriest it is time to break up."

" *Myn smoo yn cheshaght, sreaie yn chloie."*
" The greater the company, the merrier the play."

" *Stiark keayrt ta dooinney siyragh ass seaghyn."*
" The hasty man is seldom out of trouble."

" *Stroshey yn thcay na yn Chiarn.*"
" The voice of the public is stronger than the Lord of the Manor's."

" *Tra ta thie dty naboo er aile gow cairail jeh dty hie hene.*"
" When thy neighbour's house is on fire, mind thine own."

" *Ta ushag ayns laue chammah asjees sy thammag.*"
" A bird in the hand is worth two in the bush."

" *Tou er y varney veayl.*"
" Thou art upon the brink of a precipice."

" *Lesh y vioys shegin jannoo.*"
" Struggle unto death, or with life we must work."

" *Ceau eraue ayns beeal drogh voddey.*"
" Throw a bone into a bad dog's mouth."

" *Baase y derrey voddey grayse y voddey elley.*"
" The death of one dog is the life of another."

" *Cha dennee rieau yn voyrn feayraght.*"
" The proud never felt cold—some say, felt pain."

" *Ta fys ec dy chooilley ghooinney c'raad t'an vraag gortagh eh.*"
" Every man knows where the shoe hurts him."

" *Ta'n vry erskyn y churnaght.*"
" The malt is better than the wheat."

" *Ta'n yeean myr e ghooie my vel clooie er e chione.*"
" The chicken is like its kind before down is on its head."

That is, the chicken fathers itself before it is fully fledged.
" The tree is known by its fruit."

GOLD ON CUSHAGS.

> " *Ta airh er cushagyn ayns shen.*"
> "There is gold on Cushags there."

Cushag is the Manx name of the rank weed Ragwort, which grows most luxuriantly in the Isle of Man. It is an ironical expression, often used when people talk disparagingly of the island and boastingly of other places, either where they have been, or where they purpose going to. Men frequently speak of other countries as the land of Goshen, where gold is so plentiful that it can be gathered off the very weeds of the field !

> " *Mceyl-chreen.*"
> " A flesh-worm."

A worm that burrows under a person's skin, causing great itch. It is said of it—

> " *Dy beagh ee er e bolg myr t'ee er e dreeym,*
> *Shimmey mac dooinney yinnagh ee harrish y cheym.*"
> " If it were on its belly as it is on its back,
> Many sons of men would it put over the style."

It is a prevailing idea that the itch and other irritating cutaneous diseases are caused by insects, or worms, under the skin. This insect is said to lie with its back towards the flesh, and its feet, or feelers, towards the skin, under which it creeps. It is supposed that if the position of the creature would be reversed, so that the insect would have its feet, or feelers, towards the flesh, it might then burrow into the flesh, and thereby cause the death of the person affected, whereby " many sons of men " (many people) " would be put over the style "—that is, would die, and would find their resting-place in the churchyard—"*over the style* " of the churchyard.

IMITATION OF THE SOUND OF KIRK ARBORY BELLS.

"*Shenn phott shenn ghryle,*
Shenn chlooid dy choodaghey yn aile."
"An old pot, an old griddle,
An old clout to cover the fire."

BALLA-SALLA.

' Four L's, four A's, an S, and a B,
Spells a nice village, as you may see."

The village of Balla-Salla is situated two miles north of Castletown, and near it are the ruins of Rushen Abbey. It was here, about the year 1781, that Abraham de la Pryme erected the first and only mill in the Isle of Man for spinning and weaving cotton. It was given up in 1791.

HERRINGS.

"No herring, no wedding."

At first sight it would appear there could be no connection between herrings and marriage, but when it is considered the great number of young men yearly engaged in the herring fishery in the Isle of Man, with whom a successful season is of the utmost importance, not only to them but to the expectant ones who are anxiously awaiting the result of the season, for on its productiveness, or otherwise, depends whether they are to be married or not—hence the saying, "No herring, no wedding." From an examination of the church registers may be learnt whether the fishing was productive or not by the number or paucity of entries of marriages. This is not confined to the Isle of Man alone. In the fishing districts of Scotland the same result takes place, for in the returns for the third quarter of the year

1871, the Registrar of Fraserburgh states that the herring-fishery was *very successful*, and the marriages were 80 per cent above the average. On the other hand, the Registrar of Tarbert reported a steady falling off in the fishing of that creek, and consequently the quarter passed without an entry in the marriage register. The Registrar of Lochgilphead also returns that the herring-fishery has been a failure in the loch, and states that this accounts for the blank in the marriage column.

> "What we lose in dog-fish we shall have in herring."
> "As straight as the backbone of a herring."

This is alluded to in the oath taken by the Deemsters and High Bailiffs of the Isle of Man, as mentioned in the first series of *Mona Miscellany*, p. 20. According to the Report of the Committee of Legislature, 22d February 1827, they state that " herrings in summer are caught to the south of the net, and in winter to the north of it."

In addition to what has been given in the first series of *Mona Miscellany* on the proverb, " In neither barrel, better herring," the following illustration is to be met with in an old author, John Heywood's *Proverbs and Epigrams* :—

> "A foule olde riche widowe, whether wed would ye,
> Or a yonge fayre mayde, being poore as ye be?
> 'In neither barrell better hearynge,' quoth hee."

And also in Stephen Gosson's *Schoole of Abuse*, 1579—

> "Therefore of both barrelles, I judge cookes and painters the better hearing."

CHARACTERISTICS OF THE SEVERAL TOWNS OF THE ISLE OF MAN.

BY A LADY.—In the early part of the present century.

PEEL	.	.	for Antiquity.
CASTLETOWN	.	.	„ Dignity.
RAMSEY	.	.	„ Scenery.
DOUGLAS	.	.	„ Malignity.

A Manx poet, writing about this time, remarks—

"Douglas, the seat of scandal,
Sours her own cup, and blasts the joys of life."

Whatever might have led to this characteristic of Douglas at that day, it is pleasant to know that at present it is distinguished for its "urbanity."

QUAINT SAYING ON A MEMBER OF THE OLD HOUSE OF KEYS.

"*Bee oo goll as dty vussal bane ort as cha bee reg ayd dy ghra agh.*"—"I am agreeable."

Which may be thus rendered :—"Thou will be going with thy white handkerchief on thee, and thou will have nothing to say but—'*I am agreeable.*'"

This was in allusion to the easy way some of the members were led without expressing an opinion of their own. The first reformed House is no improvement in this respect.

A SAYING ON COLQUITT.

"*She boircy ny cruinncy v'ch choud as v'eh bi∂.*"
"He was the plague of the world as long as he was alive."

This is said of Colquitt, called "Keoi" (mad Colquitt), one of the persons mentioned in the ballad of "Illiam Dhône."

On Tricky Fellows.

"*Hug eh chyndaa 'sy charr.*"
"He changed his note."

This is said of a man deserting his client after having first warmly espoused his cause.

"*Crén chluic ta 'sy hoinn.*"
"What a kick in his gallop ; a quirk or tricky fellow."

"*T'ch creoighey m'oi.*"
"He grows hard against me."

"*Lhiam—lhiat.*"
"With me—with thee." An inconstant person. It is also said—

"*Chengey lhiam, chengey lhiat.*"
"Tongue with me—tongue with thee."

Weather Sayings.

"The Isle of Man seen fair and clear,
Is a sign of westerly breezes here.
This is a weather proverb at Maryport, in Cumberland.

"A fox day." Deceitful weather, not to be depended on. Is a common expression in the Island, by which is meant a single fair day is sure to be closely pursued by a rainy one.

"*Cha jean un ghollan-gheayee sourey,
Ny un chellagh cheylley geurey.*"
"One swallow does not make a summer,
Nor one woodcock a winter."

"*Sheeu kishan dy yoan mayrnt maaill bleeaney rannin.*"
"A peck of March dust is worth a year's rent in the Isle of man."

A common saying is, A peck of March dust is worth a king's ransom.

> "*Three kegeeshyn dy chegeeshyn slane,*
> *Ta voish laa'l thomys sy nollick gys laa'l Breeshey bane.*"
>> "Three fortnights, or forty-two days,
>> From St. Thomas' to Candlemas."

> "*Laal' moirrey ny gianle, lieh foddyr as lieh aile.*"
> "On Candlemas day you must have half your straw and half your hay."

>> "*Laa'l Breeshey bane,*
>> *Dy choolley yeeig lane,*
>> *Dy ghoo ny dy vane.*"
>> "By Candlemas day,
>> Fill up every drain,
>> Both the black and the white."

> "*Choud as hig y seell-ghreinney stiagh Laa'l Breeshey, hig y sniaghtey my jig laa boayldyn.*"
> "As long as the sunbeam enters in on St. Bridget's day, the snow will come before May day."

It is also said—

>> "If Candlemas day be fair and bright,
>> Winter will have another flight;
>> If on Candlemas day it be shower and rain,
>> Winter is gone, and will not come again."

> "*Laa'l Paul ghorrinagh gheayee,*
> *Ghenney er y theihll as baase-mooar sleih ;*
> *Laa'l Paul aalin as glen,*
> *Palchey er y theihll dy arroo as meinn.*"
> "St. Paul's being tempestuous and windy,
> Brings famine and great mortality ;
> But St. Paul's being calm and clear,
> Brings plenty of corn and meal."

" *Laa'l Parick arree yn dow gys e staik as y dooinney gys e lhiabbee.*"

" On St. Patrick's day, the ox to his stake, and the man from his bed."

" *Giare shecar, liauyr shiar.*"

" Short west, long east."　　Alluding to the wind.

" *Oie mooie, as oie elley sthie,*
　　Olk son cabbil, agh son kirree mie."

" One night out and another night in
　　Is bad for horses, but good for sheep."

" *Ollick roy Rhullic rea.*"

" A wet Christmas, a rich churchyard."

" *Foddee fastyr grianagh ve ec moghrey bodjalagh.*"

" A sunny evening may follow a cloudy morning."

" *Yn chiuney smoo erbee geay jiass sniessey j'ee.*"

" Next to the greatest calm is the south wind."

" *Ny three geay-ghyn s'feayrey dennee, Fion M'Cooil,*
　　Geay hennen, as geay huill,
　　As geay fo ny shiauill."

" The three coldest winds that came to Fion M'Cooil,
　　Wind from a thaw, wind from a hole,
　　And wind from under the sails."

" *Tan rayrnt chionney as yn nah ree fanncy.*"

" March tightens, and April skins."

" *Ta Eayst jesarn sy rayrnt dy liooar ayns shiaght blecancy.*"

" A Saturday's moon in March is enough in seven years."

There was an old superstition in the Island that a Saturday's new moon was unlucky, but one occurring in March still more so. Once, then, in seven years would be often enough for such an event.

" *My ta'n Ghrian jiarg tra girree teh,*
  Foddee shiu jerkal rish fliaghey."
" If the sun is red when he rises you may expect rain."

" *Lane croie cabbyl dy ushtey laa'l Yoan feeu mayl Vannin.*"
  " A horse-shoe full of water on St. John's day is worth the
  rent of the Isle of Man."

Aged Manx people, when they wish for particular weather
at the approach of the different seasons of the year, say—

" *Arragh chayccagh.*"—" A misty spring."
" *Sourey ouyragh.*"—" Gloomy summer."
" *Fouyr ghrianagh.*"—" Sunny autumn."
" *As geurey rioeeagh.*"—" A frosty winter."

MANX MOTTO.

Several remarks on the arms and motto of the Isle of
Man appeared in the first series of *Mona Miscellany.* The
following is the Manx of the motto :—

" *Quocunque jeceris stabit*"—
" *Raad erbee cheau oo eh nee eh shassoo.*"

BALLADS AND SONGS.

"I love a ballad in print."

SHAKSPEARE.

BALLADS AND SONGS.

TRADITIONARY BALLAD.

THIS is from a copy printed in Train's *History of the Isle of Man* (vol. i. pp. 50-55, Douglas, 1845), with these remarks :—
"The following curious ballad, which is now for the first time translated into English, was composed in the Manks language. The date of printing has been obliterated from the copy in my possession, which I believe to be extremely scarce ; but the writer, as appears from the last three verses, lived during the time of Thomas, second Earl of Derby, whose landing in the island in 1507 he describes. This Earl succeeded his grandfather in A.D. 1504, and died in 1521, between which dates the ballad has evidently been written."

"The translation of the lines as they stand in the Manks song is without any regard to the poetry in English."

MANNANAN BEG, MAC Y LEIRR,
NY SLANE COONTEY JEH ELLAN VANNIN;

Soilshaghey crén mayll vér ny Mannanee da Mannanan; kys ren Noo Parick eshyn y imman ersooyl as e Heshaght; kys hug Parick ayn Creestiaght; as coontey jeh ny chied Aspickyn va'syn Ellan.

Myrgeddin coontey jeh'n chied Ree va Mannin, as e Lhuight; coontey jey ny Chiarnyn; as kys kaink yn Ellan gys Clein Stanley.

I.

Dy neaishtagh shin agh rish my skeayll,
    As dy ving lhieu ayns my chant;
Myr share dy voddyms lesh my veeal,
    Yinnin diu geill dán ellan sheeant.

II.

Quoi yn chied er ec row rieau ee,
    Ny kys eisht myr haghyr da;
Ny kys hug Parick ayn Creestiaght,
    Ny kys myr haink ee gys Stanlaa.

III.

Manannan beg va mac y Leirr,
    Shen yn chied er ec row rieau ee;
Agh myr share oddym's cur-my-ner,
    Cea row ch hene agh an-chreestee.

IV.

Cha nee lesh e Chliwe ren ch ee reayll
    Cha nee lesh e Hideyn, ny lesh e vhow;
Agh tra aikagh eh lhuingys troailt
    Oallagh ch ee my geayrt lesh kay.

LITTLE MANNANAN, SON OF LEIRR,
OR AN ACCOUNT OF THE ISLE OF MAN;

Showing what rent the Manx inhabitants paid to Mannanan; and how St. Patrick banished him and his company away; and how St. Patrick established Christianity first in the island.

Also an account of the first king that was in the island, and his posterity, and how the island came to the Stanley family.

I.

IF you would listen to my story,
 I will pronounce my chant
As best I can; I will, with my mouth,
 Give you notice of the enchanted island.

II.

Who he was that had it first,
 And then what happened to him;
And how St. Patrick brought in Christianity,
 And how it came to Stanley.

III.

Little Mannanan was son of Leirr,
 He was the first that ever had it;
But as I can best conceive,
 He himself was a heathen.

IV.

It was not with his sword he kept it,
 Neither with arrows or bow;
But when he would see ships sailing,
 He would cover it round with a fog.

V.

Yinnagh ch doinney ny hassoo er brooghe,
　　Er-lhieu shen hene dy beagh ayn keead ;
As shen myr dreill Mannanan keole,
　　Yn ellan shoh'n-ayn lesh cosney bwoid.

VI.

Yn mayll deeck dagh unnane ass e cheer,
　　Va bart dy leaogher ghlass dagh blein ;
As eisht shen orroo d'eeck myr keesh,
　　Trooid magh ny cheery dagh oie-lhoine.

VII.

Paart ragh lesh y leoagher scose,
　　Gys yn slieau mooar ta heose Barrool ;
Paart elley aagagh yn leoagher wass,
　　Ec Mannanan erskyn Keamool.

VIII.

Myr shen eisht ren adsyn beaghey,
　　O er-lhiam pene dy by-veg nyn Geesh ;
Gyn kiarail as gyn imnea,
　　Ny doggyr dy lhiggey er nyn skeeys.

IX.

Eisht haink ayn Parick nyn meayn,
　　She dooinney-noo véh lane dy artue,
Dimman ch Mannanan er y tonn,
　　As e grogh vooinjer dy lich-chiart.

X.

As jeusyn ooilley dy row olk,
　　Oroo cha ren ch veg y ghrayse ;
Dy row jeh sluight ny buch-chrout,
　　Nagh ren ch strooie as coyrt dy baase.

V.

He would set a man, standing on a hill,
 Appear as if he were a hundred ;
And thus did wild Mannanan protect
 That island with all its booty.

VI.

The rent each landholder paid to him was
 A bundle of coarse meadow grass yearly ;
And that, as their yearly tax,
 They paid to him each midsummer eve.

VII.

Some would carry the grass up
 To the great mountain up at Barrool ;
Others would leave the grass below,
 With Mannanan's self above Keamool.

VIII.

Thus then did they live ;
 O, I think their tribute very small,
Without care and without anxiety,
 Or hard labour to cause weariness.

IX.

Then came Patrick into the midst of them ;
 He was a saint, and full of virtue ;
He banished Mannanan on the wave,
 And his evil servants all dispersed.

X.

And of all those that were evil,
 He showed no favour nor kindness,
That were of the seed of the conjurors,
 But what he destroyed or put to death.

XI.

Vannee ch'n cheer veih kione dy kione,
  As rieau cha daag eh boght ayn-jee ;
Dy row jeh lhiurid lhannoo beg,
  Dy dob rieau dy ve ny Creestee.

XII.

Shen myr haink y chied Chredjue Mannin,
  Ec Parick noo er ny chur ayn ;
As Creest dy niartagh aynin eh,
  As neesht myrgeddin ayns nyn gloan.

XIII.

Eisht vannee Parick Karmane noo,
  As deag eh eh ny aspick ayn ;
Dy niartagh yn credjue ny smoo as ny smoo,
  As caballyn ren eh anrick ayn.

XIV.

Ayns dagh treen balley ren eh unnane,
  D'an sleih shen ayn dy heet dy ghuee ;
Myrgeddin ren eh Keeill Charmane,
  Ta ayns y pheeley foast ny sole.

XV.

My dug Karmane er e obbyr kione,
  Hug Jee fys er as hooar eh baase ;
Myr shoyn diu hene yn chaghter chion
  Cha vel fer ain hed jeh-lesh saase.

XVI.

Hooar eshyn baase as teh ny lhie,
  Raad by vooar y treih ve cha leah er n'in im shley
Crosh dy chlagh te'e e gha chass,
  Ayns e Cheeill hene foast ayns y Pheeley.

XI.

He blessed the country from end to end,
 And never left a beggar in it;
And also cleared off all those
 That refused or denied to become Christians.

XII.

Thus it was that Christianity first came to Man,
 By Saint Patrick planted in,
And to establish Christ in us,
 And also in our children.

XIII.

He then blessed Saint German,
 And left him a bishop in it,
To strengthen the faith more and more,
 And faithfully built chapels in it.

XIV.

For each four quarterlands he made a chapel
 For people of them to meet to prayer;
He also built German church in Peel Castle,
 Which remaineth there until this day.

XV.

Before German had finished his work
 God sent for him, and he died;
As ye yourselves know that this messenger
 Cannot be put off by using means.

XVI.

He died, and his corpse was laid
 Where a great bank had been, but soon was
 levelled;
A cross of stone is set at his feet
 In his own church in Peel Castle.

XVII.

Eisht haink Maughold ayn myr beer,
　　As ghow eh Thalloo ec y Chione;
As hrog eh keeill as rollick mygeart,
　　Yn ynnyd by-vian lesh beaghey ayn.

XVIII.

Ny caballyn doardee Karmane noo,
　　D'an sleih shen-ayn dy heet dy ghuee;
Hug Maughold shiartanse jeu ayns unnane,
　　As myr shen ren eh skeeraghyn cooie.

XIX.

Hooar Maughold baase as tèh ny lhie,
　　Ayns e cheeill hene neesht ec y Chione;
As y nah aspick hank ny-yei,
　　Myr share shioune dooys she eh va Lonnan.

XX.

Connaghan yn nah er eisht haink ayn,
　　A haink Marooney reesht yn trass;
T'ad shen nyn droor ayns keill Marooney,
　　As ayns shen vees ad dy bra vaght.

XXI.

Nish lhig mayd shaghey ny deinney-noo,
　　As chymney mayd nyn Anmeeyn gys Mac Yee,
Cha nheeu fir agglish voylley ny smoo,
　　Derrey lhig ad fenish Ree dagh ree.

XXII.

Myr shen eisht ren adsyn beaghey,
　　Gyn dooinney ayn yinnagh orroo corree;
Agh goll dy gheddyn pardoon veih'n Raue,
　　Er'-derry haink eh huc Ree Gorree.

XVII.

Then came Maughold, we are told,
    And came on shore at the Head,
And built a church and yard around,
    At the place he thought to have his dwelling.

XVIII.

The chapels which Saint German ordered
    For the people to come to prayers in them,
Maughold put a parcel of them into one,
    And thus made regular parishes.

XIX.

Maughold died, and he is laid
    In his own church at Maughold Head ;
And the next bishop that came after,
    To the best of my knowledge, was Lonnan.

XX.

Connaghan then came next,
    And then Marown the third ;
There all three lieth in Marown,
    And there for ever lieth unmolested.

XXI.

Now we will pass by these holy men,
    And commit their souls to the Son of God.
It profiteth not to praise them more
    Until they appear before the King of kings.

XXII.

Thus then did they live or pass their time,
    No man that would molest or anger them ;
But going to get a pardon from Rome,
    Until there came to them King Gorree,

XXIII.

Lesh e lhuingys hrean as pooar y ree,
  As ghow eh thalloo ec y Laane ;
Shen y chied er ec row rieau ee,
  Dy ve ny ree er yn ellan.

XXIV.

Cha geayll mee dy ren eh skielley ec purt,
  Chamoo ren eh marroo ayn jee ;
Agh aym ta sis dy daink jeh sluight,
  Three reeaghyn jeig jeh Ree Gorree.

XXV.

Eisht hank ayn Quinney as haink ayn Quaill,
  Haink towse dy lheigh as reill ayn jee ;
Ny keeshyn mooarey as y mayll
  Vees dy hirrey dy bragh er dooinney dy bee.

XXVI.

My ta red erbee jannoo skielley diu,
  Cur-jee nyn mollaght er Mannanee ;
She ad by-vessey d'an ellan sheeant,
  Ec dagh drogh leigh 'yannoo ayn jee.

XXVII.

Eisht haink ayn Ollister mooar mac ree Albey,
  Lesh lhuingys hrean dy braue ayn jee ;
As er-lhiam pene dy by-voo lesh foalsaght,
  Cha nee lesh dunallys smoo chragh eh ee.

XXVIII.

Cha daag eh bio jeh sluight y ree,
  Mac ny inneen d'ymmyrkey kiona ;
Agh ad unnane myr baare dod ee,
  Hie dy hirrey cooney gys ree Goal.

XXIII.

With his strong ships and king's command,
    And came on shore at the Lhane.
He was the first that ever had it,
    To be a king of the island.

XXIV.

I never heard that he did any injury at a harbour,
    Neither did he kill any in the island ;
But I know that there came of his race
    Thirteen kings of King Gorree.

XXV.

Then there came Quinney, and then came Quayle,
    There came a measure of law and rule,
With greater taxes and greater rents,
    Which will for ever be demanded of the men that be.

XXVI.

If anything doeth you harm,
    Give your curse upon the Manxmen ;
They were the worst for the enchanted island,
    By making each bad law in her.

XXVII.

Then came great Ollister, son of the king of Scotland,
    With strong shipping he bravely came ;
But I think myself it was more by falsehood,
    And not by courage he made most havoc.

XXVIII.

He left not living, of the king's seed,
    A son or daughter to carry his head,
Excepting one, who, as best she could,
    Went to seek for help to the king of France.

XXIX.

O Albanee my vow uss feeu,
    As dy haghter oc dy heet ayn ;
Cammah nagh durree oo as ve dy ree,
    Myr vow, O ree! as mac Ree Laughlin.

XXX.

Agh s'beg eh lhiam, dy veg eh lhiat,
    Ny fee 've rock, rock erskyn dy ching ;
Agh lhig dooys loayrt jeh'n in neen gring,
    Neeayr as nagh daag oo bio agh ee ;
Haink jeh sluight Ree Laughlin,
    As v'ec inneen da Ree Gorree.

XXXI.

Chia leah as chragh y noid y cheer,
    Nagh jagh eh roish as daag eh ee ;
Myr yinnagh y sowin choo rish e quallan,
    Eh aagail ny lhie er beggan bree.

XXXII.

Cha leah as cragh y noid y cheer,
    Nagh jagh eh roish noon gys Nolbin ;
As ghow ish lhuingys neesht myr beer,
    As lhie ee rhimbee gys ree Hoocsyn.

XXXIII.

Cha leah as raink ee gys y choort,
    Ren eh j'ec soiagh dy seer choar ;
As daa ny deiney haink maree,
    Hug y ree palchey dargid's dóar.

XXXIV.

Nagh ren eh fenaght j'ee quoi v'ee,
    Ny cre vo heilkin gys e choort ;
To mish dooyrt un inneen da ree,
    Erreish ve spooilt as gyn kiannoort.

XXIX.

O Scotchman! if thou wert worthy,
    And as a messenger when thou didst come,
Why didst thou not stop and be our king,
    As thou, O king! wert son of King Laughlin?

XXX.

But I care but little, that thou thought'st it little,
    The ravens to croak, croak above thy head;
But let me speak of the mentioned girl,
    Since thou didst not leave alive but she,
Of all the seed of King Laughlin,
    And she was daughter to King Gorree.

XXXI.

As soon as the enemy spoiled the country,
    Did he not go away and leave it?
As the she greyhound would do with her whelp,
    And leave him lying with little strength.

XXXII.

As soon as the enemy spoiled the country,
    Did he not go over to Scotland?
And she took shipping, and to the best that I know,
    Went over to the king of England.

XXXIII.

As soon as she arrived at court,
    He entertained her with great kindness;
And to the men that came with her
    He gave plenty of silver and gold.

XXXIV.

He then asked her who she was,
    Or what her business to the court;
She answered, I am a king's daughter,
    I have been robbed, and without a protector.

XXXV.

She mysh dty vyghin as dty ghrayse,
　　Ta mish nish lhoobey hoods, O ree ;
Cha vel mee geearee mie ny maase,
　　Agh gecaree ort dty chymmey ree.

XXXVI.

She dty vea hooin, dooyrt ree Hocsyn,
　　As ren eh poosey ish myr beeu ;
Vee sluight Laughlin, inneen Gorree,
　　Rish Sir William dy Vountegue.

XXXVII.

Eisht Sir William va ree Vannin,
　　Cha hoie eh jee agh beggan feeu ;
Son chreck eh ee as ghow eh maase,
　　O ree red bastagh dy ren rieau.

XXXVIII.

Rish yn Chiarn Scroop chreck eshyn ee,
　　O ree, nagh moal hug saynt da maase ;
Ga ve ayns foayr mooar rish y ree,
　　Gerrit ny-yei hur eshyn baase.

XXXIX.

Agh fys nyn gooishyn cha vel aym,
　　Lhig danesyn sailliu fyfferee ;
Agh aym ta sys er shoh dy feer,
　　Dy row lane maase seihlt ec y ree.

XL.

Haink yn ellan eisht gys y ree,
　　Conaant Scroop myr shoh dy jarroo,
Nagh beagh ny sodjey echey j'ee
　　Ny veagh e vio-hys er y thalloo.

XXXV.

It is to thy mercy and thy grace,
 That I do humbly sue to thee, O king ;
I do not ask for good or wealth,
 But crave of thee for thy pity, O king.

XXXVI.

Welcome to us, says the king of England,
 And he married her very soon ;
She was of the seed of Laughlin, the daughter
  of King Gorree,
 By Sir William of Montague.

XXXVII.

Then Sir William was king of the Isle of Man,
 But he thought but little of it ;
For he sold it, and bought cattle,
 Which was a pity that ever he did.

XXXVIII.

To Lord Scroop he sold it ;
 O king, how simple to covet cattle.
Although he was in great favour with the king.
 It was but a short time until he suffered death.

XXXIX.

But their matters I do not know ;
 Let those who please prophesy ;
But this I know right well,
 That the king had a vast number of cattle.

XL.

Then the island came to the king ;
 Scroop's covenant appointed so,
That he should have no more of it
 Than during his life on earth.

XLI.

Haink yn ellan reesht gys y ree,
    As mooar y bree cha row echey ayn ;
Hug eh da Earl Northumberland ee,
    Agh cha dug eh ee da e chloan.

XLII.

Adsyn veagh dunnal ayns caggey,
    Yioghe ad giootyn mooar myr bailliu ;
Agh ayns caggey mooar Salisbury,
    Va Earl Northumberland er ny varroo.

XLIII.

Quoi hagher eisht gys y vagher,
    Agh Sir Juan Stanley cosney bwoid ;
Myr by-vannee haink er y laa,
    Lesh e chliwe geyre ve sheer goll trooid.

XLIV.

My ree, by-veg er hene nyn mea,
    Yiaragh eh dooinney sheese dyn glare ;
Varragh eh lesh un vuilley shleiy,
    Cabbyl as dooinney gys y laare.

XLV.

Cre dy aase veagh claiggin e ching,
    Gyn king cha ragh eh-aas ;
Ny cre by eillit veagh e ghreem,
    Roashagh e chliwe geyre e chress.

XLVI.

Tra scuirr y magher, as gow eh fea,
    Eisht boggey mooar ayn hene ghow'n ree ;
As deie eh huggey Sir Juan Stanley,
    Dy ghoail eh leagh jeh maase as nhee.

XLI.

The island then came to the king ;
    But he had no great authority in it,
Because he gave it to the Earl of Northumberland ;
    But he did not give it to his children.

XLII.

Those that would be courageous in wars
    Would get great presents if they would ;
But in the great war at Salisbury,
    The Earl of Northumberland was killed.

XLIII.

Who happened then to come to the field,
    But Sir John Stanley, well fitted ;
As that day proved a blessing to him,
    As he went by with his sharp sword.

XLIV.

My king, he little thought of life ;
    He would cut a man down without speaking ;
He would, with one blow of spear,
    Take to the ground both man and horse.

XLV.

Whatever growth his head might be,
    Without heads he would not go away ;
Or however harnessed his back might be,
    His sharp sword would reach his girdle.

XLVI.

When the field was quiet, and had taken rest.
    There the king rejoiced greatly himself ;
And he called to him Sir John Stanley,
    To take his pledge of cattle and goods.

XLVII.

Kyndagh dy vel us er my rere,
    Sheer cosney bwoid dooys, as dhty hene ;
Gow son dy leagh Ellan Vannin,
    Son leagh dy hogher dy bragh beayn.

XLVIII.

Shen myr haink yn ellan gys nyn laue,
    As shen myr haink Clein Stanley ayn ;
As ree lurg ree freayal shin veih gaue,
    As mooarane bleeantyn chiarnane ayn.

XLIX.

Eisht tra hooar Sir Juan Stanley baase,
    Haink reesht Sir Juan geyrt er e vac ;
Va mooarane blein heear ayns Neirin,
    Ny lieutenant feer ooasse oc.

L.

Eisht haink Thomase Derby ruggerey ree,
    Eh-hene va ceau yn cribble oar ;
Cha row un chiarn ayns Socsyn 'sthie,
    Lesh whilleen gymman-glioon cheet ny chear.

LI.

En Albanee choilleen eh clea,
    As hie eh noon gys Keel Choobragh ;
As ren eh lheid y chladdagh thien,
    Dy vel paart ayn foast gyn mullagh.

LII.

Nagh bwaagh shen dasyn dooinney aeg,
    Yn clea chooilleen my by-voar e ghraine ;
Roish haink ricau er o ghob faasaag,
    As e ghciney 'chur lesh as dy slane.

XLVII.

Because thou hast served me well,
 And gained booty for me and thyself,
Take for thy portion the Isle of Man,
 To be for thee and thine for ever.

XLVIII.

Thus the island came to their hands,
 And thus the Stanleys' name came in ;
And king after king keeping us from danger,
 And many years lords in it.

XLIX.

Then when Sir John Stanley died,
 Then came again Sir John, his son,
Who had been many years in Ireland,
 A very noble lieutenant there.

L.

Then came Thomas Derby, born king ;
 'Twas he that wore the golden crupper.
There was not one lord in England itself
 With so many knee-guineamen coming in his country.

LI.

On Scotchmen he revenged himself,
 And he went over to Kirkcudbright,
And there made such havoc of houses,
 That some of them are yet unroofed.

LII.

Was not that pretty in a young man
 To revenge himself while he was but young,
Before his beard had grown round his mouth,
 And to carry his men home with him whole ?

LIII.

Ayns un thousane queig cheead as shiaght,
    She ayns mee ny boaldiney ve ;
Ghow eh thalloo ayns Roonyssvie,
    Er boirey'n theay hug eh slane fea.

LIV.

Lheid y thie as dreill eshyn hene,
    Dy ree ny ruggerey dy hreg ny hrean ;
Cha vaik sleih lhied rish milley blein,
    Chamoo hee reesht 'syn carish ain.

LV.

Agh arragh dy voylley cha jean yms ny smoo,
    Choud as sbooie dooiney seanish my hooill ;
Er-aggle dy dagher daue rhym y ghra,
    Dy nee son leagh vein sheer brinooile.

LVI.

Agh faag-ym da'n nah ghooinney hig my yei
    Dy voylley hene myr sheagh chur da ;
Tra vees e chress ny lhie 'syn oaie,
    Yiew'n dooinney bwoid myr sheagh cur da.

LIII.

In one thousand five hundred and seven,
  And it was in the month of May,
He came on shore at Derbyhaven,
  And put a full end to the commotion of the public.

LIV.

Such a house as he kept himself,
  For a king, or down to a low degree,
People never saw for countless years,
  Neither will again in our days.

LV.

But any more praise I will not give
  So long as I live among men,
For fear they may tell me
  That it is for gain I make so much flattery.

LVI.

But I leave the man that cometh after me
  To praise him as he will find him worth.
When his crest will be laid in the grave,
  He will get the glory he deserved to have.

CUTLAR MACCULLOCH.

A DIALOGUE between a Manx housewife and her husband, wherein is shown why the Kirk Bride people eat their meat before they sup their broth ; and wherein is likewise recorded one of the surprising feats of the renowned Galloway chieftain, Cutlar MacCulloch.

Huan.—"Jean siyr * ven y thie" †—pack up and away,
    Cutlar MacCulloch will be here to-day.

Sheval.—The Galloway chief !—it never can be ;
    He's chasing the herring-boats out at sea.
        The breeze blows fresh,
        'Tis off the land—
    The sea-king hath other work in hand.

Huan.—Siyrree,‡ ven y thie, or, as I'm a sinner,
    MacCulloch will surely be first to dinner ;
    I saw his broad sail as I stood on the brow,
    And he'll only be here too soon I trow ;
        So up and away
        While yet we may,
    His flotilla stands for Ramsey Bay.

Sheval.—Augh, the breeze blows fresh, and the sea is rough,
    To-morrow will surely be "time enough !"
    Ben Varrey§ hath bound the broad beach with a chain,
    To-day is the wedding of Mylecharane !
        There's broth and there's mutton,
        The table to put on,
    And the barn floor swept, the dancers to foot on.

---

* Jean siyr.—Make haste.

† Ven y thie.—Housewife, woman of the house.

‡ Siyrree.—Make royal speed.

§ Ben Varrey.—Mermaid. Hath bound with a chain.—The myth here alluded to is, that the sunlight flashes on the ripple of the sea wavelet (as it breaks on the pebbly beach at high water) are jewels airing, and being prepared to adorn the hair of the mermaids on festive occasions. When these chains are

Huan.—O list what I say ! for 'tis no joke,
 Cutlar MacCulloch hath seen the smoke ; *
 And if you wait longer on *Traa dy-liooar,*†
 The Galloway men will darken our door,
  Seize on the victual,
  Lift all the cattle,
 And knock down the boys who show any mettle.

Sheval.—Well, haste then from church, an' I'll hurry the feast ;
 We'll eat all we can, and we'll drink of the best ;
 Then the rovers may step ashore when the tide flows,
 And be welcome to bones with a sauce of hard blows.
  There's the Dhooney Moar,
  Yourself, and a score,
 Will pin these catherans down to the floor.

Huan.—Your counsel is good, and your spirit is bold ;
 That Manxmen have faint hearts shall never be told.

in full sparkle, strict watch is kept on the adjacent cliff or crag that no marauder approach unawares. Should any monster of the sea or land prove too wary to be enticed away by the wiles of the syrens, or too strong to be successfully resisted, the mermaids instantly dive down to their sparry caves, the jewels vanish, and a dark shadow is thrown over the whole line of wave. These water-sprites and fairies will, on rare occasions, unite for the protection of some mutual interest ; moved either by enmity against such rude syren-despisers as Cutlar MacCulloch, or in a caprice of friendship for some fair daughter of earth's mould, and then the spell-bound shore cannot be approached ; but their favour is unstable as the elements. There is a similar superstition among the Arabs of the Red Sea.

* *Seen the smoke.*—The smoke from the Kirk Bride chimneys can be seen on a fine summer's day on the Scotch coast opposite. The tradition is that Cutlar and his crew watched for this proof that good cooking was going on amongst their better-fed neighbours, and at the desired signals pushed off from the shore, and generally accomplished the run across in time to seize the good cheer, for which the hospitable Manx were celebrated, and then proceeded to carry off everything that lay convenient. On more than one occasion these freebooters arrived at the identical moment described in the ballad.

† The husband's remonstrance on his wife's procrastination passed into a proverb—" Traa dy-liooar " denoting irretrievable delay.

A fig for MacCulloch! so bring out the wine,
And ask Dhooney Moar to come hither and dine.
He shall sit by Jean,
His heart's bragh queen,
And drink jough vie to his "vuddy-veg-veen."

I'll look to the corn, the sheep, and the bullock,
And keep them from witches and Cutlar MacCulloch.
How long shall the robber-chief come with his levy,
And carry off all not too hot and too heavy?
Too late to be running
When Cutlar is coming—
Sheval.—O, Ven Varrey's out, and she'll rule the tonney.*

Huan.—'Twould soften the heart of a man full of wrath,
To see your kind face and smell your good broth,
But here comes the wedding-train, blithesome and
grand,
All ready for dinner, so lend me a hand,
And here fix the table,
We'll eat all we're able;
MacCulloch may go to the fish with his cable.

The noggins of broth had gone merrily round,
The spoon was just plunged in the haggis profound,
Each trencher was stretched for a share of the cheer,
When, "Hark to the tramp, oh, MacCulloch is here!
Boys! spring to your feet;
Girls! hide all the meat,
We'll soon make the vagabonds sound a retreat."

MacCulloch stepped over the threshold the while,
And gazed on the plentiful board with a smile;

---

* Rule the tonney.—Rule the waves.

" Gudefolk, gudefolk, ye hurry too late,
MacCulloch is here, and his ship at the Yate.*
For broth he don't care,
The broth he can spare,
But haggis and mutton are MacCulloch's share."

The rovers were many, the wedding-guests few,
So the rovers sat down to the mutton and stew ;
But from that day to this, as our north custom tells,
We trust neither to wind, nor to mermaid spells,
But first of all eat
Our coveted meat,
And, over the broth, tell of MacCulloch's feat.

* The Yate is a well-known landing place in the north of the Isle of Man.

This ballad is printed in Miss Cookson's *Legends of Manx Land,* second series ; Douglas, 1859. The custom is alluded to in the first part of *Mona Miscellany.* It is the composition of an old resident, and one well acquainted with the traditions of the country.

THAPSAGYN JIARGEY.

MANX AIR.

THAPSAGYN JIARGEY.

This old song was formerly a great favourite, evidently alluding to some peculiar style of head-dress. The air to which it was sung was also adapted to a Manx dance then in vogue. A translation is given. Ree or Lord was a common name on the hills at Lezayre some sixty or seventy years ago.

I.

Yion thapsagyn jiargey, as rybbanyn green,
As Betsy veg villish, my vees oo lhiam pene.

> *Chorus.*—Robin y ree, Robin ye ree ridlan,
> Aboo, Aban,
> Fal dy ridlan,
> Aboo, Aban,
> Robin y ree.

II.

Yion thapsagyn jiargey, as rybbanyn ghoo,
Neem Queen y Thouree jeed, foddee oo loo.
Robin y ree, etc.

III.

Oh! Vetsy veg villish, nee oo brishey my chree,
Tad gra dy vel oo sooree er Robin y ree.
Robin y ree, etc.

RED TOP-KNOTS.

I.

THOU'LL get red top-knots and green ribbons,
My sweet little Betsy, if thou'll be my own.

> *Chorus.*—Robin the king, Robin the king riddle,
> Aboo, Aban,
> Fal dy riddle,
> Aboo, Aban,
> Robin the king.

II.

Thou'll get red top-knots and black ribbons,
I'll make thee Queen of May, I swear to thee.
> Robin the king, etc.

III.

Oh! my sweet little Betsy, thou'll break my heart,
They say thou art courting Robin the king.
> Robin the king, etc.

Dr. WILLIAM WALKER, LL.D.

Dr. William Walker was the son of a poor widow who lived at the south part of the island, and was educated at the Castletown academy, became rector of St. Mary's, Ballaugh, and vicar-general of the diocese of Sodor and Man. He was imprisoned in Castle Rushen, along with Bishop Wilson, in 1722, by order of Governor Horne. It was during that period they formed the plan of translating the New Testament into the Manx language. Dr. Walker lies buried in Ballaugh church, and the following epitaph, inscribed on a flat stone, was written by Bishop Wilson :—

GULIELMUS WALKER, LL.D.
HUJUSCE ECCLESIÆ RECTOR
PER ANNOS XXV.
E VICARIIS GENERALIBUS
NEC NON NOBILISS. DOMINO A CONCILIIS,
PASTOR, JUDEX, CIVIS,
QUO NEMO FIDELIOR, ÆQUIOR,
AUT BONI PUBLICI STUDIOSIOR,
MANSUM OMNIAQUE RECTORIA
EDIFICIA PRORSUS DILAPSA
PERMAGNO SUMPTU RESTAURAVIT.
OBIIT 18TH JUNII, A.D. MDCCXXIX.
ÆTAT. XLIX.

His mother, the writer of the following lines, was unfortunate in her second marriage, but continued to reside in the Doctor's house. The Rev. Hugh Stowell, in his *Life of Bishop Wilson*, 1819, speaks highly of Dr. Walker, and says "this interesting poem in the Manx language, in honour of this excellent man, of which a few fragments are yet found amongst the aged inhabitants of the parish. The composition is not altogether in the spirit of Ossian's poems, yet it has obtained its full share of rustic praise, and has been sung and sung again in unison, not with the harp of former days, but with the less melodious notes of the spinning-wheel. The following verse, so descriptive of his character, is often repeated with strong marks of approbation :—

" Bannaght ny moght, scaa ny mraane tregohe,
    Fendeilagh chloan gyn ayr,
    Da ny annooinee Dreem nagh goghe,
    Veih Treince dewil aggair.

He to the poor a blessing proved,
Their refuge and their friend ;
The orphan's and the widow's cause,
Still ready to defend."

I am enabled to give an entire version of this from an old MS. copy, with a translation by Mr. John Quirk, in which he has pretty closely followed the spirit of the original.

I am not able to record anything of her son Robert Tear. Several of that family will be found interred in Kirk Braddan churchyard, as mentioned in the *Monumental Inscriptions*, Manx Society, vol. xiv., 1868.

A SORROWFUL DITTY ON THE DEATH OF HER
TWO SONS, the Rev. WILLIAM WALKER, LL.D., Vicar-
General of the Diocese of Sodor and Mann, and Rector of
Ballaugh ; and Mr. ROBERT TEAR of Douglas.

By WIDOW TEAR of Ballaugh.

I.

Roish my row mee ricau my voir,
Lmaynrey vaar mee eisht my hraa ;
My chree gyn loght, my chione gyn feiyr,
My eddin lane dy vlaa.

II.

My aigney scyr veih laad chiarail,
Sthill aashagh oie as laa ;
Agh nish my gherjagh tér valleil
My chree ta brisht dy braa.

III.

As tra ren mee my stayd chaghlaa,
Hug Jee dou bannaght cloan ;
Hrog mee ad seose dy voddym ghra,
Nagh row nyn lheid agh goaun.

IV.

Ayns aggle yee lesh ynsagh vie
Dy aalin as dy glen ;
As yerk mee roo dy chooney lhiam,
Tra veign annoon as shenn.

V.

Dy insh jeh'n egin va mee ayn,
Troggal myr shoh my chloan ;
Cha voddym scrieu's te doillee ginsh,
Yn egin shen lesh goan.

VI.

Arkys as seme ghow orrym gremu
Haink saggys gys my chree ;
Ny-yeih cha daink my raad yn chrein,
Er-derrey daag ad mee.

VII.

Er yn edjag-sereenee Robbin va,
Ny vainshtyr ard ayns schleï ;
As v'eshyn gaase dy chooilley laa,
Ny smoo ayns coontey sleih.

VIII.

Symbyl jehn yusagh vér e lane,
Daag eh ayns banc as doo ;
Nee freayl e chooinaght fud sheeluane,
Er voalley ghial Cheeill-Chroo.

IX.

Illiam pessyn Cheeill Voirrey va,
Bochilley chiaralagh Chreest ;
Lane yesh yn Aspick, sooill yesh y theay,
Brin ny Hagglish neésht.

X.

Bannaght ny moght, scaa ny mraane hreoghe,
Fendeillagh cloan gyn ayr ;
Da ny hannoonee dreeym nagh goghe,
Veih tréanee ghewill aggair.

XI.

As ga dy row e churrym mooar,
Va e chreenaght corrym rish ;
As er goo mie e hoïltyn hooar,
Cooyrt recoil Hostyn fys.

XII.

Veih hooar eh ooashley's eunyn noa
Ny mast 'ain joarree roie ;
Lheid's nagh dooar Manninagh bio,
As scoan hooar lheid ny-yeih.

XIII.

E hoilshey ren soilshean dy gial,
Trooid magh yn Ellan Slane ;
E hampleyr skeaylley dy chooilley voayl,
E choyrle vic gys dagh ayrn.

XIV.

Gloyr Yee, as foays e helloo noo,
Va kinjagh e chiarail ;
Biallagh gys e vochilley smoo,
As veih shen jerkal faill.

XV.

Myr va e hoilchyn ooilley mooar,
Mannagh beagh eh dy bragh er ve ny smoo ;
Foast droill eh yn leigh ayns pooar,
Hug lesh meerciltys gys toyrt-mow.

XVI.

Oyr vooar ta ec ny Manninee,
Lurg lheid yn charrey choe ;
Son stiark ny vud oc ta lheid y chree
Dy reayll drogh-yannoo fo.

XVII.

Jeh Saggyrt Walker cooinagh vees,
Choud as ta Mannin ayn ;
As ayraghyn trooid mooarane eash
Vees ginsh jeh da nyn gloan.

XVIII.

Jhys hie eh seoise gys cooyrt y ree,
Noi ny kyndee brishey'n leigh ;
As ghow eh voae ooilley nyn mree,
As hooar ad lhieggey veih.

XIX.

Quoi hyrmys cisht ny jeïr ta roie,
Veih groinyn yn choiltane ;
Keayney nyn mockill ghraihagh vie,
Nagh vel öc nish er-mayrn.

XX.

Agh mish e voir tra smoo ayns feme,
Hie eh er scarrey vóym,
Troggit dy leah shagh harrish y cheim,
'Sy Rollick hrimshagh hrome.

XXI.

Keayrt va mee maynrey ayns my chloan,
Moir ghennal ren ad jeem ;
Dreill ad erskyn feme my chione,
As vad sthill dou son dreeym.

XXII.

Nish ta mee coodit lesh slane oie,
Gyn soilshey dym hiar ny heear ;
My chainle ta ass gyn saase erbee,
Dy gherjagh moir ny ayr.

XXIII.

Fo dorraghys doo, my aigney dooint,
Gyn jerkal jeh soilshey reesht ;
Ayns dinnid nagh vow acyr grunt,
Mastey yn sterrym neesht.

WIDOW TEAR'S BALLAD ON HER TWO SONS,
Dr. WALKER AND ROBERT TEAR.

Translated from the Manx by Mr. John Quirk of Carn-ny-Greie.

I.

BEFORE a mother I became,
How happy were my days ;
Nor head nor heart knew noise or pain,
To chill my blooming face.

II.

A stranger to all anxious care,
I always felt at ease ;
But they are gone, my comforts dear,
My heart forgets its peace.

III.

When I had changed my state of life,
God gave me children dear ;
I brought them up, so I might say,
But few their equals were.

IV.

Good scholars train'd in virtue's ways,
Obedient, neat, and clean ;
And these I hoped would prove my stay
When life was on the wane.

V.

To tell the straits I had to pass
To rear my children so,

Would prove a hard and heavy task,
Or more than words could do.

VI.

Trouble and want had pierced me through,
And pinch'd my heart full sore ;
But still the worst I never knew,
Until they were no more.

VII.

Among the people, Robert was
A hero at the pen ;
And day by day he gently rose
Higher in their esteem.

VIII.

A sample from his skilful hand,
Placed there in black and white,
Commemorates his worthy name,
On Kill-Chroo's walls so bright.

IX.

Will vicar of St. Mary's was,
A Christian pastor true ;
The bishop's hand, the people's eye,
And vicar-general too.

X.

To widows, fatherless, and poor,
A blessing and a shield ;
The feeble's help, who to the power
Of tyrants would never yield.

XI.

His wisdom, equal to his trust,
Still firmly bore him on ;
Till his good conduct and his worth,
At England's court was known.

XII.

That court where he was well received,
And honoured with a name ;
Such as no Manxman living had,
And ne'er may have again.

XIII.

The brightness of his light was known
Throughout the Isle of Man ;
In word and deed his lustre shone
To bless his native land.

XIV.

God's glory and his people's good
He made his constant care ;
Obedient to his heavenly Head,
And look'd for wages there.

XV.

Among his labours in our cause,
We'll long be proud to show ;
He was the man who kept in force,
The ecclesiastical law.

XVI.

Well may old Mona's sons lament
And weep 'neath such a blow :
How few are found, with hearts intent,
To keep transgression low !

XVII.

Dear Doctor Walker's name shall live
As long as Mona will ;
And fathers through succeeding years,
Will to their children tell

XVIII.

How, when at England's royal court,
'Gainst those who broke the law,
He took away their vain support,
And brought their courage low.

XIX.

Who then shall wipe away the tears,
And cheer the gloomy brow,
Of those who mourn their shepherd dear,
The flock's bereavement now ?

XX.

But oh ! when I was most in need,
I saw him hurried home ;
Pass'd o'er the stile his last retreat,
The mournful, gloomy tomb.

XXI.

Once I was happy in my sons,
A joyful mother I.
Beyond all want they cheer'd me on,
And always stood me by.

XXII.

Now cover'd with night's darkest shade,
No glimmering ray appears ;
My candle out, whilst none take heed
To cheer a parent dear.

XXIII.

My mind in total darkness kept,
All hope of light I've lost ;
Plung'd in th' unfathomable deep,
And midst the tempest toss'd.

Mr. Quirk remarks on the eighth verse :—"The stream running close by Kirk Patrick's church on the eastern side was called *Keeil-Cragh's stream*, perhaps long before the present church was erected. It is most likely that a small chapel known by that name stood near the spot where the present parish church stands. What can it mean ?"

The site of this old chapel is a small enclosure on part of the estate of Knockaloe, adjoining the highroad leading towards Ballamoore. It is laid down in the Ordnance map as "Keeil-Cragh."

ARRANE YN PHYNNODEREE.

THIS wild song appears to be a portion of some other which I have not recovered. It is evidently the malediction of some unfortunate female on her unfaithful lover, upon whose head she hurls all the evils that the whole realm of fairydom can inflict.

I.

CRED dy jinnagh yn slource as y drolloo,
Troggal seose ayns caggey cheoï,
Maidjey'n phot, as ny juistyn ooilley,
Ooilley feiyral noie ry-hoie.

II.

Maidjey'n phot, as yn vuirkin hanney
Cressad, goggan, juist, as claare,
Oilley caggey, scryss' as sanney
Tra veagh oo cleddit soue er laare.

III.

Cred dy jinnagh yn tarroo ushtey spottagh
As yn ghlashtin oo y ghoaill,
As yn phynnoderee, ghlioonagh, sphrargagh
Clioonagh y yannoo jeed noi'n voal.

IV.

Phynn M'Cowle as ooilley e heshaght,
Ferrish ny ghionney as y vuggane,
Dy jymsagh ad cooidjagh mysh dty lhiabbee
As clickal lesh oo ayns suggane.

THE PHYNNODEREE SONG.

I.

MAY the chimney-hook and the pot-hooks
  Against you rise in cruel war ;
The ladle, the dishes, and the pot-stick,
  All for the dread attack prepare.

II.

May these, when join'd with the sharp, thin bodkin,
  Crucible, noggin, and all hardware store,
All help to tear, and flay, and skin you,
  When fell'd beneath them upon the floor.

III.

Yea, may the water-bull, and the night-steed,
  And the rough satyr, come at the call ;
And when around your bed collected,
  All squeeze and crush you against the wall.

IV.

May Phinn M'Cowle, with all his fellows,
  Join with the fairy of the dale,
And all such bogles around you gather,
  And steal you off in a straw-rope creel.

CAPTAIN THUROT.—A MEMOIR.

ONE important incident in the history of Manx affairs during the middle of last century was the memorable naval action, off Bishop's Court, between Captain Elliot and Thurot, and as this has been made the subject of song, some account of Thurot will not be out of place in this collection, more particularly as during his early career the Isle of Man had for a short period been his place of residence.

In a scarce pamphlet, entitled *Genuine and Curious Memoirs of the Famous Captain Thurot*, London, 1760, written by the Rev. John Francis Durand, who was long personally acquainted with him, we find it recorded that Francois Thurot was born at Boulogne, in France (the French Biographical Dictionary says he was born at Nuits, in Burgundy, in 1727), his father and mother being both natives of the same place. He was of Irish extraction, his grandfather, whose name was Farrel, and was a captain in the Irish army under King James II., going off with that prince from Ireland, and during his residence at St. Germains married Mademoiselle Thurot, a lady of some family distinction, by whom he had one son, whose parents dying during his infancy, he was taken by his mother's relations, brought up by them, and went by their name. He was bred to the law, and married a Mlle. le Picard who died in giving birth to the subject of this memoir. Madame Tallard, a lady of great rank and fortune, was young Thurot's godmother, from whom he received many instances of friendship, and was instrumental in his ultimate promotion in the French navy.

When young Thurot was about fifteen years of age, one Farrel, an Irish smuggler, came to Boulogne and claimed relationship with the elder Thurot, and assured him that the house of the O'Farrels was still a flourishing house in Connaught, and offered, if he would let his young son go over with him, to make his fortune. This proposal was accepted, and young Thurot was equipped at the expense of his Irish cousin, set sail for Limerick, but stopped at the Isle of Man upon some business of the smuggler's. Here young Thurot, taking some disgust, refused to follow Captain Farrel any farther. Here he entered into the service of a Welsh smuggler, in whose employment he remained some time, running goods betwixt the Isle of Man, Anglesey, and Ireland. It was here Thurot acquired a knowledge of the English language, and imbibed that spirit of daring, combined with his natural great courage and love of adventure, as well as that skill in a seafaring life, which subsequently distinguished his character. He was entrusted with affairs of the greatest consequence to his employer, and was at one time stationed at Carlingford for near twelve months. From this he proceeded to Dublin, and afterwards to Scotland, engaged in similar transactions, which gave him that knowledge of the coasts which he made use of in his after career. He proceeded to London, where he spent a great part of his time from 1748 to 1752, going continually between France and England.

The hazardous life he had taken up at length brought him to a prison in Dunkirk in 1754. Having good friends, who interceded in his behalf, he was removed to Paris; and while undergoing some examinations, he convinced some people in power that should the war break out with England, which was at that time contriving (1755), he might be able to render considerable service from his knowledge of the various English and Irish channels and his perfect command of the language. He was accordingly entrusted with the command of one of the King's sloops.

In 1759, when the French ministry determined to invade England, various arrangements were made, and a large body of troops were assembled, under the command of the Duke d'Aiguillon, and the transport of these was to have been protected by a formidable fleet of ships of war, commanded by M. de Conflans, who was defeated in a general action on the 20th November by Admiral Hawke.

Thurot was appointed to the command of a small squadron fitting out at Dunkirk to make occasional descents on the Irish coast, for the purpose of distracting the attention of the English Government, and by dividing the troops facilitate the proposed invasion. This squadron consisted of—

	Commanders.	Guns.	Sailors.	Soldiers.
Le Marechal Belleisle	M. Thurot .	48	200	400
La Blond . .	Capt. La Kayee	36	200	400
Terpsichore . .	Capt. Dessauaudais	24	60	70
Begou . . .	—	36	200	400
Amaranthe . .	—	24	40	100

Two Cutters as Tenders, one pierced for 10 and the other for 8 guns.

The troops consisted of volunteer drafts from regular regiments, and were composed of—

French Guards .	Le Comte De Kersalls, Commandant.
	M. de Covenac, Colonel.
Swiss Guards	Cassailas, ,,
Regiment of Burgundy . .	De Roussilly, ,,
Regiment of Camkise . .	Frechean, ,,
Hussars	Le Compte de Skerdeck, Colonel.
Volontaires Etrangers.	

With his squadron Captain Thurot sailed out of Dunkirk on the night of the 15th of October, evading the eye of Commodore Boys, who was watching that port, and arrived at Gottenburgh on the 26th; and after procuring supplies of provisions and other stores there, put to sea on the 14th November. A strong gale dispersed Thurot's squadron in the night between the 15th and 16th, and four of his vessels only joined company the next day. The Begon returned to Dunkirk much damaged. On the 17th, his squadron anchored at Bergen, in Norway, where they remained until the 5th December, when they weighed and steered northward. After beating about for a length of time, their provisions became short, when a general council was called on the 1st January, at which it was resolved that each man's allowance should be reduced to ten ounces of biscuit and half a septier of wine or spirits per day. On the 16th February, off the coast of Islay, some provisions and cattle were obtained. The Belleisle had been seriously strained by the stormy weather, and was so leaky that two pumps were constantly kept going. The Amaranthe, having separated from Thurot's squadron on the 12th February, got back to France by the west of Ireland, and reached St. Malo on the 25th of that month, which port her crew entered, almost dead with fatigue, hunger, and thirst.

On the morning of Thursday the 21st February, Thurot's squadron, reduced to three frigates, appeared off the island of Magee, standing in shore for the Bay of Carrickfergus, when on landing, they attacked the garrison, who surrendered on the following morning. In this encounter about 50 of the French were killed. After getting provisions and fresh water on board, the troops embarked, and put to sea on Tuesday the 26th.

Captain Elliot, who commanded three frigates at Kinsale, hearing of Thurot's exploit in the north, set sail in quest of him, and at four in the morning of Thursday the 28th, got sight of Thurot's ship, and gave chase. The most authentic account of what then took place is best learnt from the logs of these vessels, as follows :—"H.M.S. Æolus. Wednesday 27th February 1760. Wind W.N.W. and N.W. Strong gales and squally.

"28th, wind N. by W., N.N.W., N. by E., N.N.E.

"Aire Point, Isle of Man. S.S.E. ½ E., distance 2 miles. First part, strong gales and squally ; latter, moderate and clear weather. Wore ship several times, by reason of the narrowness of the channel. At 8 p.m., Mull of Galloway, E. by N., 7 miles ; at 12, Copland light, N.W. ½ N., 4 leagues ; at 3 a.m., discovered 3 sails to windward cleared ship and gave chase ; at 6, discovered the chase to be the enemy's, fired two chase-guns, which they returned ; at half-past 6 got close alongside the largest of the enemy and engaged, and soon after the action became general, and continued about an hour and a half, when our antagonist struck her colours, as did the other two soon follow her example. They proved to be the ' Marshall Bellisle,' Mos. Thurott, Commander, the ' La Blond,' and ' Terpsichore.' (Being lockt with the ' M. Bellisle '), was obliged to let go our small Br. anchor, to clear us, slipt the cable, and bore away for Ramsey Bay, in the Isle of Man, to refit the ships, which were all greatly disabled in the action. We had 4 men killed, and 15 men wounded ; the enemy about 300 killed and wounded ; amongst the first was Mons. Thurott, Commodore, with several officers of distinction.

" Friday 29. Wind N.E. Moored in Ramsey Bay. Light breezes, and cloudy. At 3 p.m. anchored in Ramsey Bay. Bt. Br., and moored a cable each way. It was with great difficulty we kept the ' M. Bellisle ' from sinking, she having six foot in the hold. A. M. employed repairing our rigging, etc.

" Saturday, March 1., N.W., moored in Ramsey Bay ; ditto weather ; sailed the ' Pallas,' with five hundred prisoners for Belfast ; employed fishing, the masts being all wounded."

The log of the " Brilliant," Captain James Loggie, represents that vessel to be, on the " 28th February, distant three miles from the Point of Air, in the Isle of Man, S.E. ½ S. at 8, when the enemy struck, the point bearing S.E. by S., distant 7 or 8 miles. A lieutenant and 30 men were put on board ' La Blonde ' prize ; and the ' Pallas ' is recorded to have sailed on the 1st for Ireland, with 550 prisoners."

The log of the " Pallas," Captain Michael Clements, states that vessel to be, on " the 28th February 1760, with the Point of Air, on the Isle of Man, S.E. by E., distant two miles.

" First part, fresh gales and squally ; middle and latter, moderate and fair. At 3 p.m. unbent the mainsail, and bent another ; at 4 a.m. saw three strange ships on our weather-bow, bearing down upon us. Cleared ship, and gave them chase. They hauled their wind for the Mull of Galloway, then bore away right before it ; at daylight were almost within gun-shot ; out 3d and 2d reefs of the top-sails, got up top-gallant yards ; quarter-past 6 the ' Æolus ' made the signal for engaging. They proved to be the ' Marshall Bellisle,' ' La Blond,' and ' La Terpsichore,' French frigates. Half-past 6 began to engage, and at 8 they struck. During the engagement had one man killed and two wounded, our sails and rigging very much damaged, one shot through our mainmast, and our best bower anchor shot away. When they struck, the Point of Air, on the Isle of Man, bore S.E., distant 3 or 4 miles. At 9, the 'Æolus' made the signal to anchor, and bore away for Ramsey Bay. Sent our first lieutenant, a mate, and nineteen men, on board the 'Terpsichore.' At noon, the Point of Air, S.E. by E., distance 2 miles, the Commodore made our signal to stay by the 'Bellisle,' she having made the signal of distress."——

Captain Elliot, in his letter to the Admiralty, dated Ramsey, 29th February 1760, detailed these particulars, and stated that all the ships "are much disabled in their masts and rigging, the 'Marshal Bellisle' in particular, who lost her boltsprit, mizen-mast and main-yard in the action," and gave the number of killed and wounded, viz.—

'Æolus,'   32 guns,   4 killed,   15 wounded.
'Pallas,'   36   „   1   „   5   „
'Brilliant,'   36   „   0   „   11   „

Captain Thurot behaved with the greatest bravery imaginable; having lost one of his arms near an hour, he rejected the proposal of some of his officers to surrender, and when told that the water was fast rising through a hole pierced by a ball from the "Æolus," said, "Never mind it, go on," which was no sooner pronounced than he fell by a grape-shot through his breast. At this juncture Lieutenant Forbes, of the 'Æolus,' perceiving the 'Bellisle's' deck pretty clear of men, most of whom were below in great confusion, jumped into her, with about twenty-five sailors, struck the colours with his own hand, and found Thurot's men preparing to throw their commander overboard.

Thus fell the brave Thurot, universally lamented by all who knew him, who, even whilst he commanded a privateer, fought less for plunder than honour; whose behaviour was on all occasions full of humanity and generosity; and whose undaunted courage raised him to rank and merited distinction. His death secured the glory he always sought, he did not live to be brought a prisoner into England.

Mr. Durand, in his *Memoirs*, states that Thurot's body was taken on shore and embalmed, after which he was buried with military honours. This statement cannot be correct, for we find, on referring to Bishop Hildesley's letter to Dr. Monsey, in Butter's *Memoirs of Mark Hildesley*, p. 389, he states, "They might as well also have given the bishop the honour of having preached his funeral sermon, as he did preach at Ramsey the very day on which Thurot might be supposed to have been buried there."

That the body was committed to the deep is farther proved by the following interesting statement, published in Train's *History of the Isle of Man*, 1845, vol. ii. p. 327. The particulars were communicated by the Rev. James Black, minister of the parish of Penningham, in Wigtonshire, who witnessed the engagement, and who followed Thurot's funeral to the churchyard of Kirkmaiden, a small cemetery hard by the margin of the sea.

"Every consecutive tide, for two or three days after the action, cast a number of dead bodies ashore on the coast of Galloway. Among the last thus thrown up by the influx of the sea, was that of the French commander, whose remains were easily distinguished from the others by the silk velvet carpet in which they were sewed up. Some historians say he was thrown overboard by mistake ; but from the circumstance of his having been thus sewed up in his cabin carpet, I think that unlikely. It appeared that he had been attired in his full dress of Commodore when the engagement commenced, as his remains were clothed with all the insignia of his rank as a naval officer. He was identified most particularly by marks on his linen, and by a silver tobacco-box, with his name in full engraved on the lid. The remains of this gallant young seaman were removed from the beach to the house of a person in the vicinity, who, acting under the direction of Sir William Maxwell of Monreith, the lord of the manor, invited every respectable person in that quarter to the funeral. Sir William himself acted as chief mourner, and laid the head of that distinguished individual in the grave.

"The carpet in which the corpse was found was for a long time kept at Monreith House, and my informant supposes it to be there still. The tobacco-box was presented, by Sir William Maxwell, to the victorious Elliot, in whose family it is yet, perhaps, an heirloom. Thurot's watch, which fell into the hands of one of Sir William's domestics, is now in the possession of a person in Castle-Douglas."

Thurot was about 36 years of age, and Mr. Durand says, " he was rather robust than genteel, and he was rather comely than handsome, very brown, and extremely florid, and had a very small scar under his left eye, which was rather an advantage to him than otherwise." He is also described as of a low stature, well made, and having lively black eyes ; of a frank humour and affable disposition.

He lies in a remote churchyard, without a stone to record his name, or even to point out the exact spot where his remains were interred ; his actions alone are his monument.

It may be mentioned that Bishop Hildesley and his family witnessed the action from Bishop's Court, and that the bowsprit of the " Bellisle," two yards in circumference, which was struck off during the engagement, and came on shore not far from where he was standing, he set up on a small eminence, in the glen leading up from his palace, which he named "Mount Æolus," in commemoration of the victory ; the mount still remains, but the frail memorial of Thurot has long ago passed away.

The trade of Liverpool was ruinously interfered with by French privateers, who hovered between the mouth of the Mersey and the Isle of Man. In a Liverpool paper, under date 8th September 1758, we find the first notice of Captain Thurot, as follows :—"It is reported that the brig 'Truelove,' of Lancaster, and the brig 'Jane,' of Lancaster, had been taken off Lough Swilly by the 'Marshall Belleisle,' privateer, of St. Maloes, of thirty 12-pounders on one deck, eight 6-pounders on the quarter-deck, four on the forecastle, and four 18-pounders below. Captain Thurot, commander."

From a list, published in July 1760, it appears that in four years, ending at that date, there had been taken by the French, of vessels belonging to Liverpool alone, 143, principally engaged in the West Indian and American trades.

A print, 24 inches by 15, was made from a painting by Wright, representing the ships in Ramsey Bay, as they appeared immediately after the battle, dedicated to the merchants of Liverpool, and which may still occasionally be met with in the island.

Having, some years since, met with an aged person who had witnessed this action in his early days, and was proud of relating the fact, I was induced to enter more fully into Thurot's eventful life than I might otherwise have done, when only recording the songs which have been composed respecting him.

The following is from *Popular Songs, illustrative of the French Invasions of Ireland*, edited by T. Crofton Croker, and printed for the Percy Society, 1846, as well as many of the facts recorded in the foregoing memoir.

THUROT'S DREAM.

It is said that Colonel Cavenac informed John Wesley that Thurot, after sailing from Carrickfergus, had a presentiment of his death in consequence of a dream, which Wesley has preserved in his journal, 5th May 1760 :—"The next morning as he (Thurot) was walking the deck, he frequently started without any visible cause, stopped short, and said, ' I shall die to-day.' "

I.

The twenty-first of February, as I've heard the people say,
Three French ships of war came and anchored in our bay ;
They hoisted English colours, and landed at Kilroot,
And marched their men for Carrick without further dispute.

II.

Colonel Jennings being there, at that pretty town,
His heart it was a-breaking, while the enemy came down.
He could not defend it for the want of powder and ball,
And aloud to his enemies for " quarter" did he call.

III.

As Thurot in his cabin lay, he dreamed a dream,
That his grandsire's voice came to him and called him by
    his name ;
Saying, Thurot, you're to blame for lying so long here,
For the English will be in this night, the wind it bloweth
    fair.

IV.

Then Thurot started up, and said unto his men,
" Weigh your anchors, my brave lads, and let us begone ;
We'll go off this very night, make all the haste you can,
And we'll south and south-east, straight for the Isle of Man."

V.

Upon the next day the wind it blew north-west,
And Elliot's gallant seamen, they sorely were oppressed ;
They could not get in that night, the wind it blew so high,
And as for Monsieur Thurot, he was forced for to lie by.

VI.

Early the next morning, as daylight did appear,
Brave Elliot he espied them, which gave to him great cheer ;
It gave to him great cheer, and he to his men did say,
"Boys, yonder's Monsieur Thurot, we'll show him warm play."

VII.

The first ship that came up was the Brilliant without
    doubt,
She gave to them a broadside, and then she wheeled about ;
The other two then followed her and fired another round,
"Oh, oh, my lads," says Thurot, "this is not Carrick town."

VIII.

Then out cried Monsieur Thurot, with his visage pale and
    wan,
"Strike, strike your colours, brave boys, or they'll sink us
    every man :
Their weighty shot comes in so hot, on both the weather
    and the lee ;
Strike your colours, my brave boys, or they'll sink us in
    the sea."

IX.

Before they got their colours struck great slaughter was
    made,
And many a gallant Frenchman on Thurot's decks lay dead,

They came tumbling down the shrouds, upon his deck they
 lay,
While all our brave Irish heroes cut their booms and yards
 away.

X.

.   . .   .

 . . . .

And as for Monsieur Thurot, as I've heard people say,
He was taken up by Elliot's men and buried in Ramsey Bay.

XI.

Now for to conclude, and put an end unto my song,
To drink a health to Elliot, I hope it is not wrong;
And may all French invaders be served the same way.
Let the English beat the French by land, our Irish boys on
 sea.

BATTLE OF RAMSEY.

THUROT AND ELLIOT.

THIS song was taken down as sung by a person in Baldwin in 1869, who stated that he had often heard his old father sing it, but did not know the author. How well the record of this battle has been retained in the memory of Manxmen for more than a century, shows the great interest that was taken in the career of Thurot, who no doubt at the time had many friends in the island who were well acquainted with his exploits.

It will be observed this is the same song as that given under the name of "Thurot's Dream," which was copied from the version given by Mr. Crofton Croker in the *Popular Songs illustrative of the French Invasions of Ireland*, Part II. (Percy Society, 1846), but which appears to be defective, wanting several verses now supplied in the present copy, which, from its greater regularity of detail, is most probably the original. The various readings are only the result of the oral transmission of the song, a complete printed copy of which I have never seen. It has been considered advisable to print both versions.

I.

My very heart is broken for Carrickfergus town,
Such a fine situation as our enemy pulled down.
On the twenty-first of February, as I've heard people say,
Three French ships of war came and anchored in our bay.

II.

They hoisted up English colours, and landed at Kilroot,
As for Carrickfergus there was a furthermore dispute ;
But brave Colonel Jennings gave them powder and ball,
'Till one hundred and three of these French dogs did fall.

III.

So brave Colonel Jennings, at that very same space,
His heart was so broken for that beautiful place ;
He could not defend it for want of powder and ball,
'Till aloud to his enemies for "quarter" he did call.

IV.

On the twenty-seventh of February the wind blew nor'-west,
These three gallant ships they were sorely oppres't ;
They could not get in that night, the wind it blew so high,
But brave Monsieur Thurot, he was forced to let by.

V.

Thurot lay on his hammock, he dreamed a dream ;
A voice came unto him by night, and called him by name,
Saying, You are to be blamed, Thurot, for lying so long here ;
The English will be down to-night, the wind it blows so fair.

VI.

Thurot jumps from his hammock, and unto his men did say,
" Weigh up your anchors, brave boys, and let us be away ;
Take up your anchors, brave boys, make all the speed you
can,
And we'll steer south-south-east, straight for the Isle of
Man."

VII.

Early the next morning, when daylight did appear,
Elliot espied Thurot, and gave him a good cheer ;
Elliot espied Thurot, and unto his men did say,
" See, yonder's Monsieur Thurot ; we'll show him English
play."

VIII.

Thurot takes out his spying-glass, and spied all around,
He spied three British heroes all steering up and down,
He spied three British heroes all gathering in a swarm ;
" Hurrah ! my boys," says Thurot, " this place shall soon be
warm."

IX.

Then out spoke Monsieur Thurot, without a fear or doubt,
"Take in your hooks on board, boys, we never shall be took ;"
Then cried out Captain Elliot, and "Be it not too fast,
Give him a gallant broadside, cut down his yards and mast."

X.

Then first came up the "Brilliant," without a fear or doubt,
And gave him a gallant broadside, which made him wheel
    about ;
Then come up the other two, which gave him fire round.
"Oh, oh, my boys," says Elliot, "this is not Carrick town."

XI.

Then out spoke Monsieur Thurot, with colour pale and wan,
"Strike down your colours, brave boys, or they'll sink us
    every one ;
Their weight of shot comes in so hot, both windward, bow,
    and lee ;
Strike down your colours, brave boys, or they'll sink us in
    the sea."

XII.

Before they had their colours down, what a slaughter there
    was made,
And many a gallant Frenchman on Thurot's deck lay dead ;
And as for Monsieur Thurot, as I've heard the people say,
He was carried away by Elliot's men and buried in Ramsey
    Bay.

XIII.

To which concludes my ditty unto this mournful song,
To drink a health to Captain Elliot, I hope it is not wrong ;
And may all French invaders be served the same way—
If the Irish did not beat them on land, the English did at
    sea.

THUROT AS ELLIOT.

THE NAVAL BATTLE OF THUROT AND ELLIOT.

THIS account of the engagement between Admiral Thurot and Captain
Elliot is here printed for the first time. The translation of the Manx
has been made by Mr. John Quirk of Carn-ny-Greïe, Kirk Patrick, from
the original MS. copy, which, with the assistance of the Rev. John
Thomas Clarke, late chaplain of St. Mark's, is considerably enlarged,
and the whole rendered into a more correct historical fact.

I.

Ec balley veg Frangagh er dorrid ny bleeaney,
Flodd veg dy hiyn-chaggee ren geddyn so hiauihll ;
As chond's veagh Thurot kion-reiltagh e gheiney,
Cha bailloo ve orroo dy jinnagh ad coayl.

II.

Sheer caggey noi'n ree ain, gyn aggle ny nearey,
As roostey as spooilley yn ymmodee siyn ;
Yn gheay ren ee sheidey er ardjyn ny Haarey
As gimman ad stiagh so recriaght yn reeain.

III.

Eisht hie ad dy ghoaill Carrick-Fergus ayns nerin,
As myr vád cheet stiagh gys ny voallaghyn ayn
Ard-chaptan y valley dooyrt rish e hidooryn,
Shane dooin ad y oltagh lesh bulladyn ghurn.

IV.

Ny-yeih ayns traa gherrit ván phoodyr oc baarit,
Nagh voddagh ad shasoo as eddin chur daue ;
Eisht captan y valley dooyrt reesht rish e gheiney,
Nish shane dooin roie orroo lesh clinenyn ayns laue.

V.

Ván stayd oc danjeyragh dy cronnal ry-akin
Eisht dooyrt eh roo, shane dooin cur seose huc ayns traa,
Son foddee mayd jerkal rish baase fegooish myghin,
Neayr's nagh vel shin abyl yn noid y hyndaa.

VI.

Myr shen haink ad stiagh ayns y valley laa-ny-vairagh
Dy yannoo myr bailloo rish ooilley ny v'ayn ;
Mysh lieh-cheead dy Rangee va currit er feayraght,
Daag Thurot cheu-chooylloo nyn lhie ayns y joan.

VII.

Tra va Carrick-veg-Fergus oc spooillit dy bollagh,
Nagh chiare ad dy roshtyn yn Ellan shoh noain
Agh s'beg erree vocsyn er quoi veagh nyn rohaiailtagh,
Yinnagh yn daanys oc ooilley dys kione.

VIII.

She Elliot veeit ad rish ren orroo lhiggey,
As lesh eddin ghebejagh doad orroo aile.
Hug Thurot dy-chione lesh ooilley 'n voyrn echey,
As sheese beign da lhoobey er-boayrd yn Vellisle.

IX.

Tra haink ad dy-cheilley as gunnaghyn lhiggey,
As cronnagyn getlagh goll shiar as goll sheear.
Fuill frangagh myr ushtey dy palchey va deayrtey,
As Belleisle vooar y Thurot va tholl't myr y chreer.

X.

Ny Frangee myr eeastyn va scarr' ter ny deckyn,
Tra hir ad son Thurot sud shilley cha groun ;
Agh véshyn ny chadley ayns diunid ny marrey,
Cha lhiass daue ve moyonagh ass Thurot ny smoo.

XI.

Slane shch-feed ayns coontey dy reih gunnaghyn Rangagh
    Noi gunnaghyn Elliot gueig-feed as kiare ;
Three longyn noi three ren ad caggey dy barbagh.
    Er derrey hooar Thurot e voynyn 'syn aer.

XII.

Va oyr ec ny Frangee dy ghobberan dy sharroo,
    Son yn obbyr va jeant ayns three lich-yn oor ;
Three-cheead reesht jeh'n cheshaght va lhottit ny marroo,
    As dufsan dy cheeadyn goll stiagh 'sy thie-stoyr.

XIII.

Va gueig jeh ny Sosthynee marroo myrgeddin,
    As 'nane-jeig-as-feed gortit 'sy chah ;
Agh shimmey v'er enennaghtyn guin yn laa cheddin
    Er-bey dy ren Elliot cosney yn laa.

XIV.

Nagh dunnal yn dooinney va'n Offisher Forbes
    Ghon cullyr lhong Thurot er-boayrd yn chied er ;
As Thomson myrgeddin hie sheese ayns yn aarkey
    Dy yeigh ny thuill-vaaish eck lesh barragh as gierr.

XV.

Fir-veaghee shenn Vannin v'er cheu heear yn Ellan,
    Eer Aspick Vark Hildesley, as ooilley e hie ;
Ren jeeaghyn dy tastagh as fakin as clashtyn,
    Veih hoshiaght dy yerrey yn caggey va cloïe.

XVI.

Croan-spreïe yn Velleisle tra ve currit er shiaullay
    Ve eiyrit as immanit stiagh er y traie
Ve soit ec yn Aspick son cooinaght jeh'n chaggay,
    Er ynnyd ard-chronnal er-gerrey da e hie.

G

XVII.

Eisht mygeayrt Kione-ny-Haarey goll-rish deiney-seyrey,
　　Hug ad lhieu nyn gappee seose baiy Rumsaa ;
Ee irree-ny-greiney ny Frangee va keayney,
　　Tra honnick ad Thurot vooar currit dys fea.

XVIII.

Tra hoig shin ayns Mannin cre'n ghaue v'er n'gholl shaghey
　　As c'raad va ny deiney v'er reayll jin yn ghaue ;
Ard phobble ny cheerey, eer mraane chammah 's deiney,
　　Haink roue dy veeiteil ad dy oltaghey daue.

XIX.

Va geinsyn reih caarjyn ee theah as shiolteyryn
　　Va mooar jeant jeh'n Cheshaght ren cur lesh y laa ;
As rieau neayr's hiauill Ree Illiam dys Nerin,
　　Cha ren lheid ny laaghyn soilshean er Rumsaa.

XX.

O sleih-cheerey as shiaulteyryn trojee seose arraneyn,
　　Ny Frangee, ta'd castit er dy chooilley heu ;
Ta'n chaptan oc cadley ayns diunid ny marrey
　　Ny lhig daue ve moyrnagh ass Thurot ny smoo.

XXI.

Nish lhieen mayd yn veilley as iu mayd dy cheilley,
　　Lesh Shee-dy-vea ghennal gys Georgee nyn Ree ;
Son she ny siyn—chaggee ta shin orroo shiaulley
　　Va'n saase dreill nyn noidyn veih ny MANNINEE.

THUROT AND ELLIOT.

Translated by Mr. John Quirk, Carn ny Greïe, Kirkpatrick.

I.

From the seaport of Dunkirk to cruise during winter,
    A gallant French squadron did venture to go ;
And while the proud Thurot remained their commander,
    They proudly disdained to submit to the foe.

II.

They fought 'gainst our Sovereign with courage most daring,
    And caused 'mongst our shipping much damage and loss ;
And during a gale which blew fresh o'er old Erin,
    At length they succeeded in reaching our coast.

III.

Then as they were nearing a spot on the borders,
    E'en old Carrick-Fergus whose strength was but small,
The chief of the township reminded his soldiers
    To have them saluted with cannon and ball.

IV.

And when they had spent the last grain of their powder,
    And against the enemy they were unable to stand,
The gallant commander did issue his order,
    To rush in upon them with cutlass in hand.

V.

Then as he observed a strong force put in motion,
    He said, 'tis best to submit while we may,
Or death without mercy will soon be our portion,
    Since we are unable to drive them away.

VI.

Next day into fair Carrickfergus they entered,
  To do as they pleased with all they could find ;
About fifty men of bold Thurot's adventurers,
  Who lay stark and cold, to the dust were consign'd.

VII.

When they left Carrickfergus completely ransacked,
  Straight on for lone Mona the Frenchman did steer ;
But who should salute them they little suspected,
  To finish for ever their warlike career.

VIII.

Brave Elliot appeared with broadsides most glaring,
  And with a bold front put an end to their toil ;
Proud Thurot was caught at the height of his daring,
  Who had to submit, tho' on board the Bellisle.

IX.

When warmly engaged in this bloody action,
  The French quickly fell 'neath the thundering squalls ;
Their rigging was scattered in every direction,
  And Thurot's Bellisle was riddled with balls.

X.

The French of all classes on deck lay in masses,
  When there they sought Thurot midst carnage and gore ;
But Thurot was sleeping below in the ocean ;
  No Frenchman need boast of his courage any more.

XI.

The guns of the French were a score and one hundred,
  While Elliot's numbered one hundred and four ;
Three ships against three contended and thundered
  Until the Bellisle lost her great commodore.

XII.

One hour and a half put an end to their struggle,
    When three hundred Frenchmen fell wounded or slain,
One thousand two hundred in sorrow and trouble,
    As captives to prison were led o'er the main.

XIII.

Five men also fell on the side of the English,
    Whilst thirty-one more were hurt more or less ;
But keen had we felt the sharp sting of anguish,
    Had not the brave Elliot met with success.

XIV.

The Bellisle was taken by Lieutenant Forbes,
    The first man who boarded and brought her flag low ;
And saved by brave Thompson who dived in the ocean,
    And stopped her death leakage with tallow and tow.

XV.

The people who dwelt on the west side of Mona,
    E'en Bishop Mark Hildesley with all of his train,
Could hear the tough music as cannons were booming,
    And much of their doings could plainly be seen.

XVI.

They saw the Bellisle when deprived of her bowsprit,
    A log which soon reached the Bishop's domain,
To stand on an eminence commemorating
    The day and its deeds, with all things that came.

XVII.

Then round Point of Ayre most gallantly leading,
    They brought up their captives towards Ramsey Bay ;
At day-light's returning poor Frenchmen were mourning,
    To know their great Thurot was lifeless as clay.

XVIII.

When we understood what dangers had threatened,
  And where were the men who averted the blow,
The head-men of Mona did hasten to meet them,
  To greet and salute them as best they could do.

XIX.

To the best of our means they were treated and honoured,
  While Elliot's kindness still gladdened the place;
And ne'er since King William sail'd hence for old Erin
  The good folk of Ramsey knew ought of such days.

XX.

O landsmen and sailors, do ye all sing in chorus,
  The French are defeated behind and before;
And Commander Thurot laid low in the ocean,
  No Frenchman need boast of his courage any more.

XXI.

And now the full bumper with joy and good feeling,
  We'll drink to the health of our King and our Queen,
For the gallant vessels on which we are sailing
  Were the means to keep Thurot from MANNIN-VEG-VEEN.

EPITAPH ON M. THUROT.

From the *Gentleman's Magazine* for March 1760.

JOHN WESLEY, in his journal, May 1760, relates, on the information of Mrs. Cobham, while that lady was in attendance upon General Flaubert, after he had been wounded at the capture of Carrickfergus, " a little plain-dressed man came in, to whom they all showed a particular respect. It struck into her mind, ' Is not this M. Thurot ?' which was soon confirmed." She said to him, " Sir, you seem much fatigued : will you step to my house and refresh yourself ?" He readily accepted the offer. She prepared a little veal, of which he ate moderately, and drank three glasses of small warm punch ; after which he told her— " I have not taken any food before for eight and forty hours." She asked him, " Sir, will you be pleased to take a little rest now ?" Observing he started, she added, " I will answer life for life, that none shall hurt you under my roof." He said, " Madam, I believe you, I accept the offer." He desired that two of his men might lie on the floor by the bedside, slept about six hours, and then, returning her many thanks, went aboard his ship.

Here lies the pirate, brave Thurot,
To merchants' wealth a dreadful foe :
Who, weary of a robber's name
Aspired to gain a hero's fame :
But oft ambition soars too high,
Like Icarus when he strove to fly :
In short, Thurot with ardour fill'd,
His breast with emulation swelled,
Abjuring Sweden's copper shore,
His course to fair Hibernia bore ;
There took some peasants unprepar'd,
So struck his blow, and disappear'd ;
But luckless fate, which oft pursues us,
And when we least expect subdues us.
This scheme, how well soe'er concerted,
Into a dire mischance converted,

And made it prove, as we'll relate,
The sad forerunner of his fate :
For Æolus brave Elliot led,
Who early in his school was bred,
Cut short this champion's thread of life,
And with it clos'd the doubtful strife ;
In which Bellisle, a name we own,
Amongst ten thousand heroes known,
Of France, the wonder and the brag,
Again compell'd to drop the flag,*
Was forced such fortune to lament,
As erst her namesake underwent :
But to return to him whose glory
Is now the subject of our story,
He was no wit, nor quite an ass,
But lov'd his bottle and his lass.†
You then good fellows passing by,
Afford the tribute of a sigh
His fate lament—enough we've said,
Thurot once lived—Thurot is dead.

* The Chevalier de Bellisle, brother to the Marshal, lost his life as he was endeavouring to fix the standard on the Sardinian entrenchments at Exilles, 1747.

† M. Thurot's mistress, it is said, attended all his fortunes, and was on board the Bellisle when he was killed.

THE LAST DYING SPEECH AND CONFESSION OF A YOUTH FALSELY DONE TO DEATH BY HIS MISTRESS.

THIS ballad is from No. IV. of the MS. Collection of Ballads made by the Rev. T. E. Brown, who thinks it is either a translation or close imitation of some English ballad.

I.

Myr hie mee magh gys Sostyn,
  She redy veet mee ayn
As faill mooar ren ee chabbal dou,
  My aillin v'ee son blein.

II.

Eisht lesh ny chebbyn mooar eck
  Nagh daill mee r'ee myr shoh
Dy gholl maree gys (y) Hollant
  My veagh shin ooilley bio?

III.

Lesh dou feageil Sostyn,
  Ve gys my trimshey trome;
Tra ren my ven-ain shtyr
  Tuiltym ayns graih rhym.

IV.

"Ta aym thie as thalloo,
  Marish argid as airh waigh;
Shen ooilley reem's stowal ort
  My vee oo phoosey mee."

V.

Gur eh mie eu, ven-ainshtyr,
  Cha jargym poosey mish,

Ta mee er n'y anroo gialdyn,
  Nagh vol feer jesh ve brisht.

VI.

Ta shen rish my ghraih Sally,
  Yn ard-sharvaant en bene,
O cred shin mee, ven-ainshtyr,
  My chree ta lesh ee shen.

VII.

Nagh ren my ven-ainshtyr
  Goaill lane dy chonee rhym?
Nagh loo ee seose as vreear ee
  Dy ghoaill my vioys voym?

VIII.

Tra nagh jinnin poosey ee
  Dy ve son ben dou vene,
Ghow ee shuityn feer aggairagh
  Dy chur mee ayns pryssoon.

IX.

Va fainey er yn nair eck,
  Myr s'bollagh v'ee dyn grayee,
Slif ee eh ayns my phocket,
  Hug orrym's surrause baase.

X.

Nagh re lesh constable,
  Hie mee er chur resh,
Kiongayrt rish bing dy gheiney,
  Dy bee er my vriwnys?

XI.

Loryr mee jeh reddyn jeeragh,
    Ny-yeih, cha row couyr ayn ;
Son roo ee seose dy nel mee ee,
    Hie mee er chur ayns pryssoon.

XII.

Shinish guillyn negey
    Ta geaishtagh rhym's nish,
Ny jern-jee jeem's gamman,
    Ny craid my geayrt-y-mish.

XIII.

Son ga nagh vel mee foiljagh,
    Yn seikll shegin dou faagail ;
O bannaght ayd, ghraih Sally,
    Ayns graih rhyt neem partail

TRANSLATION OF "MYR HIE MEE MAGH GYS SOSTYN."

By J. Ivon Mosley.

I.

As I went out to England,
  A lady met me there,
And wages good she offered me,
  If I'd serve her for a year.

II.

Her offer I accepted,
  And then with her prepared
To take a trip to Holland,
  If we should both be spared.

III.

The day that I left England
  Was a woeful day to see,
For my mistress had conceived a love
  That was not returned by me.

IV.

" I have both land and houses,
  Which I'll freely give to thee,
And heaps of gold and silver too,
  If thou wilt but wed with me."

V.

I thank you, lady, kindly,
  But I cannot marry now,
For I have made a promise,
  And dare not break my vow.

VI.

It is with my Sally dear,
  Your waiting-maid so kind :
O madam, do believe me !
  My heart's with her entwined.

VII.

'Twas then my vengeful mistress
  Made a threatening display,
And more, a fearful oath that she
  Would take my life away.

VIII.

Because I did refuse her
  To be my wedded wife,
She took a wily measure
  To rob me of my life.

IX.

On her hand a ring she wore :
  I say with latest breath,
In my clothing she inserted it,
  To bring about my death.

X.

A constable she sent for,
  And I was forced to go,
To be placed before a jury,
  That I the truth might show.

XI.

Boldly then I spoke the truth,
  But this she would not own ;
She falsely swore I robbed her :
  I was into prison thrown.

XII.

Come all ye youths and listen,
　　Who are standing here, and be
Not idly thinking of my words,
　　But a lesson learn of me.

XIII.

Although I am not guilty,
　　To leave this world must I :
So blessings on thee, Sally dear ;
　　Through love for thee I die.

ARRANE ER INNEENYN IRRINEE.

JEEAGH guillyn agey sooree,
  Nagh vell cur monney geill ;
My yiow ad inneenyn aalin,
  Feallagh vees jeu pleadeil.

Yiou main inneenyn errinee—
  She shoh roo hene t'ad gra—
As giallit keead punt toghyr,
  Cha n'aggle dooin dy braa.

She giallit keead punt toghyr,
  Agh sgerrit vees ad rish ;
Kion ghaa ny three dy vleeancy,
  Bee'n scollag as eh brisht.

Bee eh shooyll ayns ny margaghyn,
  As mennick sy thie-oast ;
Ass y ven as ass y toghyr,
  Bee'n scollag jannoo boast.

Lurg coontey beg dy vleeantyn,
  Ve ceauit oc cummal hie,
Jeeagh urree gow sampleyr jee,
  Jeeagh urree goll feed thie.

Ta stoyr dy ghownyn cotton eck
  As oanraghyn dimity,
Ny lhie ayns ny corneilyn,
  Smoo feme oc er y niee.

My choyrle diuish ghuillyn agey,
  Ta geishtagh rish m'arrane

Nagh poost shiu er graih toghyr
  Choud as vees seihll ermayrn.

My t'ou uss goll dy phoosey,
  Jeeagh son sharvaant jeh'n'aill,
As chymsee pingyn cooidjagh
  As kionnee uss jee queeyl.

Sneeuys ee dhyt dy kinjagh,
  Dagh oor myr vees eck traa ;
Mannagh vou lien dy chinnagh,
  Yiow barragh er y lieh.

Dy beign er phoosey Nancy,
  Cre'n gerjagh v'ee my chree !
Veagh ben aym gys my fancy—
  As s'mie bynney lhiam ee.

Agh phoost mee er graih toghyr,
  Vy red nagh rou ricau mie—
Hooar mee toot d'inneen vooar irrinee,
  Nagh dod ricau cummal hie.

T'ee fargagh, moyrnagh, litcheragh,
  As lhie foddey er y laa,
Geam da'n charvaant eck girree
  Dy chiartagh j'ee yn tea.

T'ee goardagh yn charvaant eck,
  Ee hene soie ayns corneil,
As er y veggan foaynoo
  Y laghyn dy vaarail.

Ta foiljyn inney'n erriuagh,
  Er skeaylley lianyr as lhean,

Er vhilley ard as injyl,
 Cheusthie jeh mooarane blein.

Cha nee ayns inney'n' errinagh,
 Ny ayns yn togh'r ta'n foill ;
Feedyn nagh beeagh un skilling
 T'er phrowal chiart cha moal.

T'ad coamrit lesh fardailys,
 Wasteilagh, gee as giu ;
Ta'n traa oc ceauit gyn-ymmyd,
 Tad coyrt ny deiney mou.

Raad boallagh nyn shenn moiraghyn
 Ve cummal seose yn thie,
Tad shoh dy phluckey neose eh
 Gys t'eh er laare ny lhie.

Ah ! treih son ny mraaue mie shen,
 Dy vel ad nish cha goaun,
Ta'n veillid t'ain syn ynnyd oc,
 Coyrt naardey n slane ashoon.

Ta clashtyn ain jeh Sodom,
 Quoi haink gys jerrey treih ;
Litcheragh, moyrn, as soaillid,
 Va mhilley ec cheu sthie.

T'au chenn phadeyr Isaiah,
 Neesht cur dooin coontey plain
Scrieuit ayns yn threeoo chabdil,
 Mysh triehys moyrn ny mraane.

My sailt ve er chen cairys,
 As goll jeh'n seihll ayns shee,

II

Fow ben fegooish molteyrys,
　　Gyn foalsaght ayns e cree ;

Slane, onneragh, as jeidjah,
　　Dwoaiagh er saynt as moyrn ;
Son coyrt sampleyryn cairagh,
　　Roish sheshaghyn as cloan.

Eisht gueeyn ort my charrey,
　　Tra t'ou er gheddin ee
Er graih dy chooilley vannaght,
　　Jean dellal vie chur jee.

My shen tra vees shiu symnit,
　　Roish stoyl mooar brewnys Yee,
Coyrt coontey jeh nyn stiuirtys
　　Lhig ooilley ve ayns shee.

Son shegin ooilley shassoo,
　　Coyrt coontey yn laa shen ;
Cre'n aght ghell mraane rish deiney,
　　As deiney rish ny mraane.

A SONG ON FARMERS' DAUGHTERS.

Translated by Mr. John Quirk, Carn-ny-Greïe.

Young men commencing courting
    Too heedless oft have been ;
They look for showy lasses,
    High in the world's esteem.

We'll get a farmer's daughter !
    'Tis thus they form their plan ;
A hundred pounds as portion,
    And I'm a happy man.

A hundred pounds as portion,
    But soon its course is run ;
Two or three years being over,
    Leaves him a bankrupt man.

At fairs and at the public-house
    He is too often found,—
There boasting of the farmer's lass
    And her one hundred pound.

When two or three years have pass'd him,
    Living with her he loves,
Look at her, and take notice
    How slovenly she moves.

Her finery and dresses
    Are huddled here and there
Neglected in the corners,
    Need washing and repair.

Ye gay young men and bachelors
    Who listen to my rhyme,

O do not wed for portion
　　Within the bounds of time.

If ever you will marry,
　　And seek your future weal,
Get an industrious maiden
　　And buy a spinning wheel.

She'll prove a constant spinner,—
　　The distaff is the staff;
If flax you cannot purchase,
　　Get tow for half and half.

Had I but married Nancy,
　　How happy I had been!
The woman to my fancy—
　　And I could love her keen.

But for the sake of dowry
　　I done what now I rue,—
Married the farmer's daughter
　　Which no house-keeping knew.

She's lazy, proud, and saucy,
　　Found late in bed each day;
From whence proceed her mandates,
　　And orders 'bout the tea.

Or sitting in a corner,
　　She rules with sullen sway;
Whilst she herself is idling
　　Her precious hours away.

The faults which spoil'd these lasses
　　So many years ago,

They now pervade all classes,
   And ruin high and low.

They're not confin'd to farmer's girls,
   Nor to the pence they had ;
For scores not worth a shilling
   Will treat you all as bad.

Their vain and foolish dresses,
   Extravagance and ease ;
Their time is spent on nonsense,
   They mar their husband's peace,

There, where our ancient mothers
   Their household's weal did crown,
These who have took their places
   As surely pluck them down.

Alas ! for these good women,
   That they have got so scarce,
The mis'ries which supplant them
   Will lay the nation waste.

Who has not heard of Sodom,
   And her untimely end ?
Abundance, pride, and idleness,
   Corrupted her within.

Isaiah, the third chapter,
   If nowhere else beside,
Speaks volumes about women,
   And their distracting pride.

If e'er ye would be happy,
   And reach a blest estate,

Get partners without falsehood,
  Pure hearts without deceit ;

True, diligent, and honest,
  Strangers to lust and pride,
In all respects made worthy
  To be the household guide.

And when at length you've found her,
  And seen the happy day
For all you hold endearing,
  O give her full fair play.

So when you'll stand together
  Before the judgment throne,
You need not blame each other
  For aught that you have done.

For we must stand in judgment,
  To answer for our lives,—
How wives have dealt with husbands,
  And husbands with their wives.

MYLECHARAINE.

Translated from the Manx Song in *Mona Miscellany*, Part I., page 57,
by Mr. J. Beale, Grantham.

I.

O Mylecharaine, where gott'st thou thy store?
    Alonely didst leave thou me;
I got it not deeply beneath Curragh ground,
    And alonely didst leave thou me.

II.

O Mylecharaine, where gott'st thou thy stock?
    Alonely didst leave thou me;
I got it not just betwixt two Curragh blocks,
    And alonely didst leave thou me.

III.

O Mylecharaine, where gott'st thou what's thine?
    Alonely didst leave thou me;
I got it not just between two Curragh sods,
    And alonely didst leave thou me.

IV.

I gave my web of hemp, and I gave my web of flax,
    Alonely didst leave thou me;
And I gave my cattle-ox for the daughter's dower,
    And alonely didst leave thou me.

V.

O father, O father, I feel quite ashamed,
    Alonely didst leave thou me;

Thou art going to church in thy sandals white,
    And alonely didst leave thou me.

VI.

O father, O father, look at my decent shoes,
    Alonely didst leave thou me ;
And thou going about in thy sandals of hide,
    And lonely didst leave thou me.

VII.

Ay, one sandal black, and t'other one white,
    Alonely didst leave thou me ;
Fy, Mylecharaine, going to Douglas on Saturday,
    And alonely didst leave thou me.

VIII.

Yea, two pairs of stockings, and one pair of shoes,
    Alonely didst leave thou me ;
Then didst wear, Mylecharaine, full fourteen years,
    Alonely didst leave thou me.

IX.

O damsel, O wench, thou needst not feel ashamed,
    Alonely didst leave thou me ;
For I have in my chest what will cause thee to laugh,
    And alonely didst leave thou me.

X.

My seven curse of curses on thee, O Mylecharaine,
    Alonely didst leave thou me ;
For thou'st the first man who to women gave dower,
    And alonely didst leave thou me.

Mr. Beale remarks that Mylecharaine, in verse I., slily answers that he did not get his treasure deep in the centre of a fathomless bog. In verse II., that he did not get his stock betwixt two masses of solid matter in contact in the bog. In verse III. that he did not get his general goods between two bits of loose matter in the bog. In verse IV. that he had dowered his daughter. In verses V.-VIII. she gently upbraids him with irreverently and slovenly using sandals, while she takes pride in being shod decently ; and playfully, but respectfully, hints at the droll figure he will cut in Douglas, the largest town in the island, on Saturday, the market day ; concluding with a very telling allusion to his long-practised miserly habits. In verse IX. he consoles her with the prospect of the fortune in store for her. In verse X., for portioning her, he has a seven-double curse—" a regular fourteen pounder"—hurled at him by, we may suppose, a disappointed suitor, who had lost the hand of his daughter, and might be the questioner in the first three verses.

THE MYLECHARAINE SILVER CROSS.

It had been the intention of the editor to have given a more particular account of the family of Mylecharaine than what is stated in the first series of *Mona Miscellany*, p. 54, and considerable trouble has been taken to accomplish this, but without effect. It was desirable to obtain information as to the time when the person who is said to have found the treasure lived, and one of his descendants has repeatedly promised to look up some of their old deeds that would have given the date as to the time they first acquired property in Jurby, but has failed to do so. One thing, however, was done; the editor obtained the loan of an ancient cross, which, along with some other small valuables, had been handed down from their forefathers. This, after being cleaned from the soil and peat which filled up some parts of it, and entirely concealed the engraved portion, turned out to be silver. It had evidently lain long unused, from its blackened appearance, and probably formed one portion of treasure that had been concealed in early times when the Isle of Man was subject to so many raids from Norsemen and others, and probably was the foundation of the rise in fortune of the Mylecharaine family.

An exact drawing of this cross has been carefully made, which will no doubt be an acceptable contribution to the Manx antiquary. The small ring at the top, by which it was suspended, has been unfortunately broken; it is otherwise quite perfect. It is evidently of great age, if we may judge from its workmanship and peculiar form. It bears a very striking resemblance to the St. Cuthbert gold cross, found on his body at the opening of his tomb in 1827, a drawing of which is given in Chambers's *Book of Days*, vol. ii. p. 312. 1864. St. Cuthbert was bishop of the Northumbrian Island

THE MILNCHARAINE SILVER CROSS
FULL SIZE — FRONT & BACK

of Lindisfarne, and died in the year 688. His body, after several removals, found a resting-place in 1104 in Durham Cathedral. If the Mylecharaine cross be assigned to the same age, it will, indeed, be entitled to be called an antique.

The principal part of the property is in Kirk Christ Lezayre, part in Andreas, and part in Jurby, and being intack, bears no name, only a number in the Lord's book. The old house is not in existence. There is a field called *Galt ny thicyn*—the Field of the Houses. Mrs. Jane Cashen of the Curraghs, Jurby, is the lineal descendant or representative of Mylecharaine.

There is a tradition that Mylecharaine was an illegitimate son of one Christian of Milntown, who, fearing an invasion, hid some valuable property in the Curragh, which this son afterwards secretly took up, and from thence was called

> *Molley e chiarciel,*
> Mylecharaine,
> Deceiver of my care.

COLBAGH VRECK ER STHRAP.

This old Manx ballad has been arranged conversationally. It was taken from one written by the Rev. Philip Moore. He was a first-class scholar, and was one of the translators of the Scriptures into Manx. He was rector of Kirk Bride, and for forty-eight years chaplain and school-master of Douglas, where he was born on the 5th September 1705, and died there 22d January 1783, and was buried in Braddan Church-yard.—*Vide* Butler's *Life of Bishop Hildesley,* pp. 186-192.   London, 1799.

I.

Yn Chuyr.—Haink Shuyr ven-y-phosee stiagh,
　　　She mooie er y phling-vag v'ee ;
　　　Gra dy beign's er phoosey ayns traa,
　　　Cha beign's nish ayns stayd cha treih.

Chorus.

　　　She poost, as poost, as poost,
　　　As poost dy liooar vees shiu,
　　　Nagh nhare diu foddey ve poost,
　　　Na taggloo smessey ve j'eu.

II.

　　　Agh my-lhie my lomarcan va mee,
　　　S'beg gerjagh v'aym dy bragh ;
　　　Agh foddey baare lhiam nish,
　　　Ve poost rish guilley vie reagh,

　　　　" She poost, as poost, as poost," etc.

III.

Yn vraar.—Haink stiagh eisht braar ben-y phoosee,
　　　As loayr eh mychione e huyr
　　　Dy boan diu ee chammah as ta mish,
　　　Cha nieau-agh shin urnee son oor.

　　　　" She poost, as poost, as poost," etc.

IV.

T'ee moyrnagh, ard, as litcheragh,
As lhie feer foddey er-laa ;
Chyndaa ec hene 'sy lhiabbee,
Myr, shoh, te'e ceau e traa.

"She poost, as poost, as poost," etc.

V.

Mannagh n'oyms ben share na ish
Jeer! cha poosym's ben dy braa.
Son hem shaghey dy chooilley ven-aeg,
Fegooish cur orroo traa-laa.

"As poost, as poost, as poost," etc.

VI.

Ben-y-phoosee.—Eisht loayr roo, Ben-y-phoosee,
S'beg tushtey teu ny Reeayl ;
Dooys dy phoosey dooinney son graih
Cha vel eh agh ayns fardail.

"She poost, as poost, as poost," etc.

VII.

Dyn thie, ny cooid, ny conryn,
Carmeish, curlead, ny lhuisag ,
Tra hig boghtynid stiagh 'sy dorrys,
Nee graih goll magh er yn uinnag.

"She poost, as poost, as poost," etc.

VIII.

Yn Voir.—Haink Moir ben-y-phoosee stiagh,
As loayr ec rish e inneen ;
Traa hie mish hoshiaght dy phoosey,
Cha rou jalloo aym lhiam pene.

"She poost, as poost, as poost," etc.

IX.

Agh gooyn dy eglieen olley,
Fegooish eer smoe dy cheau ;
Agh nish ta'ym ollagh as cabbil
As palchey dy liooar ta'ym jeu.

"She poost, as poost, as poost," etc.

X.

V'aym gooyn dy eglieenolley
Marish apryn dy saloon
Quoig dy henn lieen skeddan
As bussal dy spinagyn huin.

"She poost, as poost, as poost," etc.

XI.

Yn Ayr.—Eisht dooyrt Ayr ben-y-phoosee,
Ny treig ufs rish dty ghraih ;
My te son laccal toghar,
Verym's dhyt dty haïe.

"She poost, as poost, as poost," etc.

XII.

Yiow'n cholbagh vreck er sthrap,
As nagh re oo hene vees souyr ?
As yiow'n chenn vock vane, golleig,
Dy hayrn yn arroo 'syn ouyr.

"She poost, as poost, as poost,
As poost dy liooar vees shin,
Nagh nhare diu foddey ve poost,
Na taggloo smessey ve j'eu."

ARRANE Y SKEDDAN.

By the Rev. John Cannell, Vicar of Onchan.

I.

Shicish ooilley Easteyryn neem's coontey chur diu,
Mysh Imbagh yn Skeddan ny sbrooaie cha row rieau ;
T'ain palchey dy argid cour arroo as feïll,
Foast praaseyn as skeddan she ad nyn ard reil.

II.

Tra harrish t'an Imbagh, cha-lhisagh shin plaiynt
Agh booise y chur dasyn ta freayll shin ayns slaynt ;
Slane voylley chur da, son e vannaght hooin wass,
T'an Skeddan ersooyl dys y cheayn vooar by-Yiass.

III.

Ayns shen goaill e aash, va kiarrit da rieau,
Ny ribbaghyn-vaaish s'beg choontey v'eh jeu ;
Ayns shen cean e hraa derrey cheet yn nah vlein,
Er Greeb Bal-ny howe, yion mayd eishteh'sy lieen.

IV.

Ayns flinghys dy mennick, as mennick neesht feayr,
Foast prowal as ciurr, shinney lhian churmyner ;
Tra ta caslys, vie goll, as yn eeast cheet e-ash,
Chelleeragh t'an dooan soit son y vock-ghlass.

V.

Te shilley vondeishagh, goaill prowal vie stiagh,
As s'eunyssagh y laa, dy chreck yn eeast magh ;
Dy chreck eh dy gennal rish kionneyder vie,
Goaill jough lesh arrane, as craa-laue ben-y-thie.

VI.

Lesh cappan dy yough, as greme veg dy veer,
Nee mayd beaghey cha souyr as eirrinee yn cheer ;
Lhig dooin gin dy chreeoil dys y cheshiaghtain hene,
Mastey deiney, shin s'gennal fud immanee yn lieen.

VII.

Nish jerrey y choyrt er ny ta mee er ghra,
D'ron palchey dy Skeddan ee mannin dy braa ;
Freill, freill dooin yn vannaght, O Chrootagh y theihll
As ayns booise lhig da manninee fosley nyn meeal.

THE HERRING SONG.

Translated from the Manx by Mr. John Quirk, of Carn-ny-Greïe,
Kirk-Patrick.

I.

Ye seamen of Mona, come join heart and hand,
To sing of the season which gladdens our land ;
We've plenty of money to procure bread and beef,
Yet potatoes and herrings must rule as our chief.

II.

The season being over, we should not complain,
For health, and all mercies, we'll thankful remain ;
Still praise our Preserver for blessings bestow'd,
When herrings remove to their southern abode.

III.

Their quarters prepar'd by our Maker all-wise,
The snares and the dangers they seem to despise ;
They rest for a season, and then come again,
Bal-ny-howe upon Greeba's our spot for 'em then.

IV.

Tho' oft wet and cold, both by day and by night,
We follow our business with joy and delight ;
When fish multiplies and foretells a good take,
The line and the hook are prepared for the hake.

V.

'Tis pleasant to witness good hauls coming in,
And so a fine day is, to sell it again ;
To sell to good buyers, with beer at command,
And sing with a shake of the landlady's hand.

I

VI.

With an honest got morsel and a cup of good beer,
As snug as our farmers, we'll live round the year ;
We'll heartily drink to the health of our men,
And none are more cheerful who tug at the train.

VII.

And now my dear Mona, to finish my rhyme,
May plenty of herrings for ever be thine ;
Preserve the great blessing, thou God of all grace,
And may it redound to thy glory and praise !

NAUFRAGE A DOUGLAS, ISLE DE MAN,
en 1787.

LOSS OF THE MANX HERRING FLEET,

21st September 1787.

In the first series of *Mona Miscellany*, pp. 80-85, was given an account of this disaster, in which was mentioned a French print depicting the sad event. Having received permission to copy this print, we are now enabled to present it to the members of the Manx Society.

This print, representing the scene of the disaster, was several years ago picked up by the late Rev. G. S. Parsons, of Castletown, Government Chaplain, at an old print-shop in Paris. From him it passed into the hands of the late George Quirk, Esq., Water Bailiff, and was in the possession of Richard Quirk, Esq., Receiver-General, in 1871.

The picture presents a view of the Old Fort, the Old Pier, the greater part of which was washed away in 1786, and Douglas Head. The wreck of the boats (all one-masted), the struggling of the men, the fury of the sea, and the angry appearance of the sky, from which flashes of lightning are emitted, is very spiritedly drawn. The ballads relating thereto are given in the first series of *Mona Miscellany*.

MARRINYS YN TIGER, LIORISH YUAN VOORE.

JOHN MOORE of Camlork, in Braddan, author of the following ballad, was one of the crew of a privateer called "The Tiger," which he sung so frequently, that he was himself called "Moore, the Tiger." This appellation has come down with his descendants to the present day. Mr. Moore was also the author of several Manx carvals, a specimen of which will be found in the present collection. This ballad humourously describes the history of an old vessel which the gentry of the island purchased and manned, for the purpose of assisting England in her war with France and America. On her first voyage "The Tiger" fell in with a Dutchman, and brought her into Douglas; but not being then at war with that country, complaint was made at the Court of St. James, and those concerned in this outrage were lodged in prison until satisfaction had been given to the Dutch.

I.

Ren deiney-seyrey Vannin,
　　Ayns yrgid, stayd as moyrn,
Nyn bingyn cheau dy cheilley,
　　As chionnee ad shenn lhong.

II.

Va ynnyd oc ayns Doolish,
　　As boaylyn er y cheer,
Raad cheau ad pingyn cooidjagh,
　　Dy chionnagh' privateer.

III.

Ny pingyn hie dys Sostyn,
　　Va ymmyd daue ayns shen,
Dy chionnaghey 'n chenn Tiger,
　　'Sdy choyrt ee dys y cheayn.

IV.

Hie eam magh trooid yn Ellan,
    Son guïllïn jeh ynsagh-cheayïn
Ny guïllïn roie dy ghoolish,
    Tra cheayll ad lheid y sheean.

V.

Ayns sheshaghtyn v'ad chymsagh,
    Cheet voish dagh ayrn jeh'n cheer.
Dys thie Nick Voore ayns Doolish,
    Cha liauyr as grenadier.

VI.

She Qualtragh vees nyn gaptan,
    As marish nee mayd goll.
As feiyr vooar hie fud Doolish,
    Lesh lheimmyraght as kiaull.

VII.

Caggee mayd noi ny Frangee
    As noi America.
Ta guïllïn-vie ayns Mannin,
    Nagh jean voish noid chyndaa.

VIII.

Liorish nyn jebbyn aalin,
    Ny guïllïn hayrn ad lhieu,
Ny errinee va gyllagh,
    Kys yion mayd jeant yn traaue.

IX.

Va shoh daue ard oyr aggle
    Quoi eiyragh er y cheeagh,
Dy goaun veagh guïllïn Vannin,
    Son coltar chur fo chreagh.

X.

Va Illiam vooar y Coudray
    As dooinney vooar yn Chronk,
Va'd gylläigh son ny guillïn
    Va wheesh d'inneenyn oc.

XI.

O shuish, inneenyn Vannin
    Ta dobberan ayns doo,
Gra nagh vel guillïn faagit,
    Agh paitchyn nagh vel feen.

XII.

Dy vel ad ooilley failt oc,
    Er boayrd yn Phrivateer
As scoan my ta wheesh faagit
    As roshys fer er kiare.

XIII.

As tra nagh vel wheesh faagit
    As roshys fer y wheesh,
Te foddey share ve follym,
    Cha nee fer eddyr jees.

XIV.

Giu as cloic er ny caartyn
    Chum roinyn oie as laa,
Gra blebceyn ny guillïn
    Nagh jed noi America.

XV.

Myr eginit hie mee maroo,
    As hass mee seose dys gunn,
As kinjagh va mee dobberan,
    Dy row my ghraih rey rhym.

XVI.

Ny cheayrtyn va mee smooinaghtyn
　　Nagh vaikin ee dy braa
As ceau my laghyn seaghnagh
　　Ny lhie ayns baïe Rumsaa.

XVII.

Three laa va shin er hiaulley
　　Lesh dooin faagail Rumsaa,
Tra veeit shin rish y sterrym,
　　Hug er yn eill ain craa.

XVIII.

Va deiney tooillit teaymey
　　As guillïn coayl nyn mree,
As Harry Voore va gyllagh,
　　My ghuillïn cum shui cree.

XIX.

Yn keayn va gatt as freaney,
　　Ve rastagh erskyn towse,
Yn chronnag ain va caillit
　　Cha dod shin freayl nyn goorse.

XX.

Lurg da ve tammylt sheidey,
　　Yn sterrym reesht ghow fea,
As rosh shin shenn oie Ollick,
　　Gys aker ayns Mount Bay.

XXI.

Ec kione three laa reesht aarloo,
　　Eisht hie shin son y cheayn,
As veeit shin lhong voish Holland,
　　As ghow shin ee dooin hene.

XXII.

Eisht haink shin thie dy Ghoolish
    Lesh gunneraght as kiaull,
As deiney seyrey Vannin
    Dy moyrnagh haink nyn guaill,

XXIII.

Ga blaik lhieu fakin spooilley,
    Va'd moyrnagh gyn resoon,
Loayrt baggyrtagh nyn oi ain
    Dy choyrt shin ayns pryssoon.

XXIV.

Leah hoig shin dys nyn drimshey
    Lurg dooin ve'r roshtyn thie
Yn lhong va shin er hayr tyn
    Dy row ee goit noi 'n leigh.

XXV.

Dooyrt ad dy row'n chooish din
    Trieït feanish yn Chionnooyrt,
As cha vel brin ayns Mannin
    Ne brinnys diu y choyrt.

XXVI.

Nish gow shin reue dys Sostyn
    As meeit mayd shin ayns shen
As shooïl mayd riu er thalloo,
    Ny shiauïll mayd riu er keayn.

XXVII.

Agh ta mish nish ayns Mannin,
    As vouesyn ta mee seyr
Cha vod ad mee y lhiettal
    Veih Sheshaght my ghraih gheyr.

XXVIII.

Shoh'n erree ghow'n chenn Tiger,
    Va'n oyr jeh wheesh dy chiaull,
V'ee creckit jeh son toghyr,
    Da'n lhong va shin er ghoaill.

XXIX.

Ga va shin sheshaght ghennal
    As trean ayns corp as cree,
Drogh choyrle as drogh leeideillee
    Ver naardey cooish erbee.

XXX.

Ta'n foill ta geiyrt da'n Vanninagh
    Oyr treihys fer-ny ghah,
Te'h creeney lurg laa'n Vargee,
    Agh sbeg vondeish te da.

XXXI.

O shinish my gheiney cheerey
    Ta geaishtagh rish m'arrane,
My choyrles te diu ve creeney,
    Choud's ta'n traa ermayrn,

XXXII.

Ych'n chooish ta ooilley lhie er,
    Dy ghoaill kiarail ayns traa
Roish bee loa'n vargee harrish,
    Nyn drimshey son dy braa.

THE VOYAGE OF THE TIGER.

Translated from the Manx by Mr. John Quirk, Carn-ny-Greïe, Kirk-Patrick.

I.

ONCE as the gents of Mona
    Resolv'd our foes to whip,
They threw their pence together,
    And bought a crazy ship.

II.

They had a spot at Douglas,
    And stations here and there,
Where money was collected
    To buy a privateer.

III.

These pence were sent to England,
    Where money is of use,
And so the aged " Tiger "
    Was fitted for a cruise.

IV.

A cry went o'er the island
    For well train'd men and boys ;
So boys in troops collected,
    On hearing such a noise.

V.

They gathered from all quarters,
    And places far and near,
To Nick Moore's house in Douglas,
    Tall as a grenadier.

VI.

Qualtrough will be our captain,
 The leader of our choice,
And Douglas town seem'd moving
 With mirth and joyful cries.

VII.

We'll fight both French and Yankeys,
 We'll conquer or will die ;
The loyal sons of Mona
 Will not their colours fly.

VIII.

Their terms prov'd so enticing,
 The young could not withstand ;
Our farmers cried with anguish
 " How shall we plough our land ?"

IX.

This was a source of sorrow
 Which many a man might rue,
How few were left in Mona,
 To hold the painful plough.

X.

Pity for big Will Condray
 And the great Man of the Hill,
They had so many daughters,
 'Twas sad to hear their wail

XI.

Ye maidens of old Mona
 Who're mourning for our blades,
Who cry, " No men are left us,
 But weak and worthless lads."

XII.

" For they are all enlisted,
  To hear the "Tiger's" roar,
The few who are remaining
  Won't reach us one for four."

XIII.

" We all look for a lover,
  We must have one or none,
Far better without any,
  Than two to marry one."

XIV.

At playing cards and drinking,
  We labour'd day and night,
And cried that none but cowards
  Would hesitate to fight.

XV.

I was constrained to join them,
  And stationed to a gun ;
And oft I cried, lamenting,
  My love and I are done.

XVI.

I often thought with sorrow
  I'd never see her more,
And thus I spent my woeful days
  So near the Ramsey shore.

XVII.

Three days away from Ramsey
  Upon the briny deep,
A fearful storm o'ertook us,
  Which caused our flesh to creep.

XVIII.

Our men were worn by pumping,
  And boys were like to droop,
Big Harry cried, " My Laddies,
  Pray keep your spirits up."

XIX.

The storm which burst upon us
  With its tremendous force,
Soon swept away our rigging,
  We could not keep our course.

XX.

But when the storm abated,
  We sped upon our way,
Old Christmas eve we anchored
  In safety at Mount Bay.

XXI.

In three days' time being ready,
  We sail'd 'neath pleasant skies,
And meeting with a Dutchman,
  We took her for our prize.

XXII.

We then came home to Douglas,
  With loud salutes and noise
With pomp the gents of Mona
  Soon met us with our prize

XXIII.

They much admir'd the Dutchman,
  'Tis sad to tell the tale,
Most haughtily they threatened
  To send us all to jail.

XXIV.

We soon found to our sorrow,
    And great was our surprise,
The vessel we had captur'd
    Was not a lawful prize.

XXV.

They told us that the Governor
    Our desperate case had tried,
And not a judge in Mona
    Would put it on our side.

XXVI.

Then go your ways to England,
    We'll meet you there and then ;
And go by land or water,
    The end will be the same.

XXVII.

Now I'm at home in Mona,
    And from their yoke I'm free ;
And they can never sever
    My loving one from me.

XXVIII.

But what came of the " Tiger,"
    The source of all our noise ;
They sold her off as dowry,
    Or portion with the prize.

XXIX.

Tho' we were men of valour,
    And worthy of a chance,
Misconduct and bad leaders
    Will ruin Spain or France.

XXX.

The fault which cleaves to Manxmen
　　Still ruins many a man,
Wise when the fair day's over,
　　But what avails it then.

XXXI.

All you my friends and brethren
　　Who listen to my rhyme,
I earnestly entreat you,
　　Henceforth be wise in time.

XXXII.

Yea, let the one thing needful
　　Be made our constant care,
Lest we be found lamenting
　　The day after the fair.

YN CHENN DOLPHIN.

LIORISH YUAN LEWIN, SUNDER, YERBY.

I.

Yn chiaghtoo laa jeh'n vee September,
Hie shin er shiaulley ass baie Rumsaa ;
Kiarail dy gheddyn dys geayllin Vaughold,
Dy akin caslys lane vie traa.

II.

Tra haink traa-hidee ven y gheay sheidey,
Ren y flodd gankeral ayns y vaïe ;
Tra cheu-nastyr ren y traa coural,
As chuïr yn flodd magh jeh'n chione chraïe.

III.

Duirree shin maroo cubbyl dy laghyn,
Cha row mouney ry-gheddyn ayn ;
Kione y trass laa hie shin er shiaulley
Yeh geaylin Vaughold as jiass jeh'n chione.

IV.

Hrog shin lught vie dy skeddan ayn,
As roïn lhain dy ghoolish fegooish jough ny bee
Kiarail dy gheddyn reesht dys geaylin Vaughold,
Dy akin caslys roish yn oïe.

V.

Tra ren shin roshtyn dys geaylin Vaughold
She caslys vie va ry-akin ayn ;
Chuïr shin nyn lieen marish yn chaslys,
Magh jeh Rione Vaughold as jiass jeh'n chione.

VI.

Hie shin dy yeeaghyn row'n ceast er snaue,
She caslys vie dy lughtagh v'ayn.
Hirg shin er-boayrd ee, as eisht fo-chiauil ee,
Er son Whitehaven kiarail roshtyn ayn.

VII.

Tra v'ee fo-chiauil ain, as er nyn arrey,
Dy roie by-hiar jin, as by-lesh y trvoaie ;
Cha smooinnee shin er y tidey-varrey,
Ny cre'n lhag-haghyrt va cheet nyn-yeih.

VIII.

Tra va shin er-roshtyn dys thalloo Hostyn,
Va'n thie-lossan dorraghey er kione y cheïy ;
Neu-oaylagh va shin er boayl cha joarree,
Dy roie shin nyn maatey stiagh er traïe.

IX.

Chean shin nyn aker gour y yerree,
As sniem shin y chabyl dys y cheïy my-yiass ;
Yerkal dy sauchey, son y nah hidey,
Tra yinnagh eh lhieeney, dy voghe shin ags.

X.

Lesh y lhieeney-varrey ren y gheay sheidey,
As ren yn aker sleodey dy siyragh nyn-yeih ;
Va shin eisht eginit dy eaymagh son cooney
Agglagh dy ve ceaut er y cheïy my-hrooaïe.

XI.

Paayrt jin va gaccan dy beagh shin caillit,
Paayrt elley gra, cha naggle dooin foast ;
Agh va shin eïginit dy cam son cooney
Dy heet nyn guaiyïl dy hauail nyn mioys.

K

XII.

Tra haink magh baatey hooin va shin ayns sauchys.
As hug ee thiagh shin er kione y cheïy ;
Raad va shin jeeaghyn er y chenn Dolphin,
Cheet stiagh ayns peeshyn huc er y traïe.

XIII.

Paayrt shin va gra, ta shoh feer dewill dooin,
Paayrt elley gra te dooin feer doogh ;
Steein-y-Chamaish vees troiddey creoi dooin,
Agh foddey smessey vees Steein-ny-Oghe.

XIV.

Nish ta shin reesht er roshtyn Mannin,
As ta shin sauchey veih gaue erbee ;
Yn Chonney Logh cha dooyrt eh mouney,
Agh dooinney choar v'an chenn Phoallee.

THE OLD DOLPHIN.

Translated from the Manx by Mr. John Quirk, Carn-ny-Greie.

I.

On the seventh day of the month September,
We sail'd off from old Ramsey Bay,
Resolved to steer towards Maughold's Shoulder,
And watch appearances by the way.

II.

When it was tide-time, the wind was blowing,
And many a boat near their anchor stay'd ;
But towards evening, the weather mending,
The fleet was shot near old Clay-head.

III.

About two days we continued with them,
But very little was there to be had ;
On the third day we continued sailing,
Off Maughold's Shoulder, south of the head.

IV.

We got some herrings, and sail'd off for Douglas,
And soon got ready, thence to embark ;
Resolv'd to reach to old Maughold's Shoulder,
And take up our station before it was dark.

V.

When we arrived near old Maughold's Shoulder,
Good were the signs to be seen indeed ;
We shot our nets there amidst good prospects,
Near Maughold's Shoulder, south of the head.

VI.

When we had proved how the fish was stirring,
Signs of good cargoes did soon appear ;
We soon haul'd in, and set our sails up,
Straight on for Whitehaven resolv'd to steer.

VII.

When we got sails up, we set our compass
To steer due east, and one point north ;
Without regarding how tides were running,
Or what variations they might bring forth.

VIII.

As we were nearing the coast of England,
No pier-head lights were seen on land ;
Being unacquainted, and among strangers,
We ran in our boat upon the strand.

IX.

When out, astern we had cast our anchor,
We got a cable to the Southern Quay ;
Expecting when the tide was ebbing,
We could again get safe away.

X.

As the tide rose, the wind was blowing,
We dragg'd our anchor, its hold gave way ;
We were forced to call out for assistance,
Lest we should strike on the Northern Quay.

XI.

There some were shouting, "We all must perish,"
Others expected the storm to brave ;
But we had then to look for assistance,
Some men to help us our lives to save.

XII.

When from a boat we were safely landed,
There upon the pier-head we stood once more,
Where we could witness the poor old Dolphin,
In pieces floating towards the shore.

XIII.

Some kept on saying, 'tis very serious,
While others said, 'tis bad of course ;
Steein-y-Chamaïsh behaved rather furious,
But Steein-ny-Oghe was by far the worse.

XIV.

Now we have landed on dear old Mona,
And from these perils we are safe again ;
Whilst the Conney-logh did not much blame us,
We found the old Foallee a good-natur'd man.

THE ROSE ON THE BEAM.

On Saturday the 14th December 1822 His Majesty's brig of war *Race-horse*, of 18 guns, commanded by Captain W. B. Suckling, was totally lost on Langness, Isle of Man.

It appeared that a *rose* had been painted on one of the *beams* of the cockpit of the vessel. This incident induced a gentleman, then in the island, Captain Hook, son of Major Hook of the Royal Artillery, who had resided for many years in Douglas, to write the following song, which appeared within a few days after the loss of the *Racehorse*.

THE rose is now withered and sunk in the grave,
Its leaves are now blighted and wet in the wave ;
No more through the stream the proud *Racehorse* goes,
Yet life's brightest sunshine was under the rose.

Oh, sigh not, for fancy shall picture full true
All the moments of gladness which there swiftly flew ;
And as memory shall trace her full sail down the stream,
Do you think she'll pass heedless " The Rose on the Beam ?"

Ah no ! yet time's sand must run on and decay,
And memory, like evening's last gleam fade away ;
The heart must be blighted, life's current be froze,
E're the days be forgotten—when under the rose.

Then tarry ye moments, too swiftly ye fly,
Our leaves, like the rose, must soon wither and die ;
Life quickly shall pass ('tis a feverish dream),
And too soon be forgotten, " The Rose on the Beam."

The loss of the *Racehorse* caused a considerable sensation in the island, but more particularly at Castletown. She was on her way from Millford Haven to Douglas, for the purpose of convoying His Majesty's cutter *Vigilant*, which had been considerably damaged upon " Conister," in Douglas Bay, on the 6th October preceding. She made the Calf of Man Lights at 5 P.M. on the 14th December. Some time afterwards another light was distinguished, which the pilot believed to be that on Douglas pier head. It turned out, however to be the Castletown pier-head light. The brig had at this time got into the entrance of Castletown Bay, and before Captain Suckling could get out of the difficulty he was in, the vessel struck upon a rock at the south point of Langness. It was then dark and cloudy, with a heavy sea, which caused the brig to strike violently. With considerable difficulty the cutter was got out, and every exertion used to get the stream anchor into it, with the intention of carrying it out, but owing to the heavy breakers this was found impracticable.

It was soon ascertained that the rock was through the brig's bottom, and the water flowed in until it actually lifted the lower deck. Guns were fired, rockets thrown up, and blue lights burnt, but without attracting attention on shore. The cutter, under the command of Lieutenant Mallack, and the galley, under Mr. Curtis (Purser), left the brig with orders to make for shore to endeavour to procure assistance. Being ignorant of the locality in which they were, the men must have pulled round the promontory of Langness as the galley reached "Fort Island" at 11.30, the cutter being fully an hour later. From this place the officers and men proceeded to Castletown for assistance. Several boats put off for the scene of the wreck, but only one succeeded in passing through the breakers. This boat made five trips, and brought all the crew from the brig, but, unfortunately, when nearing the shore for the last time, with Captain Suckling, the first Lieutenant Falkner, and a number of men, a sea broke on board and swamped her. Six of the brig's crew and three Manxmen perished. Captain Suckling and Lieutenant Falkner were the last rescued, and their preservation was almost miraculous.

The cool and undaunted conduct of the Captain during the whole scene was the theme of admiration and praise by all his officers and crew. Not an article of clothing or property was saved by any one, except what was upon their persons.

On the following days, Sunday and Monday, every exertion was made to save portions of the wreck, but very little was recovered. The brig went down in deep water. The Lieutenant-Governor and the gentlemen of Castletown showed the utmost attention to both officers and men; the former were accommodated at the "George Inn," and the latter in the Barracks.

The above is an extract from an account of the loss given in *The Rising Sun* newspaper of the 17th December 1822.

In a statement of "Vessels wrecked on the Coast of the Isle of Man" from 1822 to 1835, published by Robert Kelly, Esq., Notary-Public, the number of lives stated to have been lost on board the *Racehorse* was seven. The value of the vessel was set down at £15,000.

Captain Suckling was said to have been a nephew of Lord Nelson's.

MANNIN VEG VEEN.

Written from the Recitation of Mr. Harry Quilliam of Peel, 1868.

To the tune of " Barbara Allan."

I.

O VANNIN veg veen,
Tayns mean y cheayn,
Aynjee ta lane eeasteyryn ;
Tra ta'n oarn cuïrt,
As ny praasyn soit,
Goll roue dy cherragh ny baatyn.

II.

Son y Feailloin,
Bee mayd goll roin,
Dy yeeaghyn son warpyn Skeddan ;
Heear 'sy chione rouayr,
Lesh yurnaa liauyr,
Goaill neose nyn shiauill fo'n Charron.

III.

Heear ee y veaïn,
Shiaulley dy meen,
Yn tidey keayrt va noi ain ;
Stiagh dys Purt-Chiarn,
Dy yeeaghyn ny mraane,
As dy phaagey nyn myrneenyn.

IV.

Goll veih thie dy hie,
Yeeaghyn son jough-vie,
Cha ron ny lheid ry-gheddyn ;

Eisht hrog shin Shiaull,
Erskyn nyn gione,
As hie shin son y gheaylin.

V.

Heear ec y chiark,
Magh ec yn chleait,
Yn cheayn va gatt as freayney ;
Roish rosh shin tidey
Yn Chiggin vooar,
Daa ghooinney gollish teaymey.

VI.

Goll seose yn roayrt,
Ta deiney loayrt,
As mennic fluighey nyn lieckan ;
Yn fload va roïn,
As foddey voïn,
Adsyn shegin dooin y gheddyn.

VII.

Tra ren shin feddyn,
'Syn fload vy-gheddyn,
Nagh row ad shen lesk phrowal ;
Tra cheayl shin oc,
Ny skeayllyn v'oc,
Nagh cheau shin voïn yn famman.

VIII.

Tra v'an shibber eït,
As yn ushtey roït,
As ooilley jeant dy baghtal;
Hie shin dy rousagh,
Kow yn eeast veg sondagh,
Dy heet roue hoïn dy aghtal.

IX.

Roish brishey'n laa,
Hug shin magh coraa,
Cha leah's va shin er phrowal ;
Eisht yn chied saagh,
Haink hooin dy booiagh,
Dansoor shin ee dy lowal.

X.

Ec brishey-yn-laa,
Ve kinne as rea,
Va'n cheayn gol-rish traaie-gheïnnee,
Dy chooilley hiaull,
Vo'o fakin goll,
Gyllagh, jeeagh magh son wherree.

XI.

Er y vaïe vooar,
Va sterrym dy liooar,
Lesh carish fliugh as fliaghey ;
Skeddan dy glen,
Yiogh shin ayns shen,
'Bey'n ghobbag as y vuc-varrey.

XII.

Toshiaght yn Ouyr,
Bee'n oie gaase liauyr,
Faag mayd nyn mannaght ec y Chiggin
Hig mayd eisht roïn,
Dys Doolish ny lhong,
As bee giense ain ayns thie Whiggin.

XIII.

Ayns thie Whiggin vooar,
Ta jough dy liooar,
Marish palchey lhune as liggar :

As lhiabbee-vie,
Dy gholl dy lhie,
Tra vees mayd lesh nyn shibber.

XIV.

Bee paayrt cheet thie,
Fegooish niaght vie,
Ta'n snaïe ain eït ec y ghobbag ;
Ny mraane—oast hene,
Goaill chymmey jin,
'Sgra, ta caart ain foast 'sy vullag.

MANNIN-VEG-VEEN.

Translated by Mr. John Quirk, Carn-ny-Greïe, Kirk-Patrick.

I.

Hail! Isle of Man,
Sweet ocean land,
I love thy sea-girt border ;
When the barley's sown,
And the potatoes down,
We'll get our boats in order.

II.

Midsummer day,
And we are away
In earnest seeking herring ;
Contrary Head
At length is made,
Take down our sails at Charron.

III.

West at the mine,
One day being fine,
The tide against us veering ;
We then sought next
Our soothing sex,
Our sweethearts at Port Erin.

IV.

Then here and there,
We sought good beer,
But none could we discover ;
Up to the gale
We hoist our sail,
And made toward the Shoulder.

V.

Lo there and then,
Around the Hen,*
The bounding waves were jumping,
Ere we had tried
The Chickens' tide,
We lost some sweat by pumping.

VI.

We found the fleet
We sought to meet
Had left us far behind them ;
Tho' spring tides dash,
Our decks to wash,
Yet still we strove to find them.

VII.

As we came near
To where they were,
They'd proved how things were doing ;
So, when we heard
How they had fared,
Our nets were set agoing.

VIII.

Then, supper o'er,
The water store,
And all things in rotation ;
We went to test our fish and mesh,
To learn their situation.

IX.

Before the dawn
Our horn was blown—
We then knew good and evil ;

* The Hen and Chickens are rocks opposite the Calf of Man.

And the first men
Who gladly came,
We spoke them fair and civil.

X.

At early dawn,
'Twas fair and calm,
The waves forgot their fury ;
And every sail
Within our hail,
They wish'd to see a wherry.

XI.

On the big bay,
'Twas a stormy day,
The weather wet and cloggish ;
The herrings there,
In plenty were,
The sea-hog and the dog-fish.

XII.

When days curtail,
We'll bid farewell
To Calf-lands, Hen, and Chickens ;
At Douglas then
Will be our inn,
We'll have a ball at Quiggin's.

XIII.

At Quiggin's hall
There's plenty ale,
With beer and all things proper :
A goodly place,
With beds of ease,
When we are done our supper.

XIV.

Once home again,
Some may complain,
The dog-fish did not spare us ;
Land-ladies wise
Will sympathise,
And fetch a drop to cheer us.

THE "MANX FAIRY" STEAMER.

THE "Manx Fairy" steam packet made her first trip from the port of Liverpool to Ramsey on the 31st August 1853, and returned from Ramsey to Liverpool on the following morning. On this occasion the following lines were printed and sung about the streets of Ramsey.

> OH, Mannin veg veen, ta my chree sthill lhiat hene,
> As bwooishal dhyt mie son dy braa ;
> As tra hed ym, my annym goit voym,
> Bee'm bwooishal sthill mie da Rumsaa.

> Ta'n "Ferish" er roshtyn dy bieau voish shenn hostyn,
> Ny queelyn eek tappee chyndaa ;
> As laadit dy slich va shin fakin dy v'ee,
> Ooilly bwooishal cree mie da Rumsaa.

Thus translated—

> Oh, Mona, my darling, my heart is still thine,
> My blessing upon thee, I pray ;
> And when I am dead, and my spirit is fled,
> Success unto Ramsay, I say.

> The " Fairy" has come, and swiftly has run,
> Her paddles go quickly around ;
> Well loaded she were with passengers rare,
> All wishing success to the town.

DR. WATT'S "LITTLE BUSY BEE."

Translated into Manx by Rev. J. T. Clarke.

I.

Jeeagh er y chellan veg
    Cre'n aght te'e ceau e hraa ;
Te'e getlagh nish, as getlagh reesht,
    As chaglym mill gaghlaa.

II.

Cre cha jeidjagh te'e ayns traa,
    Ayns jannoo seose yn kere ;
As streeu dy creoi, dy lhieeney eh,
    Lesh stoo ny sbuigh ny airh.

III.

Ayns obbyr eisht ta mie,
    Cha bee'ms dy bragh ergooyll ;
Son dy chur mow my annym gheyr,
    T'an noid dy kinjagh shooyll.

IV.

Gys slaynt ny giootyn t'aym,
    Lhig don my aegid cheau ;
Dy voddym's choontey choyrt da yee,
    Te'r choyrt my aegid don.

CARVAL NY DROGH VRAANE.

A PRINTED copy of this carval, under the title of "Yezebel" (7 pages),
is in the editor's possession. It has four extra verses following verse
xvii., which it has been thought better to omit in the present version.

I.

My Chaarjyn gheyr as ghraihagh,
Ayns shoh jiu er veeitteil ;
My sailliu shaghney peccah,
Fo mraane nagh jin-jee reill,
Ta'n reill oc feer neu-chairagh,
Ta'n Ostyl Phaul dy ghra,
Tra haink yn Noid'sy gharey
She'n ven s'leaïe gheill hug da.

II.

She ish va'n voir ain ooilley,
Son v'ee da Adam ben,
Ny-yeih she ee ren coayl yn vaynrys
J'ee hene as da e chloan,
She ish chaill yn vaynrys,
Tra vrish ee sarey Yee,
Tra ghow ee coyrle yn noid vroghe
She shen ren molley ee.

III.

O ! Ooilley shiuish chloan gheiney,
Ta foast er-mayrn s'ythcihll
Ny cur shin saynt da aalid
Yn ven sbwa sbooïee agh ren rieau shooyll
Agh smooinnee shiuish er David
As neesht er Solomon
Thys va'dsyn cleaynit lioroo
Ny deiney creeney v'ayn.

IV.

Ta shoh sampleyr dinish aegid,
Gow shiuish kiarail ayns traa
Nagh bee-jee miolit lioroo
Nagh myr t'an Scriptyr gra
My ren shin rieau agh lhaih jeh
Mychione yn dooinney aeg,
Va shooyl dy feer almoragh,
Tra veeit eh ben 'sy traid.

V.

As lesh e chengey veeley
She 'n scoolag violee maree
Hiart myr yn voddey oakley
Yn vannan shooyll ny-yeih,
Ny myr yn chretoor valloo
Yn butchoor shooyll ny chione,
Ragh jeeragh gys yn traartys
My veg kys da cre hon.

VI.

O shimmey dooinney creeney
T'er hurrause liorish mraane,
My lhaih shin rieau j'eh Joseph,
Quoi hilg et ayns pryssoon
She olkys e ven-ainshtyr
Dreïll eh fo bottyn-yiarn,
Myr scairagh ve'h dy yannoo
Ayns feanish Yee as Tharn.

VII.

Dy smooinagh shiuish er Samson,
As, cooinagh reesht er Yob,
Cren olkys v'ayns ny mraane oc
Er-chee dy violagh ad.

Ny geayll shin rieau j'eh Naboth,
Thys hooar eh baase cha dewill,
She kyndagh rish ben Ahab,
She ish va Yezabel.

VIII.

She ish ghow spooilley Naboth
As stroie ee phadeyryn Yee
My cheayll shiu rieau jehn 'vaase eek
She moddee ren ee y ee
As myrgeddin Athaliah
Yn olkys eek va dewill,
Tra stroie ee pobble Yudah
As ghow ee hene yn reill.

IX.

O Quoi oo hene my leharrey
Veagh cleaynit liorish mraane,
Ta'd soyllit ayns yn Scriptyr
Ny smessey ny'n lion.
Ta'd soyllit dys y lion,
As dys yn dragon neesht,
As jeh'n olkys oc ny-sodjey,
Ta nearey orrym ginsh.

X.

Ny-yeih te ayns y Scriptyr
Thiongoyrt rish dagh unnane.
My ren shin rieau agh lhaih jeh,
Cre'n olkys ren rieau mraane.
Ta'n olkys oc dou trinshey
Dy smooinagh er Noo Ean,
Dy row lheid y dooinney vannee
Rieau tilgit ayns pryssoon.

XI.

O smooinnee-jee, My Chaarjyn
Er dooinney-vannee Yee,
Thys hooar ben-aeg son daunsyn
E yeearree voish yn Ree
Ean-Bashtey va yn dooinney
My cheayll shiu rieau jeh e vaase
She e chione hooar ee son daunsyn
Nagh bollagh v'ee dyn grayse.

XII.

Cha birrys da Mac Sirach
Ve loayrt nyn oi cha dewill,
Dy re drogh ven my vessey
Ye'h dagh cretoor sy theihll.
Ta'n olkys oc reesht soyllit
Ny smessey na dagh nhee,
Ta shen erskyn ny princesyn
Ta kerragh drogh-yantee.

XIII.

Nagh streih'n stayd, My Chaarjyn,
Dagh creestee er yn oor,
Dy beagh nyn yannoo soyllit,
Ny smessey na'n chretoor.
Son t'eshin as ny princesyn
Heese dooint ayns ooig dy aile,
As adsyn ver rish peccah,
Heese marish nee ad reill.

XIV.

She marish Ben as Tubal
As Meshech as Elam,
As maroo neesht ta Dives,
Ayns sheshaght rish drogh-vraane

As maroo hig oo my charrey,
As yn tutler vroghe ta shooyll,
My ver oo raad da peccah,
Roo shoh chendaa dty chooyll.

XV.

As jeeagh dy geir 'sy Scriptyr,
Dy chooilley oor yiow traa,
Cre'n kerragh ta cour peccee,
Ayns niuvin heese dy braa,
Ayns niurin heese ayns torchagh,
Ayns aile nee oo geam dy geir,
Gra s'treih yn laa haink orrym
Tra reih mee yn laue chiaue.

XVI.

Gra shoh va slane my haitnys,
Tra ghow mee eh son reih,
Ayns fidleyryn as caartyn,
Ayns feeyn as bwoalley sleih,
Ayns streepee-ys as daunsyn
Va my haitnys oie as laa,
As fark cre'n jerrey haink orrym,
Tra ren y Chiarn rhym gra.

XVII.

Nee shoh'n breearrey ren oo
Tra vow er dty ghaa ghlioon
Vow gee my cill myr arran,
As gin my nill myr feeyn,
Vow gialdyn neesht ve booisal
As bishaghey ayns grayse,
Agh sleaie ren oo jarrood mee
As geiyrt er raad Yuaase.

XVIII.

Ny-yeih ayns slane dty hurrause
Te ooilley 'n foill ayd hene
Son va me ish dy kingagh sarsy oo
Veih peccah as drogh vraane,
Myr te baghtal ayns y Scriptyr
Thiongoyrt rish cloan sheelnaue
Dy re drogh-ven by-vessey
Ye'h dagh cretoor ta snaave.

XIX.

Cre'n sorch dy vraane, My Chaarjyn,
O lhisagh shiuish y ve,
Ta geaishtagh rish ny goan shoh
Mysh olkys mraane cre te.
Ny-yeih cre va nyn olkys
Cha row myr shen agh paart,
Son she jeh Ben v'eh ruggit,
Yn charrey ghow nyn baart.

XX.

She ish va'n moirrey vannee
As neesht moirrey malaine
As Deborah ayns kiartys
Ren bleeantyn reill yn rheam
As ymmodee mraane elley,
Dy baghtal ta'n scriptyr gra,
Ren leeideil bea cha cairagh
As fer ren rieau chyndaa.

XXI.

Son te co-laik, My Chaarjyn,
Da dooinney ny da ben,
My nee ad treiggeill peccah,
As geiyrt er Creest nyn yiarn.

As geiyrt er lesh nyn aigney,
Dagh Creestee meen yiow ayrn
Jeh miljid Ainleyn flaunys,
Trooid fuill gheyr Creest nyn yiarn.

XXII.

She trooid e uill, My Chaarjyn,
She eshyn hig nyn whaail
As marish sheshaght dy ainleyn,
Ayns bingys as ayns kiaull,
Gra gloyr hoods er yn Yrjid,
As er y thalloo shee,
As aigney mie gys deiney,
Dy kinjagh myr shen guee.

CAROL ON BAD WOMEN MENTIONED IN SCRIPTURE.

Translated by Mr. John Quirk, Carn-ny-Greïe, Kirk-Patrick.

I.

Come all ye sons of mortals,
And to my words give ear,
Would ye avoid transgressing,
Of women's rule beware ; *
Their rule is fraught with danger,
As plainly may appear,
E'en in fair Eden's garden †
She was the first to err.

II.

Thus from the days of Adam
Her mischief you may trace,
And how she brought destruction
On all the human race.
There our deluded Mother,
As you may call to mind,
By hearkening to the Serpent
Did ruin all mankind.

III.

This truly sounds alarming
To all the sons of time,
For women still are women
Through every age and clime ;
Even Solomon ‡ and David,§
Those saints of former days,
Were led astray by women,
Though wisest of our race.

* 1 Tim. ii. 12. † 2 Cor. xi. 3. ‡ 1 Kings xi. 1.
§ 2 Samuel xi. 3-4.

IV.

This to the young speaks volumes,
To flee the tempter's smile,
The gross and foul seduction
Of all that would beguile.
Read in the Book of Proverbs,*
The woman in the street,
Who happens in her rambles
The thoughtless youth to meet.

V.

By her deceitful speeches
The stripling she o'ercame,
And off to swift destruction
The wolf did take the lamb,
Led as the brute creation
To slaughter or the snare,
Unmindful of the danger,
That death is dealing there.

VI.

Lo! men, the most praiseworthy,
Have suffer'd 'neath their blast.
Have you not read of Joseph?†
Upright from first to last,
The vengeance of a woman
Caused him with grief to smart;
The pangs of iron fetters
Did pierce him to the heart.

VII.

To speak of Job ‡ and Samson,§
Still women in their day

---

* Proverbs vii. 6 to end.　　† Gen. xxxix. 7 to end.
‡ Job ii. 9.　　§ Judges xvi. 6-20.

Were urg'd by Satan's power
To draw their feet astray.
With pain we read of Naboth *
How awfully he fell,
Caused by the wife of Ahab,
The infamous Jezabel.

VIII.

'Twas she who spoil'd poor Naboth ;
God's prophets she had slain,
But vengeance overtook her,
And dogs ate up the queen.†
See also Athaliah,‡
That base usurping queen,
Who shed the blood of princes
And inoffending men.

IX.

Who could be fool'd by women,
Who look at what they've done ;
The Scriptures do compare them
To lions, and so on.
Compar'd unto the lion §
And dragons ‖ in their cell,
Of their misconduct further
We really blush to tell.

X.

But still 'tis found in Scripture,
Before the sons of men,
If you be pleased to read it,
How cruel they have been.

---

* 1 Kings xxi. 13, 14, 15.   † 2 Kings ix. 36.   ‡ 2 Kings xi. 1.
§ Ezek. xix. 2-6.   ‖ Rev. xii. 3, 4, 13, 17 : Eccles. xxv. 13 to end.

Their conduct how it grieves me
To think upon St. John,
That e'en our Lord's forerunner
Was into prison thrown.

XI.

O think of this, my brethren,
This holy man of God,
Though closely barr'd in prison,
They thirsted for his blood ;
The blessed John * the Baptist
They longed to see him dead ;
A graceless wench for dancing,
In pay received his head.

XII.

Well might the son † of Sirach
On tracing women's ways,
Defy the whole creation
To furnish such a race.
Must they the whole creation
In cruelty excel,
Exceed tormentors' furies,
And fiends of nether hell.

XIII.

Astounding news, my brethren,
We scarcely ever knew,
If women the arch-rebel
In mischief can outdo.
But he with all his princes
Are doom'd to endless woe ;
All unconverted sinners
The same must undergo.

---

* Matt. xiv. 3-12. † Eccles. xxvi. 6-12, 22-27.

XIV.

With Meshech, Ben, and Tubal,*
And Elam's mighty host,
Where Dives and naughty women
Must rank among the lost.
And we'll go, my brethren,
If we in sin remain,
Where lying tongues and slanderers
Endure eternal pain.

XV.

O think of these poor wretches
For ever doom'd to dwell,
Clos'd down below the hatches
Of an eternal hell.
Think of eternal weeping
And gnashing, what it is,
And look before you leap in
To such a hell as this.

XVI.

Were you baptised a Christian,
To own your Saviour's cause,
And without fear or flinching
To fight beneath his cross?
But will you fight against him,
And flee from Jesus' fold,
And thus bring death eternal
On your immortal soul?

XVII.

If you'll despise the danger,
And rush to endless pain,
When conscience will accuse you,
You will have none to blame,

* Ezek. xxxviii. 2, 3 ; xxxix. 1.

But rue through endless ages
That ever you were born,
And o'er a day of pleasure
Eternally to mourn.

XVIII.

Now God is nigh to save you,
If you'll implore his grace,
From death, from sin, and Satan,
And women's evil ways.
'Tis plainly seen, my brother,
Before each mortal's eye,
That women stand unrivall'd
By aught that creep or fly.

XIX.

And now, my dearest sisters,
Can you despise these lines,
Which point so very piercingly
To women and their crimes ?
But still tho' great their evils,
'Tis some we have to mourn,
For e'en our blest Messiah
Was of a woman born.

XX.

The conduct of the Virgin,*
Deborah,† and Malaine,
Can scarcely be surpassed
Among the sons of men.
With many more besides them,
In Scripture still held forth,
Their conduct most praiseworthy,‡
The honour'd of the earth.

---

* Matt. xxviii. 1-5.   † Judges iv. 4.   ‡ Gen. xviii. 12. Prov. xxxi. 10-30.

XXI.

Still Jesus, our Redeemer,
For every sinner slain,
Appears the common Saviour
Of women and of men ;
And all may find salvation,
And pardon through his blood,
And walk with Christ to heaven,
And walk on earth with God.

XXII.

And follow their Redeemer
With all their heart and mind,
Till women, men, and angels
Shall in one chorus join.
To God on high be glory,
Peace and good-will to men.
Repeat the pleasing story
Till Christ appears to reign.

A NEW CHRISTMAS CAROL.

"All you who are to mirth inclined."

THIS rude old carol is from an old MS. copy of about the middle of last century, and was a favourite one in country districts. Various versions have been printed in works on Christmas Carols, but this appears to extend much farther than any I have met with.

I.

ALL you who are to mirth inclined,
Consider well, and bear in mind
What your great God for you hath done,
In sending his beloved Son.

II.

Let all your songs and praises be
Unto his Heavenly Majesty ;
And evermore among your mirth
Remember Christ and his bles't birth.

III.

The five and twentieth of December,
Great cause have we to remember,
In Bethlehem upon this morn
There was a bles't Messiah born.

IV.

The night before that happy tide
The spotless Virgin, and her guide,
Were long time seeking up and down
To find out lodging in the town.

V.

And mark how all things came to pass ;
They in the lodgings so full was,
That they could find no room at all
But in the ox's sully stall.

VI.

Wherein the Virgin Mary mild
Was safe delivered of a Child ;
According to high Heaven's decree
He was man's Saviour to be.

VII.

Near Bethlehem did shepherds keep
With watchful care their flocks of sheep ;
So, when an angel did appear,
Which filled all their hearts with fear.

VIII.

" Prepare to go," the angel said,
" To Bethlehem, be not afraid ;
There shall you see, this blessed morn,
The heavenly babe, sweet Jesus, born."

IX.

With thankful hearts and joyful mind,
The shepherds went this babe to find ;
And as before the angel told,
They did our Saviour Christ behold.

X.

Within a manger he was laid,
And by his side the Virgin stayed,
Attending on the Lord of life,
Being both mother, maid, and wife.

XI.

If choirs of angels did rejoice,
Well may mankind with heart and voice
Sing praises to the God of Heaven,
For he to us his Son hath given.

XII.

Moreover, let us every one
Call unto mind, and think upon
His righteous life, and how he died,
That sinners might be justified.

XIII.

Suppose, O man, that thou should be
In prison strong, condemn'd to die,
And had no friends upon the earth
Would ransom you from cruel death.

XIV.

Except you could some person find,
That unto you would be so kind,
As would you free redemption give,
Would die himself, that you might live.

XV.

Such was the act of Christ, when we
Were doomed to endless misery,
To save us from the gulph of woe,
Himself much pain did overflow.

XVI.

While in this world he did remain
He did not spend one hour in vain ;
To fasting, and to prayers divine,
He mostly did devote his time.

XVII.

He in the Temple daily taught,
And many miracles he wrought ;
He gave the blind their perfect sight,
And caused the lame to walk upright.

XVIII.

He cured the lepers of their evils,
And by his power he cast out devils ;
He raised Lazarus from the dead,
And to the sick their health restored.

XIX.

But yet, for all these wonders wrought,
The Jew his dire destruction brought ;
And Judas, who did with him stay,
Did, with a kiss, his Lord betray.

XX.

Then he was taken by the Jews,
Who did him wrongfully accuse,
And pass the sentence then, that he
Should suffer death upon a tree.

XXI.

They led him then unto the cross,
And thereupon he nailed was ;
They scornfully did him deride,
And thrust a spear into his side.

XXII.

Then never let us cease to sing,
With grateful hearts unto our King,
Who hath so freely shed his blood,
Only to do us sinners good.

CHRISTMAS CAROL.

TAKEN down from the recitation of boys in the south of the island, and
as it differs in some instances from the Carol given at page 102 in the
first series of *Mona Miscellany,* it is thought worthy of preservation in
this series.

WE wish you a merry Christmas and a happy New Year ;
With your pockets full of money and your cellar full of beer,
For it's in the Christmas times we travel far and near,
So we wish you a merry Christmas and a happy New Year.

You go to your stable, your mind is on your horse ;
Your mind is not on Jesus Christ, who suffered on the cross,
Who suffered on the cross, and his blessed may you be,
For you'll never do for Jesus Christ what he has done for we.
And the Lord send you a happy New Year.

You go to your cow-house, your mind is on your cows ;
Your mind is not on Jesus Christ, who gave the several vows,
Who gave the several vows, and his blessed may you be,
For you'll never do for Jesus Christ what he has done for we.
And the Lord send you a happy New Year.

You go to your haggard, your mind is on your corn ;
Your mind is not on Jesus Christ who wore the crown of thorn,
Who wore the crown of thorn, and his blessed may you be,
For you'll never do for Jesus Christ what he has done for we.
And the Lord send you a happy New Year.

You go to the meadow, your mind is on your hay ;
Your mind is not on Jesus Christ, who was born on Christmas
day,
Who was born on Christmas day, and his blessed may you be,
For you'll never do for Jesus Christ what he has done for we.
And the Lord send you a happy New Year.

You go into your chamber, your mind is on your sleep ;
Your mind is not on Jesus Christ, who for your soul did weep,
Who for your soul did weep, and his blessed may you be,
For you'll never do for Jesus Christ what he has done for we.
     ' And the Lord send you a happy New Year.

You go into your parlour, your mind is on your dinner ;
Your mind is not on Jesus Christ, who suffered for a sinner,
Who suffered for a sinner, and his blessed may you be,
For you'll never do for Jesus Christ what he has done for we.
     And the Lord send you a happy New Year.

You go to get married, your mind is on your maid ;
Your mind is not on Jesus Christ, who in the manger laid,
Who in the manger laid, and his blessed may you be,
For you'll never do for Jesus Christ what he has done for we.
     And the Lord send you a happy New Year.

We are not come to your house to beg nor to borrow ;
For we are come to your house to drive away your sorrow,
To drive away your sorrow, and his blessed may you be,
For you'll never do for Jesus Christ what he has done for we.
     And the Lord send you a happy New Year.

For we're not like dirty beggars, who beg from door to door ;
We are your neighbour's children, that have been here before,
That have been here before, and his blessed may you be,
For you'll never do for Jesus Christ what he has done for we.
     And the Lord send you a happy New Year.

God bless the master of the house, and to the mistress too,
And all the little children, around the table too ;
Around the table too, and his blessed may you be,
For you'll never do for Jesus Christ what he has done for we.
     And the Lord send you a happy New Year.

In comes the mistress of the house, a star upon her breast ;
Awake her soul to happiness, God send her soul to rest,
God send her soul to rest, and his blessed may you be,
For you'll never do for Jesus Christ what he has done for we.
    And the Lord send you a happy New Year.

We've got a little leathern bag that's worn very thin ;
And if you choose to give us a Christmas box, do line it well
    within,
Do line it well within, and his blessed may you be,
For you'll never do for Jesus Christ what he has done for we.
    And the Lord send you a happy New Year.

THE MORNING AND EVENING HYMN.

IN MANX.

By the Rev. Thomas Corlett.

THE Morning and Evening Hymns, written by Bishop Kenn, are here given as being considered pure specimens of the Manx language. They are taken from an old MS., written by the Rev. Thomas Corlett, vicar of Lezayre, in 1773. Mr. Corlett was one of the translators of the Holy Bible into the Manx language, first printed in 1772, the portion of Job being allotted to him. He also transcribed the Liturgy and Epistles, as well as the *Christian Monitor*, and superintended a Manx impression of the New Testament in London.

HYMN SON Y VOGHREY.

I.

O ANNYM, dooisht, as lesh y Ghrian,
Roie kiart dty chourse gys y vea veayn,
Crie Jeed meerioose, as irree traa,
Dy eeck da Jee, dty wooise dagh laa.

II.

Dty hraa deyr cailt, dy-leah eïe thic,
Lhig da dagh laa ve ceaut dty mie ;
Dty churrym freill gys rere dty phooar,
Jean oo hene cooie son y laa 'ooar.

III.

Bee ynrick ayns dty ghlaare dagh traa,
Dty chree freill glen myr Grian'vunlaa,
Slane traa dty vea toig kys ta Jee,
Sheer fakin smooinaght' ghowin dty chree.

IV.

O Annym, dooisht, trogg seose dty chree,
As marish Ainleyn, moyll uss Jee,
Ta fud ny hoie sheer goaill arrane,
Coyrt gloyr as booise da Chiarn dagh hiarn.

V.

Gloyr hoods t'er vreayll mee saucht 'syn oie,
As ren lesh cadley gooragh mee ;
Giall, Hiarn, tra ghooisht-ym seose veih baase
Dy voym gys Niau mârts Yee ny ghrayse.

VI.

My vreearey, Hiarn, neems yannoo Noa,
My pheccaghyn skeayl myr lieh-rio ;
My smooinaght freill uss imlee, meen,
As lhieen mee lesh dty spyrryd hene.

VII.

Coyrlee, as leeid mee yn laa Jiu,
Ayns dagh nhee yns-ym veih dty ghoo,
Lesh bree my Niart, as mooads my phooar,
Dy vod-yms gloyragh' dt' Ennym 'ooar.

HYMN SON YN ASTYR.

I.

Gloyr hoods, my Yee, nish as dagh traa,
Son bannaghtyn dty hoilshey brâ ;
Freill uss, O freill mee, Ree dagh ree,
Fo scaa dty skeean dy saucht ayns shee.

II.

Leih dou dagh peccah, Jiu, Hiarn vie,
Er graih dty Vac, eer Mac dty graih ;
Rhym penc, yn Seihel, as rhyts, O Yee,
My gadlym noght, dy vod v'aym shee.

III.

Leeid mee 'sy raad sheer lhisin 'reih,
Nagh lhiass don aggle ghoaill Jeh'n oaie ;
Kiare mee son baase, dy vod v'aym pooar,
Dy heet gys gloyr ec y laa 'ooar.

IV.

My varrant slane ta orts, my Yee,
Lesh cadley veen Jean ' ooragh' mee,
Lheid as nee yannoo mee breeoil,
Dy hirveish oo ayns aght gherjoil.

V.

Tra ta mee dooisht my lhie 'syn oie,
My Annym lhicen lesh smooinaght vie ;
Dagh Dreamal olk freill voish my chree,
Pooar'yn y Noid, nagh boir ad mee.

VI.

Dty Ainlyn noo cur hym, Hiarn gheyr,
Dy reayll mee saucht veih dagh dangeyr ;
Lesh Graih as booise, O lhicen my chree,
Dagh smooinaght broghe freill voym, O Yee.

VII.

O cuin yioym rea rish cadley'n theihll,
Ayns niau dy vod-ym mârts ve reiel,
As marish Ainlyn sheer yoaill ay'rn,
Coyrt Gloyr as booise da Chiarn dagh hiarn.

GLORIA PATRI.

Gys Jee, fer-toyrt dagh gioot, ard Ghloyr!
Moyll-Jee eh, dagh cretoor Jeh pooar!
Moyll-Jee yn tyr, shiuish Ainlyn smoo!
Moyll-Jee yn Mac 'syn Spyrryd Noo!

PSALM CXXXIX.

In Manx.

THIS Psalm was also translated by the Rev. Thomas Corlett, taken from the same MS. as the foregoing. Some of the Psalms were translated by the Revs. Robert Radcliffe and Matthias Curghey in 1761, and were, by order of Bishop Hildesley, dated at Bishop's Court, November 9, 1761, to be sung " in the several country churches of this isle." These were printed in the Book of Common Prayer in the Manx tongue, in 1777. The one here given has not been printed.

I.

T'ou, Hiarn, coyrt tastey geyre dagh traa,
Da course my vea sheir oie as laa,
My smooinaght' dowin shione dhyts, O Yee,
Roish t'ad er yentyn ayns my chree.

II.-III.

My raaidyn, Hiarn, shione dhyt dy-mie.
My skyrraght mennick voish dty leigh,
Eer goan my veeal, 'smooinaght my chree
Shione dhyts my vel ad foast ayns bree.

IV.-V.

Comba'asit lesh dty phooar veih gaue,
Er dagh cheu scrie-ym niart dty laue ;
O shleiy erskyn y roshtyn aym,
Erskyn my vaght, ta'n chreenaght veayn !

VI.

Dy goïn y daanys keayrt erbee,
Dy yiooldey rish dty leigh, O Yee.
Veih'n eanish oyds c'raad oddyn chea,
Dy gheddyn boayl dy ghoaill ayn fea ?

VII.

Dy roïn gys Niau, t'ou röym ayns shen,
Coamrit lesh soilshey sollys, glen ;
Ny foast gys niurin vroghe ta heese,
Ayns shen t'ou reill as deyrey neesht.

VIII.-IX.

Dy beagh aym skeean y voghrey hene,
As getlagh röym ass roshtyn keayn,
Ayns shen v'ein cruinnit lesh dty laue,
As roish dty phooar v'ein sthill ercreau.

X.

Ny foast dy voddin chea as roie
Veih dt' enish, Hiarn, fo scaa ny hoie ;
Un shilley voïds nee leah chyndaa
Yn dullyr dowin gys soilshey'n laa.

XI.

Ta'n dorraghys as soilshey'n laa
Ny-neesht co-laik dhyt ec dagh traa,
Yn oie ghoo hene ta sollys röyd,
As-nhee cha vod ve kellit voïd.

XXIII.-XXIV.

Ronsee, as prow mee, O my Yee,
Vel peccah broghe reill ayns my chree ;
Tra v'eem er shagh'ryn lhiat mee thie,
As leeid mee lesh dty spyrryd vie.

A LAMENT FOR THE ISLE OF MAN.

A Song written by Edward Forbes, F.R.S. 1833.

I.

Oh! lament for the days that are past and gone,
  When the sun of glory bright,
On the fairest isle of the ocean shone
  With freedom's holy light;
When the golden ship, on a field of red,
  Beamed forth on the flag of the free,
And the king of the green land bowed his head
  To the king of the ocean sea.

II.

Would the Saxon dare to draw his brand
  Were Orry with us now?
Would the Albion dare to lift his hand
  Were the crown on King Olaf's brow?
But in the sleep of death they lie;
  Their glory has passed away;
And the children of their chivalry
  A Saxon king obey.

III.

Oh! where was the blood of the kings of old,
  When Atholl sold his throne?
When our chieftain bartered his rights for gold,
  Was this like Orry's son?
Our isle is still as bright, as fair,
  Its sons are still as free,
But a stranger monarch reigneth there,
  On the throne of the kings of the sea.

OIE VIE.

ARRANE.

I.

My Chaarjyn gheyr, Slane lhieu, slanc lhieu
　　Shooill-jee 'sy chassan vie,
As grayse as shee dy row meriu,
　　Oie vie, Oie vie, Oie vie.

II.

Shegin dooin paardail ga qualtee nish,
　　As gennaght' taitnys vie,
Lhig dooin goll er dys meeit mayd heose,
　　Oie vie, Oie vie, Oie vie.

III.

Ga ayns y seihll nyn noidyn wheesh,
　　Ta gaglagh shin chieu-sthie,
Cha bee mayd treiggit liorish Creest,
　　Oie vie, Oie vie, Oie vie.

IV.

As tra nee Yeesey cheet nyn quail,
　　Dy eamagh orrin thie,
She rish yn seihll nee mayd paardail
　　Gra rish, Oie vie, Oie vie.

V.

Tra meeit mayd ayns boayl eunyssagh,
　　Eisht hee mayd gloyr e oaie,
As kiaulley jeh e ghraih flaunyssagh
　　Dyn gra dy bragh Oie vie.

GOOD NIGHT.

HYMN.

Translated by John Kelly, Ballaquine, Baldwin.   1840.

I.

FAREWELL! dear friends, adieu! adieu!
  Still in God's ways delight,
And grace and peace shall be with you ;
  Good night, good night, good night.

II.

We part, though often here we come,
  And feel a great delight ;
Still let's pursue, we'll meet at home ;
  Good night, good night, good night.

III.

Though in the world our foes are strong
  And would our souls affright ;
Yet God will ne'er forsake his own ;
  Good night, good night, good night.

IV.

And when Christ's banner is unfurl'd,
  A signal for our flight,
We then will say to this vain world,
  Good night, good night, good night.

V.

And when we'll meet in heaven above,
  And see the glorious sight,
We'll sing of his redeeming love,
  And never say good night.

NY KIRREE FO-NIAGHTEY.

THIS song was printed in the first series of *Mona Miscellany*, but was unfortunately taken from so defective a Manx version, that it has been thought desirable to reprint it in the present series. The corrections have been made at the instigation of the Rev. John Thomas Clark, late chaplain of St. Mark's. The translation was given in the first series of *Mona Miscellany*, p. 131.

I.

LURG geurey dy niaghtey as arragh dy rio
Va ny shenn chirree marroo's n'eayin beggey vio ;
   Oh ! irree shin ghuillyn, as gow shiu da'n chlieau,
   Ta ny kirree fo-niaghtey cha dowin as v'ad rieau.
      Oh ! irree, etc.

II.

Shoh dooyst Qualtrogh Rabee as eh ny thie ching*
" Ta ny kirree fo-niaghtey ayns Breid-farrane-fing."
      Oh ! irree, etc.

III.

Shoh dooyrt Qualtrogh Rabee goll seose er y lout,
Dy row my hiaght vannaght er my ghaa housane mohlt.
      Oh ! irree, etc.

IV.

Kirree t'aym ayns ny Laggan kirree Goaïr 'sy chlieau-rey
Kirree cheoie coan-ny Chishtey† nagh jig dy bragh veih.
      Oh ! irree, etc.

---

* A hollow near Penny Pot.
† A short distance from Raby, called from a stone in the form of a chest in that valley.

V.

Dirree mooinjer Skeeihll Lonan as hie ad fo shooyll,
Hooar ad ny kirree marroo ayns laggan Vaarool.
Oh! irree, etc.

VI.

Dirree mooinjer Skeeihll Lonan as Skeeihll-y-Chreesht
neesht,
Hooar ad ny kirree veggay ayns laggan Agneish.
Oh! irree, etc.

VII.

Ny muihlt ayns y toshiaght, ny reaghyn 'sy vean,
As ny kirree trome-eayin cheet geiyrt orroo 'shen.
Oh! irree, etc.

VIII.

Ta mohlt aym son yn Ollic as jees son yn chaisht,
As ghaa ny three elley son yn traa yioym's baase!
Oh! irree shin ghuillyn as gow shin dan chlieau,
Ta ny kirree fo-niaghtey cha dowin as va'd rieau.

CUSTOMS AND SUPERSTITIONS.

" By customs and traditions they do live,
And foolish ceremonies of antique date."

ABM. COWLEY.

CUSTOMS AND SUPERSTITIONS.

TWELFTH DAY.

Shenn Laa'l chebbal ooashley—the twelfth day, January 6th, being the twelfth in number from the Nativity, is celebrated as one of the most jovial for Christmas gambols and visiting of friends, before settling down to the more serious business of the year. Waldron, who wrote his description of Manx Customs early in the eighteenth century, says :—" On Twelfth Day the Fiddler lays his head in some one of the wenches' laps, and a third person asks who such a maid or such a maid shall marry, naming the girls then present one after another, to which he answers according to his own whim, or agreeable to the intimacies he has taken notice of during this time of merriment. But whatever he says is as absolutely depended on as an oracle ; and if he happens to couple two people who have an aversion to each other, tears and vexation succeed the mirth. This they call *cutting off the Fiddler's head*, for after this, he is dead for the whole year."—Waldron's *Isle of Man.* Manx Society, vol. xi. 1864, p. 50.

When the *gienys* or dance takes place, the *mainstyr*, or master of the ceremonies, appoints every man his *teyad* or valentine for the ensuing year.

There used also to be a particular pastime introduced on this day called the *Lackets*, where a number of persons were invited, both male and female, who, after partaking of a supper, commenced dancing, during which the *lavare rane* was

introduced, which created great consternation to some, and
laughter in others. It consisted either in the real head of a
horse, or one formed of wood, so prepared that the person who
had charge of it, being concealed under a white sheet, was
able to snap the mouth at any one who came in its way.
These and many other pastimes used to amuse the natives

> " At such a time
> As Christmas, when disguising is on foot,"

but are now rapidly falling into disuse.

Something of a similar custom as the last used to be observed in Cheshire, there called " Old Hob."

PERIWINKLE FAIR.

There was an old custom, now almost lost in oblivion,
called Periwinkle Fair, connected with which some old verses
were formerly extant, now, I fear, also lost, being an accom-
paniment to a dramatic scene acted by the people on the
aforesaid fair day, being the 6th of February, or St. Dorothy's
day, the burthen of which was—

> " *Kiark y Treen e Marrow.*"
> " The Hen of the Treen is dead."

Some attribute this Manx custom to St. Catherine's day,
November 25. The line evidently refers to some very early
transaction, probably connected with the church.

I have in vain endeavoured to ascertain the entire drama,
and the verses connected with it, but have been so far
unsuccessful, and merely allude to the custom in this place
in the hope it may meet the eye of some person able to
throw more light on the subject, which appears not devoid of
interest. Upon application to the late Receiver-General,
Richard Quirk, Esq., for information on the subject, he wrote

me as follows :—" I have made some inquiries on the subject of your letter, but have obtained no further information than what I was already acquainted with. Periwinkle Fair was held near the shore at Pool Vash, close to Balladoole estate. I recollect being at it considerably more than half a century ago. The chief articles of trade brought forward to attract visitors, so far as I then knew, were periwinkles and ginger-bread. The fair has not been held for forty years past. There were also on show cattle, and, most particularly, ponies of the ancient breed. I can learn nothing towards making out the song or verses you mention, but there is really no traditionary lore extant."

THE MANX "DERBY."

The hardy race of Manx small horses has been mentioned by various writers on the Isle of Man from an early date. This breed is still to be met with in some of the upland farms, and are renowned for their fleetness, as well as being sure footed, and capable of enduring any amount of hard work. Their mettle was often tried in the race from the church on a bridal morning, in the contest who should arrive first at the bridegroom's abode, and have the honour of break-ing the bridecake over the head of the bride as she entered the house.

James, the 7th Earl of Derby, " The Great Earl," suc-ceeded to the royalty of Man in 1627, instituted races on the island on a piece of land extending rather more than a mile across the peninsula of Langness, and a record in the Rolls' Office states that he gave a cup to be run for at these races, thus establishing the " Manx Derby," the precursor of that now celebrated race " The Derby," or the " Blue Ribbon" of the turf. These races were continued by the 8th Earl by command as follows :—

It is my good will and pleasure y^t ye 2 prizes formerly granted (by me) for hors runing and shouting, shall continue as they did, to be run, or shot for, and so to continue dureing my good will and pleasure.—Given under my hand att Lathom ye 12 of July 1669.

DERBY (8th Earl).

To my governor's deputy governor,
    & ye rest of my officers in my
      Isle of Man.

The following is a curious record of this early institution, with the rules on which that sport was conducted :—

> *Insula Monœ.*—Articles for the plate which is to be run for in the said island, being of the value of five pounds sterling (the fashion included), given by the Right Honourable William, Earl of Derby, Lord of the said isle, etc. (9th Earl.)

1*st*. The said plate is to be run for upon the 28th day of July in every year, whiles his honour is pleased to allow the same (being the day of the nativity of the Honourable James, Lord Strange), except it happen upon a Sunday, and if soe, the said plate is to be run for upon the day following.

2*d*. That noe horse, gelding, or mair shall be admitted to run for the said plate, but such as was foaled within the said island, or in Calfe of Mann.

3*d*. That every horse, gelding, or mair, that is designed to run, shall be entered at or before the viiith day of July, with his master's name and his owne, if he be generally knowne by any, or els his collour, and whether horse, mair, or gelding, and that to be done at the xcomprs. office, by the cleark of the rolls for the time being.

4th. That every person that puts in either horse, mair, or gelding, shall, at the time of their entering, depositt the sume of five shill. a piece into the hands of the said cleark of the rolls, which is to goe towards the augmenting of the plate for the year following, besides one shill. a piece to be given by them to the said cleark of the rolls for entering their names and engrossing these articles.

5th. That every horse, mair, or gelding, shall carry horseman's weight, that is to say, ten stone weight, at fourteen pounds to each stone, besides sadle and bridle.

6th. That every horse, mair, or gelding, shall have a person for its tryer, to be named by the owner of the said horse, mair, or gelding, which tryers are to have the comand of the scales and weights, and to see that every rider doe carry full weight, according as is mencioned in the foregoeing article, and especially that the wining rider be soe with the usuall allowance of one pound for ———

7th. That a person be assigned by the tryers to start the runinge horses, who are to run for the said plate, betwixt the howers of one and three of the clock in the afternoon.

8th. That every rider shall leave the two first powles which are sett upp in Macybreas Close in this maner following—that is to say, the first of the said two powles upon his right hand, and the other upon his left hand; and the two powles by the rockes are to be left upon the left hand likewise; and the fifth powle, which is sett up at the lower end of the Conney-warren, to be left alsoe upon the left hand, and soe the turning

powle next to Wm. Looreyes house to be left in like
maner upon the left hand, and the other two powles,
leading to the ending powle, to be left upon the right
hand ; all which powles are to be left by the riders as
aforesaid, excepting only the distance powle, which
may be rid on either hand, at the discretion of the
rider, etc. etc. etc.

July 14th 1687.

The names of the persons who have entered their horses to
run for the within plate for this present year 1687.

Ro. Heywood, Esq., governor of this isle, hath
entered ane bay-gelding, called by the
name of Loggerhead, and hath deposited
towards the augmenting of the plate for
the next year   -   -   -   £00   05   00
Captain Tho. Hudlston hath entred one white
gelding, called Snowball, and hath depo-
sitted   -   -   -   -   00   05   00
Mr. William Faigier hath entred his grey
gelding, called the Gray-Carraine, and
depositted -   -   -   -   00   05   00
Mr. Nicho. Williams hath entred one grey
stone horse, called The Yorkshire Gray,
and depositted   -   -   -   00   05   00
Mr. Demster Christian hath entred one geld-
ing, called the Dapple-gray, and hath de-
possitted -   -   -   -   00   05   00

MEMORANDUM.

28th July 1687.

That this day the above plate was run for by the foremencioned horse, and the same was fairly won by the right worshipful governor's horse at the two first heates.

17th August 1688.

Received this day the above   which I am to pay to my master to augment ye plate, by me,

JOHN WOOD.

The first English "Derby" was run for in 1780, and won by Diomede, belonging to Sir Charles Bunbury, " whose ardour for the turf was conspicuous to his last hour." By this it will be seen that the "Manx Derby" was the senior of its now more renowned namesake, by about a century and a half.*

THE TURF HARVEST.

In a country where coal has not been found, the inhabitants have to resort to other means for their supply of materials for firing. The great extent of the Manx mountains have ever afforded abundance of good turf for the cutting of it ; and for the due regulation of this " custome of long time," various enactments of the Insular Legislature have from time to time been made.

In 1577 it was given for law, "that all manner of persone or persons that goeth to my Lord his Forrest for Turff and Ling ought to pay the Forrester an ob." The ob. is frequently mentioned in the old Manx statutes, and was no

---

* An attempt has been made to revive horse races in the Isle of Man by the formation of an excellent new racecourse near Mount-Rule, Kirk Braddan, which was opened on Thursday and Friday, July 14 and 15, 1870.

doubt the ancient coin called the *obulus*, made of iron or brass. It was generally paid by a halfpenny, which small amount was levied merely to uphold the Lord's right. In 1661, it was enacted at a Tynwald Court, held at St. John's, "That no manner of person or persons shall presume to go to the mountains or commons of this Isle after the hour of five of the clock in the afternoon, or before day in the morning, for the carrying of any Turff or Ling ; for complaint hath been made, that some persons do frequent that course, and especially upon dayes of haddy or dark mist, and do purloyne and carry away neighbour's Turff and Ling at such unreasonable times ; wherein if any do offend for the future, they shall be severely fined and punished, as by the Court shall be thought fitt." By the Statute of 15 Victoria, 1852, it was ordained that, "any person cutting or removing surface sod from the commons where there is no turf, or not replacing the sod in the public Turbaries within 14 days, to pay a fine not exceeding £2 for the first, and £3 for every subsequent, offence. Turf to be removed from the commons before 1st October under penalty of not exceeding 40s. No person to cut Turf in the public Turbaries for sale, or for any other use except for fuel. Turf not to be cut before 1st May, nor after 1st July, in each year, under penalty not exceeding £3." The *Disafforesting Act* of 1860 defines the public Turbaries.

The Manx people look forward to the season of cutting their stock of Turf for the winter's supply as one of their merry junketings, and many a laughing face replies to the sly jokes that are bandied from one to the other, as they wend their way up the sides of the mountains for that purpose. It is a sort of general pic-nic day, and great are the preparations which have been previously made, so that all should enjoy it. The cutting of "Fingan's Turf" has been alluded to in the first part of these "Miscellanies." The

following description of the " Turf Harvest" is from Kennish's
Mona's Isle, London, 1844, where he no doubt had often
formed one of the happy party :—

> " Now spring is past, and idle lies the plough,
>   I'll turn my thoughts towards the mountain's brow,
>   Where many a group of peasants at the dawn
>   Are seen to move along the upland lawn,
>   Towards the north of Corna-Chesgia's side,
>   Their winter's stock of fuel to provide,
>   With lab'ring hand from Nature's ample store
>   Of turfy mould beneath the grassy moor.
>   This yearly pic-nic, mix'd with useful toil,
>   Calls forth the dame the three-legg'd pot to boil,
>   Of good hung beef that graced the chimney-cheek,
>   The winter through amongst the turfy reek ;
>   And cowry, juice of oatmeal's husky seed,
>   That in this mountain banquet takes the lead :
>   The oaten bannock, staff of Mona's food,
>   She next prepares in segments thick and good :
>   Of new laid eggs are pack'd full many a score,
>   And good fresh butter churn'd the day before—
>   With joyful glee each lusty neighb'ring swain
>   Comes flocking round to join the mountain train ;
>   The females too are summoned to attend
>   This festive day, their pleasing aid to lend ;
>   For whilst the men the best of turf select,
>   The women do their duty not neglect,
>   But cheerfully each Manx young buxom lass
>   Displays the crocks and platters on the grass.
>   When now prepared the homely welcome fare,
>   They sit them down the well-spread feast to share,
>   And while each rustic plays an eager part,
>   The sire repeats, " There's plenty in the cart

To satisfy us all I'm sure this day,
So lads eat on, and spare it not I pray."
Each bashful maid, so modest and reserved,
Takes care her own intended best is served ;
While many looks of artless love pass round,
Pure joyful mirth and innocence abound ;
The staid in years no longer can refrain
From joining chorus with the youthful train,
Calling to mind those happy days gone by,
Ere cares of life drew forth the heartfelt sigh.

When dinner o'er, and th' accustom'd grace,
Each at his labour now retakes his place,
Whilst I, the youngest of the hardy band,
Was task'd the turf to spread with aching hand,
Marking each moment, as they slowly pass'd,
Wishing each barrow load to be the last,
Until the sun sunk far into the west
Behind the summit of vast Snaafield's crest,
Throwing its shadow o'er the lowland plain,
The well-known gnomon of the lab'ring swain.
When past this day of useful toil and mirth,
Where many assignations had their birth,
They homeward wind their course along the moor,
Their wives and children wait them at the door,
And many a neighb'ring cottage lass was there,
To meet the swain the courting kiss to share ;
As careless they to hide their artless love
As the wood pigeons billing in the grove ;
For there no etiquette or worldly pride
Had taught the heart to stray from virtue's side—
Their harmless love the matron would survey,
And the pure dictates of her mind display

In giving counsel to each youthful pair,
Ending the subject in her evening pray'r,
Imploring of the Lord that they might stand
As polish'd pillars from the maker's hand
Round Zion's gates, where he delights to dwell,
And of his mercies to their offspring tell.

MARRIAGES.

" As merry as a marriage bell."—OLD SAYING.

The rites, ceremonies, and customs adopted by different people in their various localities are so great, that we may naturally expect to find some of them peculiar to the Isle of Man, yet it may be said that many are derived from the former rulers of the isle, as also adopted from intercourse with the neighbouring coasts.

Marriages of the better class are conducted much in a similar manner to what they are in England. Seldom, indeed, do we hear in any case, of banns being proclaimed for three several Sundays in the parish church ; for the most part the party interested goes to a surrogate with his friend, and obtains a licence at a small cost, and in due time proceeds to the parish church to have the ceremony performed by the parson. The bishop of the island has the power to grant special licences to marry at any convenient time or place, when the parties most interested can fix any hour most convenient to themselves. This privilege, I believe, is only possessed by the Archbishop of Canterbury.

It is at the weddings of the small statesmen, and some of the better class of labourers in the country districts, that the old customs are yet to be observed. When the lover has made up his mind to ask the consent of his sweetheart's parents, he is accompanied to the house by his most trusted friend, called in Manx his *" Dooinney-Moyllee,"* his spokesman or go-between, to talk over the old folks, and induce them to give their consent to the match, and also to make the best arrangement for a marriage portion for their daughter, as most of them have some means at their disposal, if not in ready money, by other ways. If too poor to advance money, it is often arranged that the young folks shall remain with the bride's parents for a twelvemonth or so, until they are in a position to furnish a cottage for themselves. When all these preliminaries are arranged, preparations are made for the wedding feast, for which their relations and friends send ample store of fowls, hams, etc., making up a substantial entertainment. Occasionally the expenses are paid by the men individually present.

Formerly wedding processions to the church were preceded by a fiddler playing the " Black and Grey," the only tune struck up on such occasions. It was prevalent in the time of Charles II., as is given in Waldron's *Isle of Man*, Manx Society, vol. xi. p. 314, *note*.

In proceeding to the church it was the custom for the men to walk first in a body, and the women after them, the bridegroom's men carrying ozier wands in their hands as an emblem of superiority. Before entering the church the whole party marched three times round it, but these customs are now falling into disuse, and the particular tune is now omitted, yet the fiddler still often forms one of the wedding party and proceeds with them to the church. At the present day, having grown more polite, or more probably wishing to improve the occasion of having a choice companion, they proceed arm in arm without the ozier rods, amidst showers of old shoes, firing of guns, and blowing of horns.

After the ceremony, on coming out of the church, money is thrown amongst the idlers, who generally congregate about, for which they scramble. This is also done in passing any public place on the way home. On returning home,

some of the most active of the young people start off at full
speed for the bride's house, and he who arrives there first is
considered "best man," and is entitled to some peculiar privileges in consequence. Occasionally, when the wedding party
is attended by their friends on horseback, some severe riding
takes place, and it is well if all ends without an accident.
After the feast, the remainder of the day is spent with the
utmost hilarity in dancing and other amusements.

It has been said by a learned divine that the firing of
guns, sometimes charged with feathers, " was to indicate the
vanity and vexation of spirit incident to the state into which
they have newly entered ;" but the Manx look upon the old
shoes to indicate " good luck," and the firing of guns and
blowing of horns was to drive all fairies and evil spirits
away.

THE GOB NY SCUIT BOAGANE.

One Boagane has, at all events, been quietly laid and ceased
to disquiet the minds of wanderers in the neighbourhood of
North Barrule. The "Gob-ny-Scuit," in Kirk Maughold,
had long been a terror to Manx folks by his wailings when
the wind was at a particular point, and was considered as
some disquiet spirit who had long ago come to some untimely
end, no one knew how, and had baffled the art of the great
Ballawhane himself, who was considered to have power over
the birds of the air as well as over beasts of the field.

Mr. William Kinnish (author of *Mona's Isle and other
Poems*, 1844), a native of Maughold, was determined, if possible, to ascertain the cause of these periodical wailings that
had so often disquieted the minds of the neighbouring people
when they had occasion to pass by the place in the night.
He persevered day after day in examining the rock, until at
last he found out the Boagane. It was a natural curiosity,

o

a cleft in the rock, of considerable depth in the face of the precipice. It had the music of an Æolian Harp, caused by the wind entering into the bottom of the thin fissure, and coming out at the top a little below the surface. Owing to its upper orifice being lower than the surface of the ground above, no water was admitted, and being thus hidden from observation, the cause of the sounds could not be discovered. The cascade had nothing to do with it, as was supposed by some, but nevertheless it is a very interesting and natural source of music. Thus has one of Mona's "Boaganes" been banished to the Red Sea!

Mooayer ny Booiagh.—Begrudging a Willing Consent.

There was a servant girl at Bemahague, and the mistress wanted her to go to Glen Crutchery Well to get a can of water before daylight, and afterwards she was to be allowed to go to the fair. When going to the well she met the old man of Glen Crutchery, who asked her where she was going. "Going to your well for water," she said. He asked her if there was no water in their own well? She said there was, but her mistress had sent her. He gave her half-a-crown, and told her to take water out of their own well. The girl received the money, which confirmed the charm, and then went to the fair. When she returned home the mistress asked her where she had procured the water, for she had been churning all day and had got no butter?

It is said—

> "Vervain and dill
> Hinders witches from their will."

Fairies and Water-Crochs.

The custom of filling the water crochs with clean water for

the use of the fairies, before the family would retire to their beds, was strictly complied with by the Manx in former days, which water was never used for any other purpose, but thrown away each morning.

> " They see that all the water-crochs
> Were rightly placed, and brimming full,
> That each might have a quenching pull ;
> But woe be to the sleeping maid
> Were crochs not fill'd and duly laid !"

A Charm against the Fairies.

Much has been said respecting charms in the first part of *Mona Miscellany*. The following is one respecting the banishing of fairies from the Isle of Man—

> Shee Yee as shee ghooinney,
> She Yee er Columb Killey
> Er dagh uinnag, er dagh ghorrys,
> Er dagh howl joaill stiagh yn Re-hollys.
> Er kiare corneillyn y thie
> Er y voayl ta mee my lhie
> As shee orrym feme.

Thus freely translated—

> The peace of God and peace of man,
> The peace of God on Columb Killey,
> On each window and each door,
> And on every hole admitting moonlight.
> On the four corners of the house,
> And on the place of my rest,
> And the peace of God on myself.

CAILLAGH-NY-GUESHAG.—A MANX PROPHET.

There has ever been, from all time, persons who presume to foresee and tell of future events, and what was to happen before the end of the world, and whether true or false, as they may turn out, there will always be found people who believe in them. Such a person is said to have lived in the Isle of Man, and, like Mother Shipton of old, was held in great veneration in her day. Some of her sayings have come down and been cherished amongst the country people to the present day; but who the prophet was, and where she lived, appears to have been forgotten, unless some record of her doings is to be found in the ecclesiastical archives, where it was most likely she would appear.

Mr. John Quirk of Carn-ny-Greïe, who is so well acquainted with the legends of his country, remarks on this old lady as follows:—"A small chapel, called 'Cabbal-cheeill-Vout," stood near the Foxdale river in Kirk-Patrick, between Balla-higg and Slieauwhallin, concerning which "Caillagh-ny-Gueshag" is said to have predicted as follows:—

" Tra vees Cabbal-cheeill-Vout ersooyll lesh y thooilley,
Cha bee cleïn Quirk Slieau-whallin veg sodjey."

Which may be rendered thus in English—

When the Chapel Kill-Vout is washed by the stream,
The Quirks in Slieau-whallin will no longer remain.

This prediction seems to have been very familiar with the people in the neighbourhood, perhaps for ages, and the last proprietor was often reminded of it, when he would say—"O there remains so much of it as I can cover with my big coat yet," but a heavy flood came down upon it and swept it all away. About sixty years ago the last of the Quirks of Slieauwhallin died without issue very soon after that event. Thus ended the race of the Quirks of that place, who, it is said, had occupied Slieauwhallin during twenty-five generations. These and a hundred such things are now almost lost, with all the sayings and doings about them, even in the very neighbourhood where they happened. Can any one tell who this " Caillaghny-Gueshag" was, whose name seems in former times to be on every one's tongue ? "

Other sayings are recorded of her, as—

Dy beagh chimlee chaardagh ayns dy chooilley hie roish jerrey yn theihll.

There shall be a smithy chimney in every house before the end of the world.

Dy nee ass claghyn ghlassey yioghe sleih nyn arran.

Out of grey stones people will get their bread.

She also predicted the time would come when the Manx would travel dry shod from the point of Ayre to Scotland. This is about sixteen miles to Burrow Head, the nearest portion from the island to any of the surrounding coasts. The lighthouse was originally erected on the extreme point ; it is now a considerable distance from it, so that the old lady's prediction may yet come to pass ; it is only a question of time.

Tradition states that Ragnvald I., a King of Man in the tenth century, attempted to build a bridge over this space. A saying in allusion to this place will be found in the first series of *Mona Miscellany*, p. 36, probably one of those of this Manx prophetess.

Remarkable Days.

The following remarkable days of the Calendar, as expressed in the Manx dialect, are worthy of preservation in a record of the fast-fading customs of the country.

January 1.—La Nullick beg. The little Christmas. "The Quaaltagh" is an important personage on this day, for which see an account in *Mona Miscellany*, first series, p. 135.

January 6.—Laa'l Chybbyr-ushtey. The Epiphany or twelfth day. The day of offering worship. Cregeen says it ought to be *Laa'l chebbal ooashley.*

January 25.—Laa'l-noo Phaul. The conversion of St. Paul, which took place at Damascus A.D. 37, observed both by the English and Catholic church. *Vide* Proverbs, p. 19.

February 1.—Laa'l Breeshey. The feast of St. Bridget. For the customs on this day see *Mona Miscellany*, first series, p. 137 ; also Proverbs, p. 19.

February 2.—Laa'l Moirrey ny gianle. Candlemas-day. The day of man being tied or secured. *See* Proverbs, p. 19.

February 25.—Laa'l-noo-Mian. St. Matthew's day.

March 17.—Laa'l Parick. St. Patrick's day. The apostle of Ireland, and the first to found a church in the Isle of Man, on the small island off Peel, formerly called "St. Patrick's Isle." *See* Proverbs, p. 20.

March 25.—Laa'l Moirrey ny Sansh. The Annunciation. Commemorative of the Incarnation of Christ.

April 25.—Laa-noo Mark-yn Sushtallagh. St. Mark the Evangelist's day. There were many country superstitious observances anciently attached to the Eve of St. Mark.

May 1.—Laa Baaltinn. The day of Baal's fire. On the eve of this day fires are kindled in all parts, so that the wind may drive the smoke over the corn-fields, cattle, and houses, in order to purify them. It is also the usage to put out the culinary fires on that day, and to rekindle them with some of the sacred fire. For an account of various customs observed on this day, and on old May Eve, see *Mona Miscellany*, first series, p. 138-142.

May 12.—La Baljey. The general day for letting of houses, paying half-year's rents, taking in grazing cattle, and women servants taking their places for the year, after hiring on the 28th March.

May 18.—Laa'l Spitlhin souree. The Feast of St. Spitlhin of Summer. A saint not now known. He is also recorded on the 18th November.

June 9.—Feaill Collum Cilley. St. Columba. Apostle of the Picts. Died A.D 597.

June 11.—Laa-noo Barnabas. St. Barnabas.

June 24.—Trinaig veg. Little Trinity. On this day the annual Tynwald was formerly held at St. John's.

June 29.—Laa'l Pheddyr. St. Peter's day.

July 5.—Laa'll Eoin. St. John the Baptist's festival is kept on this day, and the annual Tynwald at St. John's, at which the laws made during the year are promulgated on the Tynwald Hill in English and Manx. It is also called "Feailoin," on which day a circle or chaplet of the plant *bollan* (mugwort) used to be worn. It was called "Baal's chaplet," in commemoration of Baal, or the Sun, the God of the Celts, having completed his circle or course. These customs are from immemorial usage, and are the remains of

the heathen worship paid by the Druids and the Celtic
nations to their God Baal. For an account of this day see
Mona Miscellany, first series, p. 143.

July 12.—Laa'l Charmane. St. German, first bishop of
Man, A.D. 447.

July 22.—Laa'l Moirrey Malane. St. Mary Magdalen.

July 25.—Laa-noo Yamys. St. James the Great.

July 31.—Feoill Machold toshee. St. Maughold's chief
feast.

August 1.—Laa' Luanistyn. Lammas Day. It is otherwise called the *Gule* or *Yule* of August, signifying a festival
or holyday, and was one of the great festivals of the Druids.
The peasantry resort to the highest mountains and to wells
on the first Sunday in August. This custom is said to be
handed down from the Israelites, whose daughters went to
the mountains yearly to lament the daughter of Jephthah,
the Gileadite, as recorded in the 11th chapter of Judges. See
Mona Miscellany, first series, p. 145.

August 15.—Laa'l Moirrey thoshee. St. Mary's principal
feast.

August 24.—Laa-noo Pharlane. St. Bartholomew. *See*
Proverbs, p. 9.

September 29.—Laa'll Vaayl. St. Michael.

October 18.—Laa-noo Luke. St. Luke's day.

October 28.—Feoill Simon. St. Simon's feast.

October 29.—Laa'l Ma'el beg. St. Michael the Less.

November 1.—Laa Sauin. All Saints. Hallowmas. It
is also called Laa'll Mooar ny Saintsh. It was a great thanks-
giving or day of rest amongst the Druids, on which day they

consecrated the holy fires to distribute a light to the people. On the eve of this day it is customary for young people to pry into futurity in various ways. See *Mona Miscellany,* first series, p. 147.

November 2.—La feoill ny Marroo. The feast of All Souls, or those dead.

November 9.—Laa'l Kickle or Kial.

November 11.—Laa'll noo Vartin. Martinmas day.

November 12.—Laa'l Souney. The season or month was called "Yn Tauyn," because anciently it was the first day of the year. The general day for letting lands, payment of rents, men-servants taking their places for the year, and commencement of winter half-year.

November 18.—Laa'l Spitlhin geuraih. St. Spitlhin of the winter quarter.

November 25.—Laa'l Catharina. St. Catharine's day.

November 26.—Laa'l Machold geuraih. St. Maughold's winter feast.

November 30.—Laa'll Andreays. St. Andrew's day.

December 6.—La Catreeney. St. Catharine's day (old style). On or before this day possession must be taken on the south side of the Island of lands when intended to change occupier.

December 21.—Laa'l Thomase. St. Thomas's day. "Oiel Fingan," when the people went to the mountains and cliffs to catch deer and sheep for Christmas, and kindled large fires on the tops. *See* the Proverb in *Mona Miscellany,* first series, p. 27.

December 25.—Laa-yn Ollick. Christmas day. The eve

of this day is called " Oiel Verree," the Eve of Mary, when carols are sung in the parish churches. For an account of this custom see *Mona Miscellany*, first series, p. 157-165, and the various carols in this volume.

December 26.—Laa'l Steavin. St. Stephen's day. It is the custom to " Hunt the Wren " on this day, and parade it about with flags, etc. In Waldron's time (1726) it was observed on the 24th December. For an account of this custom, with the song, see *Mona Miscellany*, first series, p. 151-156, and also p. 184-187.

December 27.—Laa'll Eoin 'syn Ollick. St. John the Evangelist's day.

December 28.—Laa'll ny Maccain. Innocent's day.

Laa-yn-giense.—Twelfth-day. For the customs on this day, *see* p. 181.

Oiel Ynnyd.—Shrove Tuesday. The eve of the fast. For the customs on this day and proverb, see *Mona Miscellany*, first series, p. 27.

Laa I'nnyd.—Ash Wednesday. A fast, the first day of Lent.

Je-heiney Chaisht.—Good Friday. The repugnance of making use of iron in any way on this day, it may be remarked that in the north of Durham no blacksmith through-out that district will drive a nail—a remembrance of the awful purpose for which hammer and nails were used on the first Good Friday doubtless held them back. For the customs observed on this day see *Mona Miscellany*, first series, p. 137.

Laa Chaisht.—Easter. The universal Christian festival, in commemoration of Christ's resurrection.

Doonaght Kingeeish. Whitsunday.

Months of the Year.

The Manx had names of their own for the various months, which were expressed as follows:—

JANUARY. Mee s'jerree yn-gheurey. The end of the winter month.

FEBRUARY. Yn-chied vee jeh'n arragh. The first of spring, or vernal quarter.

MARCH. Mee-veanagh yn arree ; also called yn-mart. The middle of Spring month.

APRIL. Mee s'jerree yn arree; also, Yn Avril. The end of Spring month.

MAY. Yn Baaltin ; or, Yn-chied vee jeh'n tourey. The Beltein ; or, The first month of Summer.

JUNE. Mee-veanagh yn touree. The middle month of Summer.

JULY. Mee s'jerree yn touree. The end of Summer month.

AUGUST. Yn-chied-vee jeh'n ouyr. The first month of harvest.

SEPTEMBER. Mee-veanagh yn-ouyr. The middle month of harvest.

OCTOBER. Mee s'jerree yn ouyr. The end of the harvest month.

NOVEMBER. Yn-chied vee jeh'n gheurey. The first of the Winter month. Or, Yn Tauin, or Sauin, Hollantide month.

DECEMBER. Mee-meanagh yn-gheurey. The middle of the Winter month.

DAYS OF THE WEEK.

SUNDAY.	Je Doo'nee. Shut up or closed. Dies sol; dedicated to the sun.
MONDAY.	Je Lh'ein. Dies Lunæ; the day of the moon, or lesser luminary.
TUESDAY.	Je M'ayrt; dies Martinus. The day of Mars.
WEDNESDAY.	Je Crean; dies Mercurii. The day of Mercury.
THURSDAY.	Je Ard'ein; dies Joves. Jupiter's day.
FRIDAY.	Jy' Heiney; dies Veneris. The day of Venus.
SATURDAY.	Je Sarn; dies Saturni. Saturn's day.

PECULIARITIES IN NUMERATION, CURRENCY, WEIGHTS, MEASURES, DIVISIONS OF LAND, AND QUANTITIES.

A country so peculiarly situated as the Isle of Man, in the centre of Great Britain, and though under the nominal fealty of such monarchs as might be at the time predominant, yet retaining its own form of government and law for the last thousand years, may naturally be expected to have many customs and peculiarities different to their surrounding neighbours. To enumerate some of these will be interesting, and at the same time useful, as many of the terms are comparatively unknown to the rising generation, and are gradually falling into disuse, more particularly since the revestment of the Island to the British crown, which took place in 1765, and the gradual assimilation of the laws of the Island to the spirit of English jurisprudence. Some of these terms, we fear, have passed into oblivion, yet an explanation of a few may yet be embalmed in this record of the Manx Society before they entirely pass away.

NUMERATION AND MODE OF RECKONING.

The Manx mode of reckoning is by *scores*, and the enumeration in the Manx language is as follows :—

Unnane *	.	1	Kiare-jeig . .	14
Jees	. .	2	Queig-jeig . .	15
Three	. .	3	Shey-jeig . .	16
Kiare	. .	4	Shiaght-jeig . .	17
Queig	.	5	Hoght-jeig	18
Shey	. .	6	Nuy-jeig . .	19
Shiaght	.	7	Feed .	20
Hoght	.	8	Nane as feed . .	21
Nuy	.	9	Jees as feed . .	22
Jeih	. .	10	Three as feed . .	23
Unnane-jeig	.	11	Kiare as feed . .	24
Ghaa-yeig	. .	12	etc. etc.	
Three-jeig	.	13		

Jeih as feed	.	30 that is 10 and 20.	
Nane jeih as feed		31 „	1, 10, and 20.
Jees jeih as feed	.	32 „	2, 10, and 20.
Three jeih as feed	.	33 „	3, 10, and 20.
		And so on.	
Daeed	. . .	40 „	2 twenties.
Nane as daeed	.	41 „	1 and forty, or 2 twenties.
Jees as daeed	. .	42 „	2 and 40.
Three as daeed	.	43 „	3 and 40.
		And so on.	
Jeih as daeed	.	50 „	10 and 40.
Nane jeih as daeed	.	51 „	1, 10, and 40.
Jees jeih as daeed	.	52 „	2, 10, and 40.
Three jeih as daeed	.	53 „	3, 10, and 40.
		And so on.	

* Frequently contracted as " nane.

Three feed . . .	60	that is	3	twenties.
Three feed as nane .	61	„	3	twenties and 1.
Three feed as jees	62	„	3	„ and 2.
Three feed as three .	63	„	3	„ and 3.

And so on.

Three feed as jeih .	70	„	3	„ and 10.
Nane as three feed as jeih	71	„	3	„ and 10 and 1.
Jees as three feed as jeih	72	„	3	„ and 10 and 2.
Three as three feed as jeih	73	„	3	„ and 10 and 3.

And so on.

Kiare feed	80	„	4	„
Kiare feed as nane .	81	„	4	„ and 1.
Kiare feed as jees	82	„	4	„ and 2.
Kiare feed as three .	83	„	4	„ and 3.

And so on.

Kiare feed as jeih .	90	„	4	„ and 10.
Nane as kiare feed as jeih	91	„	4	„ and 10 and 1.
Jees as kiare feed as jeih	92	„	4	„ and 10 and 2.
Three as kiare feed as jeih	93	„	4	„ and 10 and 3.

And so on.

Cheead . . .	100
Daa cheead	200
Three cheead	300
Kiare cheead .	400
Queig cheead .	500
Shey cheead . . .	600
Shiaght cheead .	700
Hoght cheead	800
Nuy cheead	900
Thousane . .	1000
Jeih cheead thousane	1,000,000

CURRENCY.

The Manx appear to have had no coinage of their own, unless we may take it for granted the *leather money* to be such, which is stated was in circulation about 1577. They had mainly to depend upon what currency found its way into the Island by way of barter or otherwise with other nations ; the consequence was, much of it was of a questionable kind. The first coin of the Island is that known as " John Murrey's pence," 1668, which was nothing more than a tradesman's token, and by an order in Council, in 1679, was allowed to pass as current "until it be otherwise declared to the contrary."

The 10th Earl of Derby issued a coinage of pence and halfpence in 1709, which was the first legitimate issue of Manx coinage known. Dr. Charles Clay, of Manchester, has gone fully into the history of the "currency of the Isle of Man," in the 17th volume of the Manx Society's publications, 1869, that it is unnecessary here further to allude to the coinage of the Earls of Derby and Duke of Atholl.

During the reign of George III., from 1786 to 1813, a coinage of pence and halfpence was issued at the rate of 14d. Manx for 12d. English, but the inconvenience arising from this difference in the exchangeable value, and the debased state of the currency in circulation being found so great, an order in Council was issued, 10th April 1839, to authorise the Mint to coin One thousand pounds sterling in pence, halfpence, and farthings, for circulation in the Isle of Man, assimilating the value of the same to the copper coinage of Great Britain. This was accordingly done, and an Act of Tynwald passed assimilating the value and legalising the same in the Island, which Act was promulgated at St. John's on the 17th March 1840.*

* *Vide* Gell's *Statutes*, p. 38. Douglas, 1848.

This Act created so great an excitement and hostility, particularly amongst the poorer class and country people, who imagined they were about to be ruined entirely, that very serious riots took place in consequence in the towns of Douglas and Peel, which rendered the presence of the military necessary. This was called "The Copper Row," and was the subject of a song given in *Mona Miscellany*, first series, p. 118.

MONEY TERMS.

Punt .	a pound.
Skillin	a shilling.
Ping .	a penny.
Lhieng	a halfpenny.
Farling . .	a farthing.

The following may be taken as an example of the mode of expressing a sum of money in Manx. Say the sum is £2578 : 16 : 9¾ :—

Daa 'housane, queig keead, three feed as hoght-puint-jeig, shey-skillingn-jeig, as nuy pingyn, three farlengyn.

The following table fully explains the difference in Manx and English currency :—

TABLE OF MANX AND ENGLISH MONEY.

MANX INTO ENGLISH.

Manx £	English £ s. d. q.	7	Manx £ s.	English £ s. d. q.	7	Manx s. d.	English s. d. q.	7
100	85 14 3 1	5	9 0	7 14 3 1	5	9 0	7 8 2	2
90	77 2 10 1	1	8 0	6 17 1 2	6	8 0	6 10 1	1
80	68 11 5 0	4	7 0	6 0 0 0	0	7 0	6 0 0	0
70	60 0 0 0	0	6 0	5 2 10 1	1	6 0	5 1 2	6
60	51 8 6 3	3	5 0	4 5 8 2	2	5 0	4 3 1	5
50	42 17 1 2	6	4 0	3 8 6 3	3	4 0	3 5 0	4
40	34 5 8 2	2	3 0	2 11 5 0	4	3 0	2 6 3	3
30	25 14 3 1	5	2 0	1 14 3 1	5	2 0	1 8 2	2
20	17 2 10 1	1	1 0	0 17 1 2	6	1 0	0 10 1	1
19	16 5 8 2	2	0 19	0 16 3 1	5	0 11	0 9 1	5
18	15 8 6 3	3	0 18	0 15 5 0	4	0 10	0 8 2	2
17	14 11 5 0	4	0 17	0 14 6 3	3	0 9	0 7 2	6
16	13 14 3 1	5	0 16	0 13 8 2	2	0 8	0 6 3	3
15	12 17 1 2	6	0 15	0 12 10 1	1	0 7	0 6 0	0
14	12 0 0 0	0	0 14	0 12 0 0	0	0 6	0 5 0	4
13	11 2 10 1	1	0 13	0 11 1 2	6	0 5	0 4 1	1
12	10 5 8 2	2	0 12	0 10 3 1	5	0 4	0 3 1	5
11	9 8 6 3	3	0 11	0 9 5 0	4	0 3	0 2 2	2
10	8 11 5 0	4	0 10	0 8 6 3	3	0 2	0 1 2	6

The parts of Manx into English are seven parts of a farthing.

ENGLISH INTO MANX.

Eng. £	Manx £ s. d. q.	6	Eng. £ s.	Manx £ s. d. q.	6	Eng. s. d.	Manx s. d. q.	6
100	116 13 4 0	0	9 0	10 10 0 0	0	9 0	10 6 0	0
90	105 0 0 0	0	8 0	9 6 8 0	0	8 0	9 4 0	0
80	93 6 8 0	0	7 0	8 3 4 0	0	7 0	8 2 0	0
70	81 13 4 0	0	6 0	7 0 0 0	0	6 0	7 0 0	0
60	70 0 0 0	0	5 0	5 16 8 0	0	5 0	5 10 0	0
50	58 6 8 0	0	4 0	4 13 4 0	0	4 0	4 8 0	0
40	46 13 4 0	0	3 0	3 10 0 0	0	3 0	3 6 0	0
30	35 0 0 0	0	2 0	2 6 8 0	0	2 0	2 4 0	0
20	23 6 8 0	0	1 0	1 3 4 0	0	1 0	1 2 0	0
19	22 3 4 0	0	0 19	1 2 2 0	0	0 11	1 0 3	2
18	21 0 0 0	0	0 18	1 1 0 0	0	0 10	0 11 2	4
17	19 16 8 0	0	0 17	0 19 10 0	0	0 9	0 10 2	0
16	18 13 4 0	0	0 16	0 18 8 0	0	0 8	0 9 1	2
15	17 10 0 0	0	0 15	0 17 6 0	0	0 7	0 8 0	4
14	16 6 8 0	0	0 14	0 16 4 0	0	0 6	0 7 0	0
13	15 3 4 0	0	0 13	0 15 2 0	0	0 5	0 5 3	2
12	14 0 0 0	0	0 12	0 14 0 0	0	0 4	0 4 2	4
11	12 16 8 0	0	0 11	0 12 10 0	0	0 3	0 3 2	0
10	11 13 4 0	0	0 10	0 11 8 0	0	0 2	0 2 1	2

The parts of farthings are reduced to the number placed over.

P

WEIGHTS AND MEASURES.

Some peculiarities in these are yet to be met with in the various transactions of trade, but they are gradually assimilating to those in England both in capacity and name. Various acts of Tynwald have from time to time been passed to regulate these, as may be seen on reference to the statutes of the island. In the Act of 24th June 1637, whereby it is enacted that all weights and measures should agree with "the assize of the Lords' weights and measures," etc. In the Act passed after the revestment to the British Crown, it was enacted in 1777 that all weights and measures should be according to the standard of His Majesty's Exchequer in England.

Bolley—Boll.—This term is in general use for the sale of grain, etc. Cregeen in his *Manx Dictionary*, 1835, gives the following meaning to this measure. "*Bolley*—a boll, a measure of 6 bushels, or 24 kishens of barley and oats, 4 bushels or 16 kishens of wheat, rye, pease, beans, and potatoes."

Farlane—Firlot, is half a boll, and is a term frequently used in measuring corn. That this measure was looked upon in early days as of importance is evident, as appears from the following declaration at a Tynwald court holden "on Tuesday next after the Feast of St. Mary, 1429." "Also that all measures of your land of Mann be made all after one, that is to say, Firlett and quart be justly and truly ordained and made."—*Mill's Statutes*, p. 11.

Lioarlhan.—A measure equal to half a *Firlot* or a quarter of a boll.

Windle.—A measure of 3 bushels. A *Peel Windle* is mentioned in one of the Earl of Derby's household accounts, 1561, *

* The Stanley Papers, part 11, Chetham Society, vol. xxxi. pp. 1 and 2, 1853. The editor, the Rev. F. R. Raines, states that the "windle is an old Lancashire measure containing a mett, or two bushels."

but I have not been able to learn its exact capacity. This term for a measure of corn is still in use in various parts of Lancashire, but the measure appears to have been variable. A windle of wheat was 210 to 220 lbs., or 3 bushels. At Preston oats were sold by the windle of 313 lbs.

Kaire Chistrauyn—Bushel.—A tub of 4 kishens or pecks.

Tubbag—Tub.—Is the term usually applied to a bushel. It contains 4 kishens or pecks. The term is commonly applied in the sale of coals.

Stoandey—Barrel.—This term is applied both for dry and liquid use. According to an English Act (13th Elizabeth, cap. 11), the barrel of herrings ought to contain 32 gallons wine measure, equal to about 28 gallons old standard, containing about 1000 herrings; the half barrel or firkin according to the same rate. Lime at the kiln is sold by the barrel at the rate of 8 barrels to the ton of 30 cwt., being $3\frac{3}{4}$ cwt. to the barrel.

Tyld.—The quantity or weight implied by this term appears to be uncertain. In the regulations for the supply of the Lords' garrisons in Peel Castle and Castle Rushen, A.D. 1561, we find that each soldier was allowed "the third part of a *tyld of beefe*, and a canne of beere of two quarts, for his supper."—*Mill's Statutes*, p. 37.

Kishan or *Kishen.*—A measure containing 8 quarts equal to one peck. This was commonly used in the sale of corn, potatoes, coals, etc. In point of weight the contents of a kishan of potatoes was estimated at 21 lbs. A kishan of coals, it is said, ought to weigh $21\frac{1}{1}\frac{4}{7}$ lbs.

Kaire Chaartyn—Gallon.—A measure containing 4 quarts.

Podjal daa Chaart—Pottle.—A measure containing 2 quarts. This is referred to in the regulations as to Peel Castle and Castle Rushen in 1561. "A canne of beere of two quarts" is also mentioned as sufficient drink for a sick soldier's supper.—*Mill's Statutes*, p. 36.

In an indenture between the Bishop of Man and others, made in the year 1532, "the clergy allege that they had taken, and ought to have of right and custome of every person brewing any ale, in recompence of the tith thereof, certain *Pottles of Ale.*"—*Mill's Statutes*, p. 30.

This custom of the Manx clergy has evidently a close connection with the custom of the "Parish Brewing-pan," of which mention was made in *Mona Miscellany*, first series, p. 36.

Caart or *Kaart*—Quart.—This has two significations—1st the well-known liquid measure—2d, a weight equal to 7 lbs. by which wool was formerly, and occasionally at the present time, sold. The Manx term for the latter is *Caart-ollcy*, for which, in the *Manx and English Dictionary*, 1866, the following meaning is given: "A weight containing 7 lbs., and used only in weighing wool, from *caart* a quart, and *ollan* wool."

Butter was formerly sold by the quart, calculated as equal to 2½ lbs. In making up salt butter in *crocks* (*crockan*, an earthen vessel), the quantity was calculated at so many quarts. A crock containing say 2 gallons or 8 quarts, ought to hold 20 lbs. of butter ; that is allowing 2½ lbs. of butter to a quart of liquid, which was the ordinary allowance.

Pynt Lich Caart—Pint.—Half a quart.

Naggin.—A measure equal to half a gill, or the fourth part of a pint. It is still in general use in the purchase of spirits and other liquids. The word (which is as common a one as can be met with), is not given in either *Cregeen* or the dictionary published by the Manx Society. Under the term *gill* in the latter, *naggin* is given as the Manx of the word.

Half a naggin.—Is equal to a glass.

Cropper.—Was a term formerly used by the common people in calling for *half a glass* of spirits at a public house.

It is still occasionally made use of, and in *Betsy Lee*, the finest and most pathetic epic of the day descriptive of Manx manners, just published by Macmillan, we find it used, as—

> " Here goes the last copper,
> And into a house to get a *cropper*."

Sniper.—This was also a common term for a *dram* or a *drop* of spirits, and almost invariably to a morning drink. *A nip* is occasionally used. It does not mean any particular quantity but usually something under a glass. It is equivalent to what is generally understood as " a hair of the old dog," or " a hair of the dog that bit you," terms totally unknown to the *Good Templars* of the present day.

These two latter words are not Manx, but provincialisms or slang terms.

In an old drinking song which is sung on completing the carrying of the barley harvest in Devon and Cornwall, the following measures are mentioned :—

> " We'll drink it out of the ocean, my boys.
> Here's a health to the barley-mow !
> The ocean, the river, the well, the pipe,
> The hogshead, the half-hogshead, the anker,
> The half-anker, the gallon, the pottle, the quart,
> The pint, the half-a-pint, the quarter pint,
> The *nipperkin*, and the jolly brown bowl ! "

*Standayrt—*Yard.—*Cregeen* gives the following meaning : —" A yard. This might be the Manx of standard, and perhaps right, as this (the yard) was the only standard measure in use, therefore called *Standayrt* (standard)." The Manx yard was 1½ inch longer than the English one, being 37½ inches.

In measuring out old intacks for instance, the Manx yard was used, and, as will be at once seen, the dimensions of the ground licenced by the lord to be enclosed (being the intack—

intake or intaking), would in modern times appear to be much greater than the actual measurement would warrant. As, for example, if a licence had been granted, say 150 years ago, to enclose a parcel of commons 100 yards in length by 80 yards in breadth, the proper dimensions of the ground, if measured at the present day, and according to the English standard, would be 104 yards and 6 inches long, by 83 yards and 1 foot wide.

For want of this knowledge or inattention to the rule, much trouble has been caused in surveying intack and other lands in late years, and in reconciling the apparent discrepancies in these measurements.

The use of the Manx yard was not of course confined to the measurement of land, but was applied to all materials. The use of the Manx yard was discontinued by weavers upon the assimilation of the currency. Within the last thirty years it was customary for country weavers in attending fairs, or in going from house to house to sell flannel or cloth, as was a usual practice, to carry with them a Manx yard measure. In addition to this, the breadth of the thumb was given in to each yard measured.

Cass—A foot.—Inasmuch as a Manx yard consisted of 37½ inches, it is not unreasonable to suppose that the foot in old times was equal to 12½ inches, the half-inch to each of the 3 feet in a yard making up the amount.

Carlagh—An inch.

Acyr—A Manx acre, is 5042 yards, measured at 37½ inches to the yard.

Feigh—A fathom.—*Cregeen* says it was so named as being probably the greatest measure formerly in use.

Raaish—A span.—*Cregeen* says this ought to be the Manx for a cubit—*craue-roih*, the length of the arm-bone.

Kesmad—A step or pace.—A measure equal to about 20 inches.

DIVISIONS OF THE ISLE OF MAN.

The Island is divided into various districts under the denomination of sheadings, parishes, treens, quarter-lands, and ballas or estates, as follows :—

Sheading or *Sheadin* is the name given to the six districts into which the Island has been from time immemorial divided. The term is evidently derived from the words *shey* (six) and *rheynn* (division or distribution). Each sheading forms a coroner's district, and contains, with one exception, three parishes. They are designated as follows :—

Glanfaba sheading, which takes precedence, as does its coroner, who has the peculiar right to execute his office in any part of the Island, and to make summonses upon and enforce judgments against the other coroners in case of need. It contains the parishes of Patrick, German, and Marown.

Michael sheading, contains the parishes of Michael, Ballaugh, and Jurby.

Ayre sheading, the parishes of Lezayre, Andreas, and Bride.

Garff sheading, the parishes of Maughold and Lonan.

Middle sheading, the parishes of Onchan, Braddan, and Santon.

Rushen sheading, the parishes of Malew, Arbory, and Rushen.

In *Chaloner's Description of the Isle of Man*, Manx Society, vol. x., at pages 30-32, an account is given of the sheadings ; the distribution of the parishes is not, however, quite correct.

Skeeyll—a parish. *Cregeen* considers the word is derived from *Scarrey*, a separation or division. Dr. Kelly (see his *Manx and English Dictionary*), on the other hand, says it is a contraction of the words *skerrey* (the parish), and *keeyll* (of the church). Be this as it may, the word is the prefix to fifteen out of the seventeen parishes in the island, thus :—

Skeeyll-y-Pharic	Parish of	Patrick.
Skeeyll-y-Charmane	„	German.
Skeeyll-y-Mayl	„	Michael.
Skeeyll Andreays	„	Andreas.
Skeeyll-y-Vridey	„	Bride.
Skeeyll-y-Chreest-ne-Heyrey .	„	Christ Lezayse.
Skeeyll-y-Maghal	„	Maughold.
Skeeyll Lonnan	„	Lonan.
Skeeyll-y-Chonnaghan	„	Onchan.
Skeeyll-y-Vraddan	„	Braddan.
Skeeyll Marooney	„	Marown.
Skeeyll-y-Stondane	„	Santon.
Skeeyll Malew	„	Malew.
Skeeyll-y-Chairbre	„	Arbory.
Skeeyll-y-Chreest Rushen	„	Rushen.

The two parishes to which the word is not annexed are—

Yourby	Jurby.
Ball-ny-Laaghey	Ballaugh.

Treen is another familiar term signifying a division or apportionment of lands into thirds. Each parish contains a number of treens, which, in their turn, are subdivided into quarterlands.

For further particulars respecting treens and treen chapels, the reader is referred to vol. xv. of the Manx Society's publications, pages 76, *et seq.*

Quarterlands.—For the facility of reference in the Lords' Books, the Isle of Man has been divided into various quantities, under the denomination of Quarterlands, Cottages, and

Intacks, with the abbey and other barony lands, with the mountains or "forest lands."

According to a survey made by Mr. Hooper in 1608 in the Rolls Office, the number of quarterlands of Lord's Land was as follows :—

Kirk-Patrick	35½
German	39½ and 4th part.
Michael	45½
Ballaugh	34½
Jurby	18½ and 4th part.
Andreas	58
Bride	42
Lezayre	33 and 4th part.
Maughold	38
Lonnan	52½
Conchan	40
Braddan	38
Marown	30½
Santan	35
Malew	26 and 4th part.
Arbory	32
Rushen	40
Total	639½ quarterlands.

Besides these there are above 2700 cottages and intacks, all which are Lords' land, with 79 mill rents. Also quarterlands formerly belonging to the dissolved monastery of Rushen, called Abbey Lands, of which there are in—

Malew	52
German	13
Sulby in Lezayre	10
Skinsco in Lonnan	5

| Braddan | 18 |
| Rushen | 1½ |

| | Total | . | . | 99½ |

Besides 6 mills and 77 abbey cottages.

Barony of Bangor and Sabal, in Kirk-Patrick, consists of 7 quarterlands, but computed to only 6.

Bishop's Barony, belonging to the Lord Bishop, 19¾ quarterlands.

Barony of St. Trinions, in the parishes of German and Marown, consists of 5 quarterlands.

Portion of land in Kirk-Maughold, said to be a barony called Ball Ellen, computed to half a quarterland, with a parcel of heathy land and hough or strand, is rated in the parish accounts to one quarterland.

A small portion in Kirk Maughold, called Staff Land—

The "Forest," commonly known by the name of the Commons, were disafforested in 1864, and the Commissioners made their award on the 13th March 1865 as follows :—

| Total acreage of the Forest | . | 25,113 | 0 | 27 |

| Allotment to the Crown . | . | 8,055 | 1 | 29 |
| Do.   to the Commoners | . | 7,908 | 3 | 4 |

The remainder was sold for making new roads, expenses, etc. etc.

Cagliagh—A boundary.—When a mere ditch or boundary hedge had to be made up between the lands of the Lord and the lands of any Baron, such as the Bishop or Abbot, the Lord was exempt from giving any portion of the soil in making up such fence, the whole of which had to be made up by the adjoining party. But a portion of the land of the Lord was liable to be taken to make up the boundary fence ;

such portion was described to be as follows :—The Barons' tenants should have as much earth or soil at the Lord's side of the fence as a man "can cutt, joining his heele to the said hedge, and reach with his spade, holding his foot thereon." — *Deemster Parr's M.S. Abstract.*

This would extend to the space of, on an average, about a yard and a half.

Preban.—A waste piece of land is so called ; hence, in right of superiority in such land or common, comes the term *Preban-y-Chiarn,* the Lord's waste, as he had also the first choice in waifs and strays.

Keirroo-balley.—A quarterland ; ploughed land, amounting to about 100 acres.

The estate of Gordon, in the parish of Kirk-Patrick, consisting of 222 acres, is said to be the largest quarterland in the Island.

Balley or Balla means a town, estate, place, or farm. The greater proportion of the estates in the Island is called Balla.

QUANTITIES.

Achlish or *Aghlish*—Such a quantity of anything as can be carried under the arm—an armful ; as much as can be carried under the *oxter*.

Boandey Sundeyn—Sumner's Band.—Amongst other perquisites payable to the Sumner, or Summoner of each parish (the officer who executes the precepts and orders of the Spiritual Courts), is what is known in Manx as *Boandey Sundeyn,* the Sumner's Band, or, as it is commonly designated in English, as "the Sumner's Corn," or "the Sumner's Sheaf." In some parishes it is called "the Dog Sheaf," *Boandey Voddey* being the Sumner's perquisite for whipping the dogs out of church on a Sunday.

It is thus described in the *Book of the Spiritual Laws :—*
" As concerning the Sumner's duty of corne, he must have a
band of three lengths of three principal cornes porcion alike
paid from every husbandman, and he must call within the
church, with the advice of the vicar or curate, all such things
as he is requested of the parish that is gone or lost, and
ought to stand at the chancell door at time of service to whip
and beat all the doggs."*

In the present day this due is usually commuted for three
sheaves, or into a money payment, but that is of course op-
tional with the Sumner, as he may insist upon having it rendered in kind. Many parties have from time to time tried
to get rid of the payment or rendering of this duty, but the
Ecclesiastical Court has invariably upheld the officer, and
given judgment for the delivery of the corn in terms of the
old law.

The mode adopted is for the Sumner to draw three long
or principal stalks of corn, tie them together so as to form a
band, and whatever quantity of corn can be enclosed in such
band (making allowance for the tying of the ends), forms the
sheaf or corn-duty to which the Sumner is entitled. When
the corn is at all rank and the stalks long, the size of the
sheaf and quantity enclosed in the " Sumner's band" is something considerable.

Bunney—A sheaf of corn.

Dash—In thrashing corn with flails the corn as it was
thrashed was put on one side in a heap as a bulk against the
side wall, or on the floor, if large enough ; this was called
the dash.

Daymouth or *Daymoth*—A well-known Manx term denoting a defined quantity of land, but more generally applicable
to the measurement of meadow or hay land.

* Mill's *Statute Laws*, p. 51.

The origin of the term is supposed to have represented the quantity of hay that an ordinary man could cut down in a day. A Daymouth has however been long understood to be 60 yards each way, or 3600 square yards, being as nearly as possible equivalent to ¾ of an acre.

In numbers of old deeds of sale and wills, whereby lands were conveyed and the particulars of extent given, the number of Daymouths are named instead of acres, thus—a meadow containing 3 acres would be described as "That meadow containing by computation four Daymouths."

Dooraght or *Dhooraght*—Although perhaps strictly speaking, this term does not come under the heading given, yet as it is so intimately associated with the purchase and sale of all commodities, whether by bulk, weight, or measure, it may not be out of place to refer to it.

If a man purchases an estate, a quantity of grain, or even a horse or cow, it was usual for him, upon paying the price stipulated to give to the seller *a dooraght*, that is something over and above the actual price, out of good will, and to make up to some extent the amount that had been at first demanded by the seller, for as a general rule there is much haggling between buyer and seller before an actual sale takes place. If a good bargain had been made by the purchaser, the extent of the *dooraght* would be proportionately greater. It bore some analogy to, but also differed from a *luck-penny*, which, as is well known, is a return made by the seller of an article to the purchaser out of the price by way of good will.

Cregeen defines the word as "a perquisite, something given over and above the settled price, undoubtedly called so because often given in the dark."—(*Doo*—black—dark).

In the English and Manx Dictionary the following definition is given to the word, "importunity, boot, good-will, a gratuity, luck-penny; but none of these do properly explain the original, nor do I know of any word in the English language that corresponds to it. When a person buys any goods and pays his money, he demands a *dooraght*, and what it is the custom to ask it is usual to give."

Duill or *Deyll-lieen*—A bundle of hemp, etc., twenty-four of which make a *troo*—about a handful each.

Evik—A small stack or rick of corn, hay, etc.

Foillin—Mulcture or multure.—This is a toll to which millers are entitled out of corn ground in lieu of a money payment. In ancient days the Lord, who held all the mills (except those belonging to the abbey), claimed the whole of the "mulcture, toll, and token of all corn and graine ground within the Island."—(*Mill's Statutes*, p. 89).

It was usual for the Lord to grant licences to erect mills upon payment of certain rents (generally tolerably high), and other special conditions. The tenants of these mills were enabled to take *mulcture*, and questions not unfrequently arose as to the extent of this toll. Deemster Parr (who was Deemster from 1696 to 1712), in his *Abstract of the Customary Laws of the Island*, referring to the matter, speaks of it as "being the 24th pt. thereof," *i.e.* of the grain ground.

In 1723 the tenant of the Abbey Mill in Malew was presented by the great Enquest for taking the 16th kishen as mulcture of shelled corn, and Deemster Mylrea then gave for law that the 24th kishen was the due mulcture. The mulcture taken at the present day is the same as of old, but now usually commuted into a money payment.

According to the law of Scotland,* "some mills have attached to them an exclusive privilege of grinding the grain of a particular district, termed the *thirl* or *sucken*. The remuneration or tax to the miller is termed the *multures*; it is divided into *insucken* multures, which is the taxed remunera-

---

* *Manual of the Law of Scotland*, by John Hill Burton. 1839.

tion for grinding; *outsucken* multures, or the remuneration paid by those who, not being astricted, send their corn voluntarily to the mill; and *dry multures*, or a tax paid to the miller whether the grain be ground or not. *Knaveship* or *sequels* are a customary allowance to the miller's assistant. There are different grades of thirlage, as constituted by the original gift, or by prescription, viz.—1st. Of *grana crescentia*, or all corns grown upon the lands, not including purchased corn. 2d. Grindable corn, or the corn which it is requisite to grind for the use of the thirl. 3d. *Invecta et illatva*, or all grain growing within the thirl, as well as all that is brought within its bounds." By statute the proprietors of lands thirled, or of mills, may have the tax commuted into a money payment by adopting certain proceedings.

The Manx law was in many respects similar to the Scotch. To many of the mills in the Island there were a certain number of bound tenants, who, if they neglected to go to the mill to which their estates were pledged, were liable to a fine. The *Soken* mentioned in the orders before alluded to, 1636, was the toll from those tenants who were bound to a certain mill, or the inthralled ground. This custom is mentioned by Sir Walter Scott in describing Hob Happer the miller's visit to the Tower of Glendearg (in the *Monastery*) to look after his dues. Every miller was formerly sworn by the Deemster to deal honestly to the public. It was part of the duty of the Great Enquest to see to this. Every old mill in the Island was furnished with a large box or chest called the "Multure Chest," in which the miller kept the multures, which he sold out to the public.*

It appears that Manx millers were no honester than their

---

* It was usual for the farmer's wife or domestic to assist in dressing the meal, who threw into this chest a handful or two, as an acknowledgment to the miller's wife for her trouble in cooking for them while engaged in the mill.

brethren in other countries, as they were required to be
sworn to deal with some degree of fairness in this matter of
mulcture; but for all that, they were not exempt from the
ridicule of the song writer, as will be found by the following
humorous specimen, printed by the *Percy Society*, London,
1846.

A version of this song is given in Harland's *Ballads and
Songs of Lancashire*, 1865, in which he states it to be a
favourite about Chipping, nine miles from Clitheroe.

THE MILLER AND HIS SONS.

There was a crafty miller, and he
Had lusty sons, one, two, and three ;
He called them all, and asked their will,
If that to them he left his mill.

He called first to his eldest son,
Saying, My life is almost run ;
If I to you this mill do make,
What toll do you intend to take ?

Father, said he, my name is Jack,
Out of a bushel I'll take a peck,
From every bushel that I grind,
That I may a good living find.

Thou art a fool ! the old man said,
Thou hast not well learned thy trade ;
This mill to thee I ne'er will give,
For by such toll no man can live.

He called for his middlemost son,
Saying, My life is almost run ;
If I to you this mill do make,
What toll do you intend to take ?

Father, says he, my name is Ralph ;
Out of a bushel I'll take a half,
From every bushel that I grind,
That I may a good living find.

Thou art a fool! the old man said,
Thou hast not well learned thy trade ;
This mill to thee I ne'er will give,
For by such toll no man can live.

He called for his youngest son,
Saying, My life is almost run ;
If I to you this mill do make,
What toll do you intend to take ?

Father, said he, I'm your only boy,
For taking toll is all my joy !
Before I will a good living lack,
I'll take it all, and forswear the sack !

Thou art my boy ! the old man said,
For thou hast right well learned thy trade ;
This mill to thee I give, he cried,
And then he closed up his eyes and died.

Glaick—Such a quantity of hemp in stalks as can be held in the hand or grasped, making a small sheaf, tied up like a sheaf of corn.

Jeebin—A quantity of herring net. *Cregeen*, says it is " a deeping of nets." It also means the thread used in making nets. In the Herring Act of 1610 it is enacted, that all the Lord's or Baron's tenants within the Isle shall have in readiness for the fishing, "out of every quarter of ground, *eight fathoms* (16 *yards*), containing *three deepings* of nine score meshes upon the rope."—*Mill's Statutes*, p. 501. Before the introduction of the very long trains now in use, a *jeebin* con-

Q

stituted the *one-sixteenth* part of a piece of net. It was 18 yards long (33 meshes being counted to the yard), and 52 meshes deep; and 4 in length and 4 in depth, joined together, formed the *piece* of 16 jeebins.

Kybbon—In the Act of Tynwald, 1610, relative to the herring fishery, amongst other orders connected with the water bailiff, it is enacted, " The water bailiff shall have out of every boat, as oft as they fish, a certain measure called a *kybbon-full of herrings;* and whosoever refused to give the same, or twelve pence in money in lieu thereof, shall be excluded from the fleet."—*Mill's Statutes*, p. 503. The capacity of this measure does not appear to be now known.

Lane-doarn—A handful.

Mam.—A measure, as much as will lie upon the palm of the hand, or rather upon both hands.

Meaish—Mease (Maze, as spelt in some of the old statutes).—The common term used in counting or referring to a particular quantity of herrings. A mease is calculated to consist of 500 herrings, but in reality the number is 620, and which is made up as follows :—A hundred means what is known as the long hundred (six score), or 120, but to each hundred is added four fish, *warp* and *tally.*

In counting herrings from a boat, two of the fishermen are almost invariably employed, each of whom alternately takes up a *warp* (namely three fish), and throws them into a basket, calling out aloud in Manx the number of warps thrown in. Thus, the first man calls out, as he throws in his warp, " *unnane*" (or, as it is generally contracted, " *nane*"), the second calls " *jees,*" the first " *three,*" the second " *kiare,*" and so on, until the number reaches 40, or " *daeed,*" whereupon the first man throws in three extra herrings, calling out " *warp,*" and the second, throwing in a single fish, cries out, " *as tally,*" that is, " and tally."

The rapidity with which a couple of experienced men will count out a large quantity of herrings is surprising. The counting in English is attended with the same forms—40 warps of 3 fish, and the extra 4 to the hundred.

In 1817 an Act of Tynwald was passed, prohibiting the sale of herrings by *tale*, and providing that they should only be bought or sold by measure called *cran* or half cran. The particular dimensions and mode of construction of these measures were given in the Act, and it was declared that the cran should contain 42 gallons English wine measure—the half cran being 21 gallons.

The provisions of this Act not having been found at all suitable, it very shortly fell into disuse, and herrings are now sold by tale as heretofore.

Minjeig—A bundle of heather, ling, fern, hay, etc., made up into two packs ; the exact quantity is not defined.

Paggey-traagh—A truss of hay.

Pellick or *Pellag*—A bulk or quantity, the exact extent of which does not, however, appear to be well defined. *Cregeen*, in his " Manx Dictionary," spells the word *pellag*, and thus defines it, " A small division of something, generally applied to the division of a cart-load in small heaps or parts."

Various cases have from time to time engaged the attention of the courts of law with reference to what is called *an Executor's crop*, that is, whether the heir-at-law of a deceased landed proprietor or the executor of his will, should be entitled to the crops of corn, the seed of which had either been sown, or was in *preparation* for being sown at the time of the death of the ancestor. With respect to the case where seed had actually been sown, there could be no doubt as to the executor's right to it.

A noted case bearing upon the subject, and which was long contested both at common law and before the House of Keys,

arose in the year 1807. The style of the cause was, Thomas
Harrison *v.* William Clark. Many of the most noted Manx
lawyers of the day were employed, and the case was presided
over by Deemster Lace, who was supposed to be a great
authority on the old common law of the country.

During the trial it was asserted that the old common law
was, that, " if three pellicks of dung were laid out, and three
furrows ploughed before the testator's death, the executor
would be entitled to the crop." Other parties stated the law
to be, that " if three horse-loads of manure were spread," the
executor should have the crop. The meaning in both cases
was, that if the ancestor had made certain arrangements and
preparations for a crop, and thereby exhausted a certain portion of his means, the executor should reap the benefit. The
legal question, however, is not now in issue.

The term *pellick* was described to mean such a quantity
as a man could carry in a *creel* on his back. Now creels,
which are a kind of pannier or dossel formed of straw rope,
netwise, are of various sizes—some to carry turf, potatoes, or
other articles, on the shoulders and back of men and women
(as may be often seen in the present day at farm-houses in
the country), and others much larger, which were slung saddle-
bag fashion over the backs of horses or asses.

Ping-Ecarlys—An earnest penny.—It was always customary, and indeed still is, in bargaining for the sale of any com-
modity (other than actual goods in a shop), for the purchaser
to give to the seller a piece of money as earnest to bind the
bargain. A penny was formerly the amount given, hence the
term. No bargain was considered valid without the passing
of earnest.

In the hiring of servants, too, it is still almost invariably
the custom to give earnest.

Ping-jaagh—Smoke Penny.—This is a very old due annually payable to the several parish clerks. By the old law (still in force) he is entitled to a groat (4d.) for each plough used in his parish, should it only be used to plough three furrows, and those parties who do not keep ploughs, but "keep smoke," that is householders, have to pay one penny. See *Mill's Statutes*, p. 57.

Ping-Vrinshee—A luck penny.—This is too well known a term to call for any explanation. It does not mean the return of a penny merely, but of a portion of the price of an article sold by way of luck or good will. See also the term *Dooraght*.

Snoad—Snooid or Snoaid.—Is the length of several horse hairs twisted or spun together, and then knotted at each end. When a number of *snoads* are thus prepared, and are joined together, they form a strong line used in the sea fishing—and which line, thus made, was called a *darrag*. The length of a *snoad* depends, of course, upon the length of the hair used. They generally run from eighteen inches to two feet. In the *Manx and English Dictionary*, the term is thus defined, "a hair-line, or rather, the length of a hair, from *snicu;* that is, as much as is spun at a time."

Sthook or *Stook*—A pile of sheaves of corn. The old *sthook* consisted of twelve sheaves. There were three modes of making up a *sthook*. The *sheeig* or pile was made up as follows :—

1*st*. Eight sheaves were set up on end in two rows of four, a sheaf at each end, and two on the top, tapering from the centre.

2*d*. Ten sheaves in two rows of five at a side, and two on the top.

3*d*. Three sheaves in three rows each, two on the top as a covering, and one as the crown of all.

The last was the old Manx mode of forming a *sthook*, and

was considered the best mode of protecting the corn from the weather when it had to remain any length of time before it was carted home.

Thow—A line to which buoys or corks are attached, and which holds up or suspends the herring nets when in the water. It varies in length according to the fishing ground.

Tooran or *Thurran*—A stack either of corn or hay of any figure, but more particularly when round or pointed.

A Spade's Cutting of Turf—In former days it was by no means unusual for a landowner, possessing a quantity of *curragh* or turf-producing land (and which abounds more particularly in the northern parishes of the Island), in arranging his affairs, to provide that some particular member of his family should have *a spade's cutting of turf*, either yearly or at intermediate periods during his life, the object being to secure fuel (coals being comparatively unknown) for the person to be benefited. The extent of this turf cutting was not unfrequently a question of strife and ill-will in the family.

Even so late as forty years ago the question of the *legality* of a grant of "a spade's cutting of turf" was solemnly tried at common law, and by appeal to the House of Keys, in which body was then reposed the appellate jurisdiction over the verdicts of jurors at law. Besides the issue as to the legal effect of such a grant, the question as to the *extent* of a "spade's cutting" was raised, and, as will be seen from the evidence adduced, there was considerable discrepancy between the witnesses upon this point.

The action arose in the parish of Ballaugh. Thomas Nelson sued Ann Mylecharane for trespass, the charge being that she had wrongfully entered into his meadow, and dug and carried away soil, etc. The defendant justified her entry into the plaintiff's lands under the provisions of a deed, whereby *a spade's cutting of turf* was granted to her for her life. The case was tried at a common law court held at Ramsey on the 14th February 1832, when the jury found a verdict in favour of the plantiff, giving £1 : 17 : 6 damages against Ann Mylecharane, whom they found to be a trespasser.

The old lady, however, *traversed* (that is appealed) from the verdict to the House of Keys, who, by their judgment dated 1st March 1833, reversed the jury's verdict, and dismissed the action, thereby upholding the right of the defendant to her "spade's cutting of turf" for her life.

The evidence as to the *extent* of the spade's cutting was as follows :—

Thomas Christian proved that it was 42 yards in length, 1¾ yard in breadth, and 3 turves in depth.

John Cry stated the length and breadth to be as described by the former witness, but gave the depth as from 20 to 23 inches.

John Caley defined the extent as 60 yards long, 2 yards wide, and 3 turves of 9 inches each deep.

John Clark, John Quayle, another John Quayle, and John Craine, severally proved the dimensions to be 60 yards in length, 2 yards in width, and 27 inches in depth, corroborating in other words the evidence of John Caley.

It may therefore be fairly assumed that the extent given by the five last-named witnesses truly represented what a spade's cutting really was.

(The proceedings in the case will be found *in extenso* in *Liber Plitor*, 1831, No. 29, parish of Ballaugh, in the Rolls Office, Castletown.)

Size of Custom Turf.—Amongst other charges upon the lord's tenants (the owners of the land paying rent, etc., to the lord) was that of supplying the garrisons of Peel Castle and Castle Rushen with turf, so many cars to the quarterland.

By certain resolutions of the Earl of Derby in 1593, it

was declared "That the custome turff be allowed according to law and custome, that is 52 turves of one cubit long and three inches square in the middest, and those to be allowed for one able carr within the houses of Castle Pecle."—*Mills*, p. 76.

The proprietors of abbey lands were in like manner bound to supply the bishop or abbot with turf, and Deemster Parr, in his *Abstract of the Customary Laws*, gives the sizes as above.

PECULIAR CUSTOMS WITH REFERENCE TO FOOD, DRINK, ETC.—

Several peculiar customs still linger in some of the out-of-the-way places in the island, but the great influx of summer visitors, with the gradual intercourse thereby created, is fast obliterating them.   We may allude to the following :—

Amvlass—A drink composed of milk or butter-milk and water.

Binjean—New milk turned to curd with rennet, and sweetened with sugar; eaten with preserves; is a great favourite during the summer season.

Braghtan—A mixture of food by no means unpalatable, partaken of as a kind of luncheon, or even at dinner.   It is a veritable sandwich.   One mode of preparing it is as follows :—

Take a piece of barley cake and spread it over with fresh butter, add a layer of potatoes bruised, then a coating of salt herring nicely picked and free from bones; upon this spread another layer of potatoes, and cover with barley cake and butter.   It is needless to add that the *Braghtan* should be eaten hot.   A seasoning of pepper is an improvement.

Cregeen thus defines the word—"Braghtan (no doubt from *breck* or *brack*), spotted, smeared, or streaked with something spread on bread, as honey, butter, herring, etc."   "*Braghtan eeymey*—a butter-cake, or a cake spread or spotted with butter or any other eatable."

Broish consists of broken pieces of oat-cakes soaked in pot-liquor or dripping ; also used for breakfast.

Cowree—A kind of food made of oatmeal steeped in water.

Jough—Drink, but usually applied to *common ale*. From this is derived the well-known term "Jough-y-dorrys," the parting drink or stirrup cup.

No social meeting of Manxmen is supposed to end fairly or friendly without having the *Jough-y-dorrys*, no matter how much had previously been drank.

Sollaghan.—This is a kind of food made of oatmeal and the liquor in which meat has been boiled. It is generally used for breakfast among the country people. For an allusion to this, see *Mona Miscellany*, first series, p. 26.

Keear-Lheeah—Two colours of wool spun and wove into cloth are so called, a dark grey colour, which cloth was formerly the garb generally worn by the Manx peasantry.

Loaghtyn—A mouse brown colour in the wool of Manx sheep, of a fine staple, was formerly a great favourite for making cloth, but that breed of sheep is now almost extinct.

Kiare-as-feed ; or, *Yn-chiare-as-feed*—House of Keys.— The explanation of this term has been so fully given in the *Manx and English Dictionary* of Dr. Kelly (Manx Society, vol. xiii.), that it is best to repeat it here in his own terms :— " The Keys, or Parliament of the Island, are so called from their number, as they consist of twenty-four persons. But as it is used as a proper name in conversation, it has therefore the article prefixed ; as, *Yn-chiare-as-feed*. This is supposed by the ingenious Rev. Wm. Fitzsimmons to be a corruption of *cor-an-phaid*, the company of the prophets, wisemen, or rulers ; for no doubt that *cor* is choir or company, and *phaid*

phadeyrys, prophecy. The government of the Island consisted
of two parts, the executive and the legislative. The King was
vested with the whole executive power, and had the sole
appointment of his own officers and council. The power of
making and repealing laws rested with the Keys, who were
obliged, in conjunction with the other power, to call annually
a Tynwald, or meeting of the people, where all new laws
were publicly proclaimed three times, otherwise they were of no
force, and a man could plead in court the *ignorantia legis*. I
could never find whether the people had any other negative
upon the promulgation of an unpopular law, except force, to
which, according to several traditional accounts, they were
frequently obliged to have recourse, and were always successful
in the application of it. This is not to be wondered at, as the
Keys were self-elected, and when a member died they chose
two men out of the body of the people, and presented them
to the King for his approbation of one of them. And besides,
they, as well as the court, were exempt from most of the
duties and taxes the people laboured under ; and together
exercised an arbitrary power, as an instance of which I shall
only mention, that whenever any of them wanted servants,
they had a right to *yard*, that is, to compel, by virtue of a
statute or *slattys*, and force into their service the best servants
in the Island, wherever they were to be found, and without
allowing them common wages. Yet, notwithstanding this
connection between the parliament and the court, it has been
found that when the Court has attempted any innovation, the
Keys have uniformly joined the people. When the Earl of
Derby endeavoured to remove the people from their posses-
sions, and to consider the soil as his property, the people and
Keys united, and at last obtained from the Insular Legislature
the Act of Settlement, A. D. 1704, which confirmed every man
in the possession of his estate, and made his possession his
property. Notwithstanding the Island is annexed at present

to the Crown of England, the laws and manner of government continue with little variation, except that the Governor, who is appointed by the Crown of England, acts in most instances in the place of the former Kings of Man. It appears, both from history and tradition, that at first the *Kiarc-as-feed* were chosen by popular election from each of the six *sheadings*, but that afterwards, on the death of one of the body, they presented two commoners to the King, and he was obliged to elect one of the two."

For the custom of "yarding," alluded to above, see *Mona Miscellany*, first series, p. 26. By the Act of 1763, "the wages due by law to yarded servants is found to be very insufficient. It is therefore enacted, that henceforth yarded servants' wages shall be augmented, and that a man-servant shall be intituled to have and receive the sum of forty shillings, and a maid-servant shall have twenty shillings for their year's servitude, any former law or custom to the contrary hereof notwithstanding." This custom has now fallen into disuse.

LEGENDS AND MISCELLANIES.

" Like an old wife's tale, with trifles light as air."

LEGENDS AND MISCELLANIES.

— ◆ —

THE RUINED CHAPEL IN ST. MICHAEL'S ISLE.

A LEGEND.

AT a distance of about a mile and a half from Castletown, the metropolis of the Isle of Man, round the head of Derby Haven, lies St. Michael's Isle, on which are to be met with the ruins of the little chapel of St. Michael (in Manx, *Kccihll Vaayl*), from which it takes its name, and which has been in its present roofless state for more than two hundred years. The length of the chapel is 31 feet, and the breadth 14 ; the height of the side walls 10 feet ; and the date of the building may be about the 12th century. There is an ancient grave-yard attached to it, which is now principally used as a place of interment by the Roman Catholics.

Many years ago there was a famous priest, who gave up all that he possessed, and came to teach Christianity in these parts. He was not a Manxman, though he could talk with the people in their own tongue. He lived in a poor house at Derby Haven, but for all that there was not a sick or needy person near but what he helped with medicine and food, as well as spiritual advice. Along with a kind heart he had a kind face and voice, so that the little children would run out to laugh and kiss his hand when they saw him pass. For a long time he used to gather the people together in the winter evenings in one of the largest rooms in the hamlet, while in the summer he would preach to the fishermen and their families on the sea-shore.

After some years of this intercourse, he proposed to the men that they should build a small church on the Island. St. Michael, he said, had appeared to him in a vision, and pointed out a chapel on a flat space upon the grass close to the rocks; he had seen it, he said, quite plain in his dream; the light was shining out of the windows; he had crept up under the wall, and looked in, and lo! he saw himself kneeling before a beautiful costly altar, and he recognised the congregation as themselves.

Now, while they were full of admiration at this dream, the good father bade them rise up and follow him to the place where he had seemed to see the chapel, and lo! when they got there they found the ground marked out where the foundations of the chapel now stand, and a border drawn some distance around on which that wall was built, which you can now trace in the grass, just as if some one had turned up a furrow on the bare earth, and then laid a carpet of turf upon it. And when the men of the place saw the marvel, and how truly the good father's dream had been from Heaven, he bade them kneel down there at once, while he prayed to St. Michael and all angels that these people would not leave off the good work till they had built a chapel to him. Thus they were led to begin, and promised to give a portion of their time till the little church should be finished.

There was abundance of stone close by, and the architecture of the edifice was of the simplest kind. Four plain thick walls, with a roof, was all they aimed at. Now, this part of the work was comparatively easy; but Father Kelly began to be sore perplexed as it approached completion, how he should furnish it within, and so fulfil the dream in providing such a costly altar as he was persuaded he ought to build. The poor people had neither silver nor gold. They had already offered such as they had — strong hands, and hours taken from their rest or work. Night after night Father Kelly used to repair to the chapel, now roofed in, and pray to St. Michael to help him in this strait. One dark evening he was there later than usual ; he had fallen down with his face upon the ground before the spot in which he hoped to put the altar. While thus prostrate in prayer, and longing for a continuation of his former dream, he heard some footsteps close outside the chapel walls. Having his face upon the earth, the sound came quite distinctly to his ear. They stopped, and a voice said, "This is the chapel, let us lay them here, 'tis just the place for a burial."

"Very well," replied another ; "how does she lie! Here goes, mate, by the north-east corner."

Then came the sound of digging and pauses, as if men were stooping down to lay something in the ground ; after that Father Kelly heard the mould put back, and some one stamp it down. Though the church had not been furnished, two or three funerals had taken place in the graveyard, one of which he had himself celebrated only that afternoon.

What could be the object of these strange night visitors? They had not disturbed the dead—they did not remain long enough for that ; their work, whatever it was, seemed to be accomplished in a quarter of an hour, for after that time he heard a slapping of hands, as if some one were cleaning them of the dusty earth, and a voice saying, "There! that is done ; and as dead men tell no tales, we may trust the present company."

"Ay, ay," replied the other, "I trust them so much, I don't think we need wait any longer."

"What ! art afraid, man !"

"Not I : but there is foul weather coming, and the sooner we clear off these cursed rocks the better."

" Well, come along ! "

Then Father Kelly heard them walk down towards the
water, and presently distinguished the grating of the boat's
keel as she was pushed off ; then the double sound of the oars
in the rowlocks died away, and all was still.   He got up
from the floor and walked out of the chapel.   It was a midsummer night.   The air was warm and motionless ; clouds,
however, had crept up so plentifully as to cover the sky.
While he stood there outside the chapel, the moon, which was
about a week old, became obscured, and the darkness drew
close to his eyes.   He could not see a yard before him ; he
listened, but heard only the slow wash of the swell as the
rising tide carried it into the clefts among the rocks, with now
and then a liquid flap, as a wave ran into a sudden angle and
fell back upon itself.   He felt for his lantern, and got out his
steel to strike a light.   Having dropped his flint, in groping
about to find it he forgot the direction in which he had stood ;
and when he got upon his feet again, after an unsuccessful
search, felt himself so utterly at a loss, that after walking a
few steps with his hands stretched out before him, he determined to wait for the morning, rather than risk a fall over
one of the slippery rocks in his attempt to return home.
When he had sat there for some time, the rain began to fall
in large though few drops ; these were, however, but the
splashes from the bucketfuls which were soon poured on his
head.   The wind, too, was loosed at the same time, and rushed
on him with such violence, that though he dared not search
for shelter lest he should fall over the rocks, he was glad to
sit down on a large stone which he felt at his feet.   The first
flash of lightning, however, showed him the chapel itself, not
more than ten yards off.   He groped towards it immediately
in the gloom, with his hands stretched out before him, right
glad when he felt its rough stones.   The wall once found, he
soon discovered the path with his feet, and when he got home
was glad to go to rest at once.

He had not slept many hours before he was roused to visit a dying man in one of the neighbouring houses. Hurrying on his clothes, he hastened to the place, where a crowd was gathered about the door, many of them dripping from the sea. The storm which he had seen the evening before had grown into a terrible tempest, during which a ship had been driven on the rocks, and utterly wrecked. All the crew were drowned but one man, whom they had dragged out of the surf, and carried to Derby Haven. He had apparently, however, been saved from death in the water to die on the land, for he was so grievously bruised and cut by the rocks on which he had been thrown, that life was ready to leave him altogether. When Father Kelly came in, he found him lying on the floor, wrapped up in such dry clothes as the people had at hand. He had begged them to fetch a priest. His back, he said, was broken, and he knew he could not live another hour ; so the people fetched Father Kelly, as we have seen, and left the two together.

"Father," said the dying man, "will you hear the confession of a pirate and a murderer ?"

The priest, seeing there was no time to lose, signified his assent, and kneeling down by his side, bent his ear to listen.

Then the man, with strange breaks and ramblings in his speech, told him of murders out in the wide seas, and horrible recollections of cruelty and rapine.

We took a Spanish ship some weeks ago, added the man, and came in here to water, being a safe place ; when I—God forgive my soul !—I committed my last crime, and stole from the captain, a box of gold he took out of the Spaniard. Another man and I were in the secret. We brought it with us, and buried it in the graveyard of your little chapel, intending to make our escape from the ship on the first opportunity, find our way over here, recover, and enjoy the booty we had got.

" To whom did it belong ? " said the priest.

" God knows ;" replied the man ; " to me now, I suppose. Those who owned it can use it no more : the ship from which the captain took it went down with all on board ; we burnt her."

" What was her name ?" asked Father Kelly.

" Name," said the dying man, " There, take the gold, and shrive me ; I have confessed !"

Then, without another word, he died. The people buried him, and gathered up some few pieces of timber from the wreck of his ship, but nothing came ashore to show whether she was laden or not. They never knew her name, nor, for a great while, what she was, the priest not conceiving himself bound to tell them even so much of what he had heard in confession. Many years afterwards the whole story was found in a book which the priest left behind him when he died.

The words "take the gold" haunted the good Father long after the man who died in uttering them had been committed to the ground. The chapel was finished, but not furnished ; the fulfilment of the dream was incomplete. Many a night the priest lay awake, arguing with himself the lawfulness of a search among the graves for the treasure, which, he had no doubt, was hidden there. Suppose he could find it, should he credit the pirate's word about the death of its owner ? Could he conscientiously appropriate it, not, indeed, for his own use, but to that of the chapel ? He thought of the terrible sentence which fell on those who put unhallowed fire in their censers ; he thought of the accursed thing found in the Jew's tent, which brought trouble upon the whole people to which he belonged. Then, again, it looked as if the sin attached to the appropriation of this gold had been punished in the persons of the pirates who had taken it. It looked as if it were rescued from the service of the world, to be devoted to that of the church—snatched from the devil himself, to be given to St. Michael, his chief enemy.

On the whole, he decided upon using the gold, if he could find it. He must, however, be cautious in the search; he would not trust the people to look. It might not be there, and then he would be ashamed. There might be more than he thought, and they might be tempted to take some; or, if not that, be jealous at his retaining the possession of it himself. He would search alone. The conversation he had heard outside the chapel, while he listened on the eve of the storm, indicated the spot on which he should look.

Having, therefore, waited for a suitable moonlight night, he went very late to the churchyard with a spade. There was no one there. The shadow of the building fell upon the likely spot; he could work unperceived, even if the late returning fishermen were to pass by that way. Half ashamed of the errand, he had not removed many spadefuls of earth from the grave he suspected, before he struck upon something hard. Stooping down, he felt for it with his hands; it was a heavy box. He took it up, smoothed down the soil, carried it straight home, double locked his door, and broke it open. It contained broad shining pieces of gold. They made such a heap on his table as he had never seen before. There was, moreover, in the box, a necklace of large pearls, gold for the chapel, jewels for the Madonna.

The church was furnished, the altar was decked, the image was brought, and round its neck he hung the string of fair large pearls.

Father Kelly saw his dream fulfilled, and as success often produces conviction, he thanked St. Michael and all angels for having turned the robber's booty into sacred treasure. So it was written in his book, but he told no one whence these riches came. Some of the simple folk thought the virgin herself had brought these jewels to the father. He, however, many a time, while he sat on the rocks by the chapel, looking out to seaward, and watching the white sails go by, wandered back to the question whence these riches came, and whether, after all, they might not hide some after-curse or other.

One evening as he sat there, a vessel came round the point, and dropped anchor in the haven. She drew his attention as being unlike any of the common coasting ships, or even of the traders which ventured on more distant voyages. She carried more canvas in proportion to her hull, and had her sails furled almost as soon as she had swung round with the tide.

Presently a boat came off from her, and was rowed to the shore, just beneath the spot where he sat. Two men, apparently officers, got out, and walking up to him, begged him to accompany them back to the ship, as they said one of their crew was dying, and needed the offices of a priest. He went with them at once without suspicion ; a man who had been with him, and heard the summons, returned to Derby Haven.

The ghostly summons, however, was a ruse ; this was the sister ship of the pirate who had been wrecked here in the storm—now some months ago. The new comers had learned her fate, and had landed to search for traces of the treasures she had on board. They had first taken the priest, as they thought, with much probability, he could tell them whether the inhabitants of the village had plundered the wreck, and also whether any of her crew survived.

What they learned from Father Kelly, no one ever knew. Some of the men, returning to the shore, strolled into the chapel, and doubtless recognised the necklace as one of the costliest items of their lost treasure. The next morning the ship was gone, and the people, searching for their priest, who had not returned home at night, found the chapel sacked, and his corpse set over the altar in the place where the image of the Madonna had been, with a knotted cord, like a necklace, tightly twisted round his throat.

The superstition of the natives never permitted them to use the chapel again. It gradually became a ruin; the roof fell in; the storms lashed the walls within as well as without; until at last it passed into the state in which it is to this day. Even now, whoever struck the walls and listened, could hear a moan within, and a noise like the jingling of money. You can try it yourself, and find whether I have told you the truth.

THE GLASHTYN.

THE Glashtyn is a goblin or sprite who wore no clothes, and was hairy; said to frequent rivers in their lonely secluded spots, and is useful or otherwise as the caprice of the moment led them, assuming various shapes, and occasionally performing kind offices for the farmer, something in the way of the Scottish Brownie or the Manx "Phynnodderee," as mentioned in the first part of *Mona Miscellany.*

In Campbell's *Tales of the West Highlands*, he relates the following, which was told him by a woman who lived near the Calf of Man, who said:—

"Did you ever hear tell of the Glashan?"

"No; tell me about the Glashan."

"Well, you see, in the ould times they used to be keeping the sheep in the folds, and one night an ould man forgot to put them in, and he sent out his son, and he came back and said the sheep were all folded, but there was a year-old lamb, *oasht* playing the mischief with them, and that was the Glashan. You see they were very strong, and when they wanted a stack threshed, though it was a whole stack, the Glashan would have it threshed for them in one night. And they were running after the women. There was one of them once caught a girl, and ha' a hould of her by the dress, and he sat down and he fell asleep, and then she cut away all the dress, you see, round about, this way, and left it in his fist, and ran away; and when he awoke, he threw what he had over his shoulder, this way, and he said something in Manx. Well, you see, one night the ould fellow sent all the women to bed, and he put on a cap and a woman's dress, and he sat down by the fire, and he began to spin; and the young Glashans they came in, and they began saying something in Manx that means ' Are you turning the wheel? are you

trying the reel?' Well, the ould Glashan he was outside, and
he knew better than the young ones; he knew it was the
ould fellow himself, and he was telling them, but they did
not mind him, and so the ould man threw a lot of hot turf,
you see it was turf they burned then, over them, and burned
them; and the ould one said (something in Manx). You'll
not understand that now?"

"Yes, I do; pretty nearly."

"Ah, well. And so the Glashans went away, and never
came back any more."

"Have you many stories like that, guidwife?"

"Ah!" said she, "there were plenty of people that could
tell those stories once. When I was a little girl I used to
hear them telling them in Manx over the fire at night; but
people is so changed with pride now that they care for nothing."

THE ENCHANTED ISLAND AT PORT SODERICK.

NUMEROUS are the allusions that are made respecting the notion of a land under the waves. Waldron relates a remarkable story of an adventurer in search of treasure off the coast of Man having descended to a great depth in a " bell made of glass," and saw unheard of riches. It is believed by many that there exists a superb city with many towers, and numerous gilded minarets, near Langness, in Castletown Bay, on a place now covered by the sea, and which is sometimes seen to rise up in all its former magnificence. The Manx sailors relate they often hear the tinkling of the church bell under the sea on a Sunday morning.

It is stated that Cardigan Bay was once the site of a submerged city ; that the renowned chief O'Donoghue continues to reside in a splendid mansion under the Lake of Killarney, over which he is seen to glide on May day morning, riding on a milk-white steed. Many other instances might be given of a similar belief, "traditions common to many nations which bear upon that of the mysterious western land hidden in the mist, which was once the Isle of Man, and is now to the westward of Man." These are all founded upon incidents which have been woven into popular tales ever since man began to speak.

The septennial appearance of the submerged island near Port Soderick is looked forward to with some degree of interest by many in the Isle of Man. Many a time and oft had Nora Cain heard her old grandsire relate the tradition of this enchanted island at Port Soderick while sitting spinning by the turf fire on a winter's evening. It was in the days of the great Fin Mac Coul, that mighty magician, who, for some insult he had received from the people who lived on a beautiful island off Port Soderick, cast his spell over it, and submerged it to the bottom of the ocean, transforming the inhabitants into blocks of granite. It was permitted them, once in seven years, to rise to the surface for the short space of thirty minutes, during which time the enchantment might be broken if any person had the boldness to place a Bible on any part of the enchanted land when at its original altitude above the waters of the deep.

On one occasion, it was about the end of September on a fine moonlight night, Nora was sauntering along the little bay in sweet converse with her lover, when she observed something in the distance which continued to increase in size. It struck her to be none other than the enchanted isle she so often had heard of. It continued gradually rising above the surface of the water, when, suddenly disentangling herself from the arm of her lover, hastened home with all the speed she could, and rushed into the cottage, crying out, breathless with her haste, "The Bible, the Bible, the Bible!" to the utter amazement of the inmates, who could not at the moment imagine what had possessed her. After explaining what she had seen, she seized hold of the coveted volume and hastened back to the beach, but, alas! only just in time to see the last portion of the enchanted isle subside once more to its destined fate of another seven years' submersion.

From that night poor Nora gradually pined away, and was soon after followed to her grave by her disconsolate lover. It is said, from that time no person has had the hardihood to make a similar attempt, lest, in case of failure, the enchanter in revenge might cast his club over Mona also.

THE UNIVERSAL PRAYER,

By Alexander Pope, is here given in order to bring before Manx
readers the translation of Mr. Kewley. Long were the critics divided
on the morality of Pope's verses, and bitter were their controversies,
and at length they were wisely suffered to expire.

I.

Father of all ! in every age,
    In every clime adored,
By saint, by savage, and by sage,
    Jehovah, Jove, or Lord !

II.

Thou Great First Cause, least understood,
    Who all my sense confined
To know but this, that Thou art good,
    And that myself am blind ;

III.

Yet gave me, in this dark estate,
    To see the good from ill ;
And binding Nature fast in fate,
    Left free the human will.

IV.

What conscience dictates to be done,
    Or warns me not to do,
This, teach me more than hell to shun,
    That, more than heaven pursue.

POPE'S UNIVERSAL PRAYER.

Translated into Manx by Mr. Kewley, of Ballafreer. This translation is from a MS., written about the year 1812, and has not, I believe, been printed. It is considered a good specimen of Manx versification, and is thus given for the facility of easy reference.

I.

Rieau er dyn chroe Ayr jeh dagh nhee,
    Sheer dhyts ta ooashley ermayrn,
Yn Noo, Ashoonagh, as Chreestee,
    JEHOVAH, JOVE, ny CHSARN!

II.

Ard Oyr dagh teshiaght mie as sie,
    'Sbeg shione dooin mooads dty phooar,
She uss ny lomarcan ta mie,
    As shin ayns dellid wooar ;

III.

Son ooilley shen Tou er nyn rheyre,
    Lesh tushtey as resoon ;
Ayns kianley dooghys kiart as chair,
    Daag reamys-aighey dooin.

IV.

Shen ta cooinsheanse roym dy leedeil,
    Ny noi resoon cur raue,
Shoh soilshagh dou nurin hregeil,
    Shen geearree gerjagh Niau

V.

What blessings thy free bounty gives,
  Let me not cast away ;
For God is paid when man receives ;
  To enjoy is to obey.

VI.

Yet not to earth's contracted span
  Thy goodness let me bound,
Or think thee Lord alone of man,
  When thousand worlds are round.

VII.

Let not this weak unknowing hand
  Presume thy bolts to throw,
And deal damnation round the land,
  On each I judge thy foe.

VIII.

If I am right, thy grace impart,
  Still in the right to stay ;
If I am wrong, O teach my heart
  To find that better way !

IX.

Save me alike from foolish pride,
  Or impious discontent,
At aught thy wisdom has denied,
  Or aught thy goodness lent.

X.

Teach me to feel another's woe,
  To hide the fault I see :
That mercy I to others show,
  That mercy show to me.

V.

Maynrys dty vannaghtyn foayroil,
    Lhig dou gyn lhiggey sheese ;
Son JEE nie boggey jou y ghoaill ;
    Ghoys soylley 'yioot lesh booise.

VI.

Cha nee gys shoh 'lhig dooys y hayrn
    Dty vieys wooar cha cruin,
Chiarn chammah dooin as da thousane,
    Dy heihll mygrayrt-y-mooin :

VII.

Niartee m'annoonid ommijagh
    Nagh jeanym briwnys creoie,
Ny seylagh coayl-anmey-dy bragh,
    Danesyn erlhiam ta dt'oi.

VIII.

My ta mee chairagh, our dou grayse,
    Dy voddym geiyrt d'an chair ;
My ta mee olk, O, insh dou saase
    Dy voddym gaase ny share !

IX.

Saue mee veih moyrn fardail y theihll,
    Veih scayhyn as anvea,
Gymmyrkey lhiam ayns dagh failleil,
    Shier freayll my chassan rea.

X.

Lhig dou gys irimshey bradr chyndaa,
    As cheillyn fooil sheelnaue :
My noidyn s'dewil ta d'olk gimraa,
    Leih dooys myr leihym's daue.

XI.

Mean though I am, not wholly so,
    Since quicken'd by thy breath :
O lead me wheresoe'er I go,
    Through this day's life or death !

XII.

This day be bread and peace my lot :
    All else beneath the sun,
Thou know'st if best bestow'd or not,
    And let thy will be done.

XIII.

To thee, whose temple is all space ;
    Whose altar, earth, sea, skies ;
One chorus let all being raise !
    All nature's incense rise !

XI.

Ga ta mee treih foast ta my vioys,
    Paart jeh dty obbyr vie :
O leeid mee sthill ayns keeayll as foays,
    Derrey nee oo m'eamagh thie !

XII.

Jui dy row beaghey cooie my chren ;
    Freill mee veih oyr dy phlaynt,
Shione dhtys ere ta mee er my hon,
    As dty aigney's dyrew jeant.

XIII.

Hoods ta dty Hiamble feayn gyn aione :
    Dty altar, ooir, as aer ;
Ardveylley dooghys as ny tayn !
    Dy row dy bragh dty chair !

FESTIVITIES IN CASTLE RUSHEN IN 1643 and 1644.

A.D. 1643. The Right Hoble. James Earle of Derbie and his Right Honble. Countesse invited all the Officeres, temporall and sperituall, the Clergie, the 24 Keyes of the Isle, the Crowners with all theire wives, and likewise the best sort of the rest of the Inhabitance of the Isle, to a great maske, where the Right Hoble. Charles Lo. Strange, with his traine, the right hoble. Ladies, with their attendance, were most gloriously decked with silver and gould, broidered workes, and most costly ornaments, bracellets on there hands, chaines on there necks, jewels on there foreheads, earings in there eares, and crownes on there heads, and after the maske to a feast which was most royall and plentifull, wth. shuttings of ornans, etc. And this was on the twelfth day (or last day), in Christmas, in the yeare 1644. All the men just with the Earle, and the wives with the Countesse, likewise, there was such another feast that day was twelve moneth at night beinge 1643.

Per me Tho. Parre, Vicr. of Malew.

The Honble. Charles was at this time about 16 years old, having been born the 19th Jany. 1627.

This Thomas Parr was styled " Surrogate," and was vicar of Malew in 1641 to 1691, and died in 1695.

A list of some of the principal characters present at these festivities would be curious. We presume this worthy vicar of the parish must have been present in his capacity of Register, taking note thereof.—P. B.

Taken from P. B's. MS. Extracts from the Episcopal Register, etc., p. in MS., 33.

THESE masques were very popular about this time, and were acted both at Court and at the mansions of the nobility. Mr. Parr, unfortunately, has not recorded the name of the masque acted at Castle Rushen in these years; probably it was *Chlorindia*, one of the many written by Ben Jonson, and performed at Court, by the Queen's Majesty, and her ladies, at Shrovetide, 1630, in which Charlotte de la Tremouille, Lady Strange, was one of the fourteen nymphs who sat round the Queen in the bower of Chloris. Their dresses are thus described in Jonson's *Works*, vol. viii. London, 1816, p. 109:

—"Their apparel white, embroidered in silver, trimmed at the shoulders with great leaves of green, embroidered with gold, falling one under the other. And of the same work were their bases, their head-tires of flowers, mixed with silver and gold, with some sprigs of ægrets among, and from the top of their dressing a thin veil hanging down." The Derby family were constant encouragers of these masques in England, hence the introduction of them in their territory of Man, to beguile the tedium of winter.

To any one curious to know the names of the masquers who personated the nymphs in the masque above named, they are thus given by the poet :—

1. Countess of Carlisle.
2. Countess of Carnarvon.
3. Countess of Berkshire.
4. M. Porter.
5. Countess of Newport.
6. M. Dor. Savage.
7. Countess of Oxford.
8. Lady Howard.
9. Lady Anne Cavendish.
10. M. Eliz. Savage.
11. Lady Penelope Egerton.
12. M. Anne Weston.
13. Lady Strange.
14. M. Sophia Cary.

15. The Queen.

THE SLIEAUWHALLIN BOAGANE.

THE mountain mentioned in the following legend is situated on the south side of St. John's Valley, overlooking the Tynwald Hill, and is mentioned by old writers as the place from whence those suspected of witchcraft or other dark practices, were hurled down from its northern summit, finding a watery grave in the depths of the *Curragh-Glass*, the Gray-Bog, which in those ancient days lay at its foot. The Rev. J. G. Cumming, in his *Isle of Man*, 1848, speaking of the severe statutes enacted against witchcraft both in England and Scotland, says, " in an island like that of Man, where the wind howls over heathery wilds, the lightning plays upon the summit of cloud-capped mountains, the thunder-peal rolls along dark and deep valleys, and is re-echoed against an iron-bound coast, mingling with the roar of the stormy billow in sea-worn caves and fearfully dismal chasms, we need feel no surprise that in such an Island persons should be found seeking gain by practising on the superstitious and awestruck feelings of the ignorant, or that laws should be enacted to suppress, if possible, such dark practices."

The legend here given is from the pen of Mr. John Quirk, of Carn-ny-Graie, Kirkpatrick, of whose poetical talent various specimens have been given in *Mona Miscellany*, who, from his mountain residence, has no doubt heard those echoes of the wailing winds which have been so often said to proceed from troubled spirits of former days, calling forth many a legend, wierd and wild, that Mona's sons delight to hear recorded while assembled around their winter's hearth. He considers the name of Slieauwhallin to be derived from Slieau, mountain, and aalin, fair and beautiful—" The beautiful mountain." Others ascribe it to Slieau, a hill, and Whallin, a whelp —" the whelp's hill," while the Rev. J. T. Clarke says the real origin of the word " Slieau-whallin " is Slieau-Whialliam, the hills of Quilliam, the oldest family name on record as the proprietor of that hill.

WILL any person now undertake the task of furnishing a true, or even a fabulous account of the rise and progress of the " Slieauwhallin Boagane," so famous in former days ?

How an apprentice, or a young journeyman tailor, living with his master, in the vicinity of Glenaspet, was said to be suspected of murdering his master's wife, how he was accused, tried, and condemned to suffer a horrible death, by being thrust into a barrel thickly stuck with spikes or nails, with their sharp ends pointed inwardly, and rolled down the precipiece from the heights of Gob-ny-beinney, above Mullin-é-Chloie. How, from first to last he pleaded his innocence of the crime laid to his charge, and told his accusers that if he was not guilty, a thorn-tree would grow at his head where he was buried, and that a well or spring of water would be found at his feet, which said well and thorn-tree are said to be seen to this day. And, moreover, how he warned his persecutors that as sure as he suffered wrongfully, he would continue to frequent and trouble the locality as long as grass continued to grow, or water to flow, and being faithful to his word, how he continued to annoy and terrify the neighbourhood in past ages.

His tremendous yells proceeding from the Monapian Sinai, frowning upon the Tynwald Hill, were said to be truly awful, often reverberating amidst the surrounding hills as far as the Greeba rocks. Sometimes a solitary scream is heard; at other times they are repeated in pretty quick succession, and uttered with indescribable vehemence and fervency, having some resemblance to the cries of a man shouting at the top of his voice when tortured by the keenest agonies of terror and pain, somewhat smothered and suppressed by partial strangulation. Whether he hath varied or enlarged his sphere of action or not since the commencement of his career, would now be difficult to ascertain, but the mode of his proceeding during the last generations appears to be somewhat as follows :—His first alarming note is commonly heard near the spot where he suffered; then he takes his flight, like a bird of passage, along the Slieauwhallin ridge of hills, shouting at intervals as he goes, passing over Arracy or Arrey-dee. Steering in the direction of Cronk-yn-irree-laa, the echoes of his finishing scream are to be heard dying away among the solitudes of the Dalby mountains.

These are some of the fragments handed down to us by our forefathers, the truth of which were seldom if ever questioned among them, but the whole seemed to go down with them as palatable as the history of the Illiam Dhône tragedy, or any other story equally well attested. Many were to be found in days gone by, who were ready to bear witness to the truth of something like that which I have been endeavouring to describe, and some sensible men are to be met with at this day who appear to be perfectly satisfied of the verity of the case, by having at one time or another had an opportunity of hearing for themselves, though it may be admitted that these opportunities are now few and far between when compared with the tales of the last century. I have never heard with any certainty what was the name of the poor tailor who suffered, as it may be presumed from the sequel, innocently; the letters W. Corran, are to be found cut in a rock near the place of execution, but whether this was the young tailor's name or not, it is now impossible to ascertain.

It is almost astonishing, after so much has been said, that little or nothing to my knowledge hath ever been written concerning this, one of the most popular of our insular boaganes. Is any account to be found among the records of old Mona concerning the days of spiked barrels, if ever such days shone upon the island; or is anything there to be met with which could throw some light on these stories or how they originated?

It may be remarked that *Arreyderyn* is a Manx word signifying watchers or watchmen, *Cronk-yn-irree-laa* "The day Watch Hill." Both these places seem to have taken their name from the constant watch kept there by our forefathers in times of danger.

A QUIET RETREAT FOR DEBTORS.

THE Isle of Man was at one time the refuge for debtors from Great Britain and Ireland, as no debt contracted off the island could be sued for in it In consequence of this it became the resort of a great number of persons who came over to elude the payment of their debts, particularly after the breaking out of the French Revolution, when the Continent ceased to be their refuge. Many of this class were of extravagant habits and of doubtful character; this led to great excess and frequent quarrels towards the end of last century and the commencement of the present. A law was consequently promulgated on the 24th March 1814, being " An Act for the more easy recovery of debts contracted out of the limits of the Isle of Man." This was looked upon by many as ruinous to the best interests of the island, but the result proved the contrary.

Mrs. Bullock, who resided in the island at the time, gives a graphic account of the doings of these gentry in her *History of the Island*. The writer of the following lines, Miss Gulindo, was no doubt one who availed herself of this privilege :—

> Welcome ! welcome ! brother debtor,
>   To this poor but happy place,
> Where no bailiff, dun, or gaoler,
>   Dares to show his dreadful face.

MUTINY OF THE "BOUNTY."

THE circumstances attending the mutiny of the "Bounty" have a peculiar interest to the natives of the Isle of Man, as one of her sons was most painfully and unfortunately connected with it. The history of that event has been so repeatedly published, that it is only necessary briefly to notice it here in order to record how Mr. Heywood became implicated in the transaction.

"The Bounty," under the command of Lieutenant William Bligh, had been fitted up by Government under the care of Sir Joseph Bankes for the purpose of conveying the bread-fruit and other plants from Otaheite to the West Indies, to which place she sailed from Spithead on the 23d of December 1787. Peter Heywood, the fourth son of Peter John Heywood, Esq., Deemster of the Isle of Man, was born at the Nunnery, near Douglas, on the 6th June 1773, entered the naval service on the 11th October 1786, and made his first voyage as a midshipman in the "Bounty." The vessel having so far accomplished the object of her voyage, was on her way home, when, on the morning of the 28th April 1789, the unhappy catastrophe took place. From various causes disputes and dissatisfaction had arisen in the vessel, and Mr. Christian, the master's mate, who had for some time been doing lieutenant's duty, having received some insulting words a few days before from his commander, conceived the idea of seizing the ship, which he accomplished with the aid of a portion of the disaffected crew, and placed Lieutenant Bligh and eighteen companions in a small boat with only a very scanty supply of provisions, who, after suffering most extreme hardships, only twelve out of their number lived to reach their home.

Young Heywood, having gone below for the purpose of getting some clothes, was forcibly detained, and was thus prevented joining Lieutenant Bligh in the boat. Upon the news of the mutiny becoming known to His Majesty's government, the Pandora frigate, Captain Edwards, was at once dispatched to Otaheite in search of the mutineers, and on her arrival out on the 23d March 1791, Heywood at once went on board and reported himself to her commander, who instantly placed him in irons. After taking twelve more of the "Bounty's" men on board, the Pandora was wrecked, when four of the prisoners and thirty of the crew were lost. Undergoing a variety of hardships, young Heywood arrived at Spithead on the 19th June 1792, and was placed in the Hector, seventy-four, to await his trial, which took place on the 12th September, and following days, along with the other prisoners accused of mutiny. Heywood was condemned, but recommended to the King's mercy, and on the 24th October the King's warrant was despatched from the Admiralty, granting a full and free pardon to Heywood and two of his companions.

The particular details connected with Heywood in this affair are to be found in Tagarts' *Memoirs of Captain Peter Heywood, R.N.*, 8vo, London, 1832, in which work are also those admirable letters of his sister, Nessy Heywood, emanating as they do from a pure and heroic soul, are an honour and a credit to her head and heart, so affectionately devoted was she to her brother. Mr. Heywood afterwards re-entered the navy, in which service he became honourably distinguished, and ultimately retired from the service in 1816 on the arrival of the Montague from the Mediterranean, of which vessel he was captain, being, as was the emphatic expression of one of his shipmates, "perfectly adored."

He married, on the 31st July 1816, Frances, only daughter of Francis Simpson, Esq., of Plean House, Stirlingshire, by whom he had no family, and died on the 10th February 1831, in the 58th year of his age.

The following lines, written by his affectionate sister during the time he was awaiting his trial, show how much her fond mind was fixed on her unfortunate brother.

On the arrival of my dearly-beloved brother, Peter Heywood, in England, written while a prisoner, and waiting the event of his trial on board His Majesty's Ship Hector.

Come, gentle muse, I woo thee once again,
Nor woo thee now in melancholy strain ;
Assist my verse in cheerful mood to flow,
Nor let this tender bosom anguish know ;
Fill all my soul with notes of love and joy,
No more let grief each anxious thought employ !

Return'd with every charm, accomplish'd youth !
Adorn'd with virtue, innocence, and truth !
Wrapp'd in thy conscious merit still remain,
Till I behold thy lovely form again.
Protect him, Heav'n, from dangers and alarms,
And oh ! restore him to a sister's arms ;
Support his fortitude in that dread hour
When he must brave suspicion's cruel pow'r ;
Grant him to plead with eloquence divine,
In ev'ry word let truth and honour shine ;
Through each sweet accent let persuasion flow,
With manly firmness let his bosom glow,
Till strong conviction, in each face exprest,
Grants a reward by honour's self confest.
Let thy Omnipotence preserve him still,
And all his future days with pleasure fill ;
And oh ! kind Heav'n, though now in chains he be,
Restore him soon to friendship, love, and me.

NESSY HEYWOOD.

Isle of Man, *August* 5, 1792.

ADDRESS TO DOUGLAS.

THY lovely bay, thy noble pier ;
Thy woodland scenes, thy waters pure and clear ;
Thy breezes soft, imparting health's sweet balm,
To cheer the mind, the body's pain to calm.
Thy lofty hills, with emerald verdure crowned,
Thy cattle feeding on the sloping ground ;
Thy peaceful valley, dotted o'er with sheep,
Thy own pure river flowing to the deep ;
These, and a thousand charms, my heart beguile,
O how I love thee ! Douglas of the Isle.

Thy rock of refuge, too, with beacon tower,
For hapless seamen, wreck'd in peril's hour ;
What words can tell the thoughts within me raised,
Of bliss bestowed, as on it I have gazed ?
To soothe each being who the storm outlives,
This little tower a welcome refuge gives ;
Where oft the home-bound skiff, in times of yore,
Hath struck upon the rock in sight of shore !

Oh, Hillary ! thy philanthropic heart
In love hath raised this magic piece of art ;
The bay's chief ornament, with use combined.
It stands the beacon, too, of thy great mind !
In chaste simplicity it rears its head,
Nor heeds the spray, nor wildest storm doth dread !
Secure within its sea-girt islet rock,
Its modest walls may brave Time's latest shock.

Thy scenes I still retrace, they still beguile
My heart to love thee ! Douglas of the Isle.

A POETICAL ADDRESS.

THE following correspondence between Bishop Ward (who was an Irishman) and the Duke of Atholl, about a site for a new church in Douglas, produced the accompanying poetical address. The author appears to be unknown.

Bishop's Court, July 23d, 1829.

My Lord Duke—I flatter myself your Grace will excuse my communicating the accompanying appeal. Your Grace knows the deplorable state of the poor of Douglas with regard to church room, which I know your Grace had long wished to remedy by promoting the building of a new church, had not the people marred the good purpose and hindered their own blessings. I have a fair prospect of being enabled by the public bounty to build a new church in that town. But we are greatly at a loss for an eligible situation. There is not one suitable spot except a small timber yard by the bridge, which is in your Grace's possession. Archbishop Cranmer, it is said, was never so happy as when he had an opportunity of exercising the Godlike principle of doing good to his enemies. I will not say the Manx are your Grace's enemies ; but they may have given your Grace cause of vexation, and used the Bishop worse. But as that is all over, and can never recur, and you are never more to meet, till you meet before the tribunal of the Great Judge at the last day, I am persuaded your Grace would like to have a memorial in the island of your forgiveness and good-will, and help them to a new church.

What I have to request of your Grace is an exchange of the timber-yard by the bridge for the enclosed piece by the Seneschal's office, which the Crown will grant me for that purpose. There is very little difference in the quantity of land, nor perhaps in the value.

The piece at the bridge is about 100 or 120 feet square. The church there would be a beautiful object on entering the harbour, and from the road coming in and out of Douglas to and from the country. It could never be surrounded by buildings, being close on the banks of the river, and flanked by the bridge and the highway. It would stand as a beautiful and sacred memorial of your Grace's munificence long after you were gone to receive your reward in the church triumphant in heaven. And though many of the present generation might not feel the obligation as they ought, yet as we do not build churches for the present race alone, generations yet unborn would bless your posterity, and I would most gratefully pray God to bless you and reward you a thousand fold as long as I lived.— I have the honour to remain, your Grace's most faithful and humble servant, W. SODOR & MAN.

To his Grace the Duke of Atholl.

Dunkeld, 28th July 1829.

My Lord Bishop—I have the honor to acknowledge the receipt of your Lordship's letter of the 23d inst., relative to the spot of ground near Douglas bridge, which you consider a suitable place for the erection of a church, and proposing to give in exchange the enclosed piece, adjoining the Seneschal's office. In reply, I beg leave to inform your Lordship that a few days since I wrote to Mr. M'Crone, desiring him to accept an offer of £600 from Genl. Goldie for the piece of land, at the same time to give the refusal of it to your Lordship, which before time I suppose has been done, but in consequence of your letter I have this day again written Mr. M'Crone, desiring him, in case he has not closed with General Goldie's offer, to defer doing so until he receives further instructions, and that he should make me a report upon your Lordship's proposal, which, as soon as I receive, I shall write you again on the subject.—I have the honour to be, etc. etc.

ATHOLL.

Dunkeld, 10*th August* 1829.

My Lord Bishop—With reference to the Duke of Atholl's letter to your Lordship of the 28th July, in reply to yours of the 23d, relative to the spot of ground adjoining Douglas bridge, which your Lordship wishes to have for the site of a new church, I am directed by the Duke to inform you, that having communicated your Lordship's proposal to Mr. M'Crone, who had received previous instructions to offer the ground to Genl. Goldie for £600, giving, however, the refusal of the ground to your Lordship, he finds Mr. M'Crone has gone too far into negotiation with Genl. Goldie to have it in his power to comply with your wishes.—I have the honour to be, etc. etc. R. C. CARRINGTON.

MY LORD BISHOP TO MY LORD DUKE.

I'm head of the church in Sodor and Man,
You, the great chief of a mighty great clan ;
You wear the kilt, I wear the cassock,
You pray, sans culotte—I on a hassock.
But most of my flock, they pray not at all,
For the sinners are many—the churches are small.
And och ! botheration o'ertake them I say,
From *their* Lord, and *your* Bishop, they went far astray ;
Scorn'd your rank and your power, his mitre and wig,
Disputed your rights, and refused his tithe pig ;
For which awful sins they're in danger to go
Where they'll broil, and torment, and roast them below.

I've a scheme in my brain (in my wig if you please),
More churches to build, and chapels of ease ;
If you'll join in this plan, we'll remove all complaints,
And the next generation we'll turn into saints.

We've both got our saints in story who shine,
Saint Andrew is yours, Saint Paddy is mine ;
And we've each gotten grace—of a different sort,
For mine's of the Church, and yours of the Court ;
Your grace from below, my grace from above,
Your anger and rage, my mercy and love ;
We'll join in one plan to gain our own ends,
And the Duke and the Bishop continue good friends.
The children we'll save from all that is evil,
The parents we'll send just plump to the devil ;
On earth you'll ne'er meet them, but this is my text,
If they scape you in this world, you'll meet in the next.

LINES COMPOSED BY MISS MARCIA CLARK, OF JURBY, DURING HER LAST ILLNESS, MARCH 27, 1828.

I.

AND must your sister Marcia die,
   And leave you all to weep?
And must she to her Father fly,
   And bow at Jesus' feet?

II.

And shall you never hear her voice
   In conversation, as before?
Ah! no; she'll soon be lost in death,
   And you shall see her here no more.

III.

Your loss is her eternal gain,
   To heaven by angels she'll be brought;
'Tis there she'll never suffer pain,
   Nor have one bad or evil thought.

IV.

In heaven her side will never pain,
   Her aching head will be at rest,
Her panting heart will cease to beat
   And she shall dwell among the blest.

V.

In heaven she'll meet her brothers dear,
   And sisters who are gone before;
And Oh! what glory shall appear,
   When she shall land on Canaan's shore.

VI.

Oh! then her Saviour shall appear,
    With glory shining in his face ;
He'll reach his hand to draw her near,
    To dwell within that happy place.

VII.

My dearest mother thinks it hard
    To part with me and let me go ;
O ! yes, my mother, we must part,
    And I must leave you here below.

VIII.

O Jesus, bless my parent dear,
    My mother who will sigh and weep,
Teach her to say " Thy will be done,"
    And sit like Mary at Thy feet.

IX.

O mother, mind you'll watch and pray,
    And then you shall sweet comfort find ;
Jesus will guard you every day,
    And cast your troubles all behind.

X.

My father dear, what shall I say
    To urge you to return to God,
O read your Bible, watch and pray,
    And we'll meet in his blest abode.

XI.

Lord bless my brothers, sisters dear,
    And all my friends that prov'd so kind ;
O may you all to God draw near,
    And stop not one dear soul behind.

T

XII.

I soon shall bid you all farewell,
 My blessing I do leave with you ;
In paradise I soon shall dwell,
 And bid the world and all adieu.

LINES ON PEEL.

By Mrs. Griffith, 1839.

WONDER and anger oft I feel,
When *would-be-wits* depreciate Peel ;
To hear pert folly simpering say—
" If of the world you're tired, pray
Don't hang or drown—but only give
The world up, and to Peel go live !"
This heartless taunt, this senseless ire,
Levell'd at thee, made me inquire
Why, Peel, such mockery and scorn,
So long, unjustly, thou hast borne ?
I find that 'tis in *wealth* alone,
The neighbouring towns have thee outshone,
To *nature's* gifts and beauties, see,
With lavish hands bestowed round thee.
Thy daughters modest, wise, and fair,
Ingenuous, artless, kind, sincere—
Patterns of rectitude through life,
As mother, daughter, friend, or wife.
Thy sons, for talents, worth, and sense,
Must surely claim pre-eminence !
Who've without wealth or interest risen,
To the first rank to Manxmen given.
Thy schools have taught those first who stand,
In worth and wealth throughout the land,
Though now alas ! they ruined lie,
Sad cause for philanthropic sigh !
Thy scenes around more beauties boast
Than any part on Mona's coast ;
Thy sloping hills, thy valleys green,
Thy shore and bay, where oft are seen

Thy busy fleet, with plenty crowned,
Whilst cheerful hum is heard around.
Thy fine old ruin bids us sigh,
Musing on greatness long gone by ;
For kingly pomp and mitred care
Lie buried and forgotten there !
Yet shall the kind benevolent mind
This generous exaltation find,
That halls where prince and prelate reigned,
Are not by prisons now profaned.
The felon's chain, the debtor's moan,
Are there alike unheard, unknown ;
We view with pleasing admiration,
It's greatness, even in desolation !
On summer's eve how calm to stray
When the last sunbeams quivering play,
And tinge with gold the silvery spray,
Along the shore, or climb the height,
Where sun and landscape charm the sight.
Then ask, what world must I forego
To enjoy this fair expanse below ?
Here peace and nature seem to tell
Of fairer worlds where spirits dwell.
Here, then, may I in life's decline,
Ambition, folly, pride, resign ;
Here strive to learn and tread the way
To heaven ! and oh ! may all who stray
From that blest path, repent, and give
Their world up—*Come to Peel—and live.*

INVITATION TO THE DOUGLAS BAZAAR.

In aid of the Funds for the House of Industry, August 1843.
By Paul Bridson, Esq.

PRAY, stop my good friend, for a moment attend,
    Assist us in helping the poor ;
Ah ! I see by your smile you will tarry a while,
    And cheerfully join us, I'm sure.
Very useful the task which we venture to ask,
    And easier than many by far,
Then list to my verse, wide open your purse,
    And buy at our Douglas Bazaar.

Bless me ! what a sight ! 'tis quite a delight,
    Such a store of nice things to behold ;
Let us visit each stall, and look at them all,
    And a few of them turn into gold.
With happy beguiling the ladies are smiling,
    Each one like a beautiful star ;
We must yield to their sway, and please them to-day,
    For they rule at our Douglas Bazaar.

Now what will you buy ?—to please you I'll try,
    Bags and baskets, we have them by dozens ;
All shapes and all prices—very clever devices—
    They'll do for your sisters and cousins.
I'm sure you may find something quite to your mind,
    Grave or gay, or whatever you are ;
For the ladies intend to suit every friend,
    Who may visit our Douglas Bazaar,

Pincushions abound, flat, oblong, and round,
    And in truth there's no lack of good purses ;
Even caps, I declare, for the babies are there,
    So carry them home to your nurses.

Racks, screens, cigar cases, and sweet little faces
　　On dolls that have come from afar ;
'Tis really quite funny to see how the money
　　May be spent at the Douglas Bazaar.

There ! look at that stall, it is just what I call
　　A display of real beauty and taste ;
And here you may find some food for the mind,
　　These volumes are temptingly placed.
The drawings I mention, as worth your attention,
　　Sure a trifle will never debar—
Or check your desire from being the buyer
　　Of these—at our Douglas Bazaar.

We have some things for using, and others amusing,
　　As you'll easily see by these lines ;
Clever puzzles to wit, and slippers to fit,
　　And cases and bands for divines.
Gay aprons and shawls may be bought at the stalls,
　　Turkish cushions and urn rugs there are ;
And worsted work rare, nicely wrought by the fair,
　　For the good of our Douglas Bazaar.

And should you but wish to partake of a dish
　　Of choice fruits or other refection,
Just look you around, and a stall may be found
　　Replete with the nicest confection.
Of ices a store, and many things more,
　　Too numerous to mention by far ;
So sit down if you please, and be quite at your ease,
　　In the midst of our Douglas Bazaar.

And again, after all, view that beautiful stall,
　　Replete with the choicest of flowers ;
For here you may buy a charming bouquet,
　　For the ball when the evening lours,

There's the post-office, too, with letters for you,
 From your friends and admirers afar ;
And if you'll but pay the high postage this day,
 You'll assist much our Douglas Bazaar.

Then, ladies, come view, and gentlemen too,
 Our wares of all sorts and all sizes ;
And when Christmas shall come, you'll find out
  that some
 Will suit well for presents and prizes.
Now look at them well, I am sure they must sell,
 And won't let them stay where they are ;
So open your heart, and refuse not to part
 With your cash at our Douglas Bazaar.

That my rhyme is spun out, you cannot now doubt,
 And my verse 'gins to falter and jar,
My brain's in a mist, so kind patrons list
 To the laureate of Douglas Bazaar.

LINES UNDER THE PORTRAIT OF JAMES SEVENTH EARL OF DERBY.

> WHILE Stanley's life-like face you scan,
> You recognise the King of Man ;
> But learn his death from history's pen,
> And then you see the King of Men.

It was also written of this renowned nobleman and ruler of Man—

> An Isle in antient times renowned by fame,
> Lies full in view, and Mona is the name ;
> Once bless'd with wealth, while Derby held the sway,
> But now a broken, rough, and dangerous way.

This Earl of Derby was unjustly beheaded at Bolton, Lancashire, on the 15th October 1651. Upon his coffin being conveyed to a house in the town, there was thrown into it a piece of paper, on which was written these lines—

> Bounty, Witt, Courage, here in one lye dead,
> A Stanley's hand, Vere's heart, and Cecil's head.

THE ISLAND PENITENT.

A Legend of the Calf, by Miss E. Nelson.

THERE is a tradition that a little ruin on the island, called the "Calf of Man," was formerly tenanted by a man who retired to this wild spot in the reign of Queen Elizabeth, imposing upon himself a solitary residence as a penance for having killed a beautiful woman in a fit of jealousy.

FAR 'mid the rocks of Man's wild shore,
　　An aged sinner dwelt—
But earthly tongue might never speak
　　The pangs that sinner felt.
Far in a cavern by the shore,
　　Of dark Castrooan flood,
A fearful voice wail'd evermore,
　　" Old sinner, blood for blood! "

Yet many a day had that old man mourn'd
　　Through a weary pilgrimage ;
But can hard fare, or penance drear,
　　Guilt's burning pangs assuage ?
The tears of heartfelt penitence
　　Are registered in Heaven ;
But that grey man ne'er shed a tear,
　　That old man was unshriven.

O ! he bare a deadly sin I ween,
　　The voice wail'd—"blood for blood!"
And the islesmen said, misdeeds had been
　　By dark Castrooan's flood.
And that old man's harp was the white, white bone,
　　Its strings were soft golden hair,
And the sinner in his sleep would moan,
　　" Dead ! dead ! although so fair ! "

And the simple islemen, many a day,
   Held marvel of the same ;
And many a mother bless'd herself,
   For thoughts she might not name ;
And many a maiden's cheek was pale,
   To cross the gloomy strath—
Alas ! there was a weary curse
   Upon the old man's path.

There is a headland bare and bold
   By Mona's lovely isle ;
And there the wanderer may behold
   A solitary pile ;
The hoary sinner rear'd that pile,
   That time-worn " cruciform,"
And there full many a day mourn'd he,
   Above the mist and storm.

There is a cave within the rock,
   As dark as evil thought ;
When winds howl'd loud, and waves dash'd light,
   Its gloom the sinner sought.
Where not a ray of heaven's light,
   Could that wild temple pierce ;
Oh ! he would mock the mad tempest
   With laughter loud and fierce !

Oh, what is elemental wrath
   To the deep mental strife ?
Alas ! the sinner's bitter laugh,
   With agony was rife ;
It mock'd, yea mock'd the elements,
   It mock'd his own sad soul ;
Woe, and alas, for evil hearts
   And minds that spurn control !

And years went by, and from his cave
    The sinner pass'd away ;
None knew the wherefore, when or how—
    None know it to this day !
Where'er he went, whate'er his fate,
    All dark Castrooan's flood
Could never from his conscience cleanse
    The memory of blood.

Go, view those monuments of old,
    They tell a fearful tale
Of deeds that blanch the cheek, and make
    The stoutest hearts to quail.
Alas ! there was doom for the sinner grey,
    That passeth not with time,
Oh ! well may the islemen, shuddering, pray
    " Lord ! save us from all crime."

FAREWELL TO MONA.

By the Rev. J. L. PETIT.

MONA, farewell! the bark is manned,
To bear me to another strand,
And other scenes, and other skies,
By morn's grey dawn must greet my eyes;
Yet shall my memory love to dwell
On the lone isle of rock and dell,
Chafed by the ocean's whirling foam,
Within whose deep secluded home
The busy world is all unknown;
Or marked by distant peaks alone,
To him who haply gazes round,
From giant Sneafell's topmost mound.
What time the morning's ruddy light,
Gleams fresh on Cronk-na-Irey's height,
When the brisk sea-breeze, clear and cool,
Sweeps o'er the crest of bold Barrule,
And circling round Slieauwhallin's falls,
The tutelary mist dispels.
If nature's charm, and fancy's thrill,
Can chase the spirit's cheerless chill,
If records of the past can bear
Our minds from present scenes of care;
If the rude cross and sculptured stone
Brings visions of an age unknown,
If Peel's grey towers and ruined walls
A wondrous train of saints recall;
If yet the fairy loves to dwell
On the green brink of Maughold's well,
O let me often roam again
Through thy brown heath and rugged glen.

Or list to Foxdale's fitful roar,
Or wrapt in legendary lore.
Linger at eve and muse awhile
In Trinian's dark and ruined aisle,
Where the stout tailor undismayed,
Throughout the twilight's deepening shade,
In spite of goblin, fiend, or witch,
Plied boldly the creative stitch,
E'en in the very face of him,
Whose spectral image, swart and grim,
Scares the lone wanderer on his path,
And heedless of his threatened wrath,
A neat habiliment began,
And finished, for the nether man;
Then fled unscathed, and refuge found,
Beyond the streamlet's mystic bound.
But hark! I hear the warning bell,
Land of the rock and glen, farewell,
And if thy bard should tempt again,
The perils of the stormy main,
O let his welcome be as free
As that which he hath met from thee;
May kindly heart and friendly smile
Receive him back to Mona's Isle.

ERRATA in Mona Miscellany, First Series.

The reader is requested to note the following errata in Manx, which appeared in the first series of *Mona Miscellany*, corrected by the Rev. J. T. Clarke, late chaplain of St. Mark's.

Page xii. line 19.—*For* Ghaelgagh, *read* Ghailckagh.
Page xiii. lines 21, 22.—*For* fo-sniaghtey, *read* fo-niaghtey.
Page xiv. line 1.—*For* houiney, *read* houney.
Page 23, line 18.—*For* Gorree, *read* Ghorree.
Page 26, line 9.—*For* Gilley-Gliash, *read* Guilley-ghliash.
Page 27, line 2.—*For* mooar moayney, *read* vooar voancy.
Page 27, line 8.—*For* olty, *read* olt.
Page 27, line 9.—*For* traaste, *read* traisht.
Page 27, line 25.—*For* Ta, *read* Ta'n.
Page 28, line 15.—*For* kiark, *read* chiark.
Page 28, line 20.—*For* chice-mean, *read* chiu-vean.
Page 29, line 2.—*For* roo, *read* ro.
Page 29, line 18.—*For* chaa-croie, *read* cheh-creoï.
Page 29, line 24.—*For* oo us choyrle, *read* yiow uss coyrlee.
Page 30, line 3.—*For* chaa-croie, *read* cheh-creoï.
Page 30, line 7.—*For* innen-slooid, *read* inneen-sloo.
Page 31, line 20.—*For* jeeah shin, *read* Jee shiu.
Page 33, line 6.—*For* clogh na-dthy, *read* clagh ny-dty.
Page 33, line 14.—*For* clag-kiclain, *read* clagg-kiaullane.
Page 33, line 22.—*For* derry bought, *read* derrey voght.
Page 36, line 2.—*For* Marrey, *read* Varrey.
Page 38, line 30.—*For* nyne kenghey, *read* dty hengey.
Page 57, line 1.—*For* Ghaelgagh, *read* Ghailckagh.
Page 66, line 5.—*For* nyrgedelin, *read* myrgeddin.
Page 67, line 12.—*For* Theah, *read* Theay.
Page 75, line 2.—*For* air, read aer.
Page 75, line 3.—*For* voaugll, *read* voayl.
Page 76-77.—The spelling of the Manx is given as in Bishop Wilson's Works.
Page 106, line 11.—*For* gig, *read* jig.
Page 106, line 17.—*For* Kaad, *read* Raad.
Page 106, line 17.—*For* dyraghyn, *read* ayraghyn.
Page 115, line 8.—*For* Ta traa goll ne raad, *read* Te traa goaill y raad.
Page 117, line 31.—   Same.   Same.
Page 136, line 3.—*For* skaddan *read* skeddan.
Page 137, line 13.—*For* thie, *read* hie.
Page 147, line 23.—*For* Oie houiney, *read* Oie houney.
Page 177, bottom.—Aggym, leave out.
Page 182, line 29.—*For* Creest y Chrosh, *read* Creest er y Chrosh.
Page 183, line 3.—*For* dy ghrach, *read* dy ghra ch.
Page 183, line 5.—Ghra eh, leave out.
Page 183, line 20.—*For* shoh *read* dy.
Page 227, line 21.—*For* Townley *read* Blundell.

THE MANX SOCIETY

FOR THE

PUBLICATION OF NATIONAL DOCUMENTS.

U

RULES.

—◆—

1. That the affairs of the Society shall be conducted by a Council, to meet on the first Tuesday in every month, and to consist of not more than twenty-four members, of whom three shall form a quorum, and that the President, Vice-Presidents, the Hon. Secretaries, and Treasurer shall be considered *ex officio* members. The Council may appoint two acting Committees, one for Finance and the other for publication.

2. That a Subscription of One Pound annually, paid in advance, on or before the day of annual meeting, shall constitute Membership ; and that every Member not in arrear of his annual subscription be entitled to a copy of every publication issued by the Society. That no member incur any pecuniary liability beyond his annual subscription.

3. That the Accounts of Receipts and Expenditure be examined annually by two Auditors appointed at the annual meeting, on the 1st of May in each year.

4. That Six Copies of his Work be allowed to the Editor of the same, in addition to the one he is entitled to as a Member.

5. That no rule shall be made or altered except at a General Meeting, after due notice of the proposed alteration has been given as the Council shall direct. The Council shall have the power of calling Extraordinary Meetings.

PUBLICATIONS OF THE MANX SOCIETY.

——◆——

FIRST YEAR, 1858-59.

Vol. I.—An Account of the Isle of Man, with a Voyage to I-Columb-kill, by William Sacheverell, Esq., late Governor of Man. 1703. Edited, with Introductory Notice and Copious Notes, by the Rev. J. G. Cumming, M.A., F.G.S. Pp. xvi.-204. Pedigree.

Vol. II.—A Practical Grammar of the Ancient Gaelic, or Language of the Isle of Man usually called Manx. By the Rev. John Kelly, LL.D. Edited, together with an Introduction, Life of Dr. Kelly, and Notes, by the Rev. William Gill, Vicar of Malew. Pp. xlviii.-92.

SECOND YEAR, 1859-60.

Vol. III.—Legislation by Three of the Thirteen Stanleys, Kings of Man, including the Letter of the Earl of Derby, extracted from Peck's "Desiderata." Edited, with Introduction and Notes, by the Rev. William Mackenzie. Pp. xix.-224. Plate.

Vol. IV.—Monumenta de Insula Manniæ, or a Collection of National Documents relating to the Isle of Man. Translated and edited, with Appendix, by J. R. Oliver, Esq., M.D. Vol. I., pp. xv.-244. Plate.

Vol. V.—Vestigia Insulæ Manniæ Antiquiora, or a Dissertation on the Armorial Bearings of the Isle of Man, the Regalities and Prerogatives of its ancient Kings, and the original Usages, Customs, Privileges, Laws, and Constitutional Government of the Manx People. By H. R. Oswald, Esq., F.A.S., L.R.C.S.E. Pp. ix.-218. Ten plates.

THIRD YEAR, 1860-61.

Vol. VI.—Feltham's Tour through the Isle of Man, in 1797 and 1798, comprising Sketches of its Ancient and Modern History, Constitution, Laws, Commerce, Agriculture, Fishery, etc., including whatever is remarkable in each Parish, its Population, Inscriptions, Registers, etc. Edited by the Rev. Robert Airey. Pp. xvi.-272. Map. Four plates. Three woodcuts.

Vol. VII.—Monumenta de Insula Manniæ, or a Collection of National Documents relating to the Isle of Man. Translated and edited by J. R. Oliver, Esq., M.D. Vol. II., pp. xxi.-250. Map.

Vol. VIII.—Bibliotheca Monensis ; a Bibliographical Account of Works relating to the Isle of Man. By William Harrison, Esq., H.K. Pp. viii.-208.

Fourth Year, 1861-62.

Vol. IX.—Monumenta de Insula Manniæ, or a Collection of National Documents relating to the Isle of Man. Translated and edited, with Appendix and Indices, by J. R. Oliver, Esq., M.D. Vol. III., pp. 272.

Vol. X.—A Short Treatise of the Isle of Man, digested into six chapters. By James Chaloner, one of the Commissioners under Lord Fairfax for settling the affairs of the Isle of Man in 1652, and afterwards Governor of the Island from 1658 to 1660. Published originally in 1656 as an Appendix to King's Vale Royal of England, or the County Palatine of Cheshire. Edited, with copious Notes and an Introductory Notice, by the Rev. J. G. Cumming, M.A., F.G.S., Rector of Mellis, Suffolk, late Warden of Queen's College, Birmingham, and formerly Vice-Principal of King William's College, Isle of Man. Pp. vii.-138. Map. Four plates. Five pedigrees.

Fifth Year, 1862-63.

Vol. XI.—A Description of the Isle of Man : with some Useful and Entertaining Reflections on the Laws, Customs, and Manners of the Inhabitants. By George Waldron, Gent., late of Queen's College, Oxon. Printed for the Widow and Orphans, 1731. Edited, with an Introductory Notice and Notes, by William Harrison, Esq., Member of the House of Keys, Author of " Bibliotheca Monensis." Pp. xxv.-155. Plate.

Vol. XII.—An Abstract of the Laws, Customs, and Ordinances of the Isle of Man, by Deemster Parr. From an unpublished MS., supposed to be written about 1690. Edited by James Gell, Esq., H.M.'s Attorney-General, Castletown. Vol. I., pp. xvi.-241.

Sixth Year, 1863-64.

Vol. XIII.—Fockleyr Manninagh as Baarlagh Liorish Juan y Kelly. Edited by the Rev. W. Gill, Vicar of Malew. Part I.

An English and Manx Dictionary prepared from Dr. Kelly's Triglott Dictionary, with alterations and additions from the Dictionaries of Archibald Cregeen and John Ivon Mosley, by the Rev. William Gill, Vicar of Malew, and the Rev. J. T. Clarke, Chaplain of St. Mark's. Part II. Pp. 432.

SEVENTH YEAR, 1864-65.

VoL XIV.—Memorials of God's Acre ; being Monumental Inscriptions in the Isle of Man, taken in the summer of 1797, by John Feltham and Edward Wright. Edited, with an Introductory Notice, by William Harrison, Esq., Author of "Bibliotheca Monensis." With six plates of the old churches. Pp. xv.-132.

Vol. XV.—Antiquitates Manniæ, or, a Collection of Memoirs on the Antiquities of the Isle of Man. Edited by the Rev. J. G. Cumming, M.A., F.G.S. Pp. viii.-140. Twenty-four plates and eleven woodcuts.

EIGHTH YEAR, 1865-66.

VoL XVI.—Mona Miscellany. A Selection of Proverbs, Sayings, Ballads, Customs, Superstitions, and Legends, peculiar to the Isle of Man. Collected and edited by William Harrison, Esq., Author of *Bibliotheca Monensis.* Pp. xv.-241. With the music to three songs.

Vol. XVII.—Currency of the Isle of Man, from its earliest appearance to its assimilation to the British Coinage in 1840 ; with the Laws and other circumstances connected with its History. Edited by Charles Clay, Esq., M.D., President of the Manchester Numismatic Society, etc., assisted in the Paper and Card Currency by John Frizzel Crellin, Esq., M.H.K., Orrysdale, Isle of Man. Illustrated extensively with photographs, lithographs, and woodcuts. Pp. xi.-215.

NINTH YEAR, 1866-67.

Vol. XVIII.—The Old Historians of the Isle of Man—Camden, Speed, Dugdale, Cox, Wilson, Willis, and Grose. Edited by William Harrison, Esq. With three maps and thirteen plates. Pp. xiv.-199.

TENTH YEAR, 1867-68.

Vol. XIX.—Records of the Tynwald and St. John's Chapels in the Isle of Man. By William Harrison. With an Appendix, containing an Account of the Duke of Atholl taking possession of the Isle of Man in 1736. Also, a Lay of Ancient Mona. Pp. xiv.-148. Fourteen plates.

ELEVENTH YEAR, 1868-69.

Vol. XX.—Manx Miscellanies. Vol. I.
(Nearly ready to be issued.)

TWELFTH YEAR, 1869-1870.

(No Works issued for this Year.)

THIRTEENTH YEAR, 1870-71.

Vol. XXI.—Mona Miscellany. A Selection of Proverbs, Sayings, Ballads, Customs, Superstitions, and Legends, peculiar to the Isle of Man. Second Series. Collected and edited by William Harrison, Esq., Author of *Bibliotheca Monensis*. Pp. xvi.-285. Two plates. With the music to one song.

www.ingramcontent.com/pod-product-compliance
Lightning Source LLC
Chambersburg PA
CBHW060541030726
47498CB00004B/1280